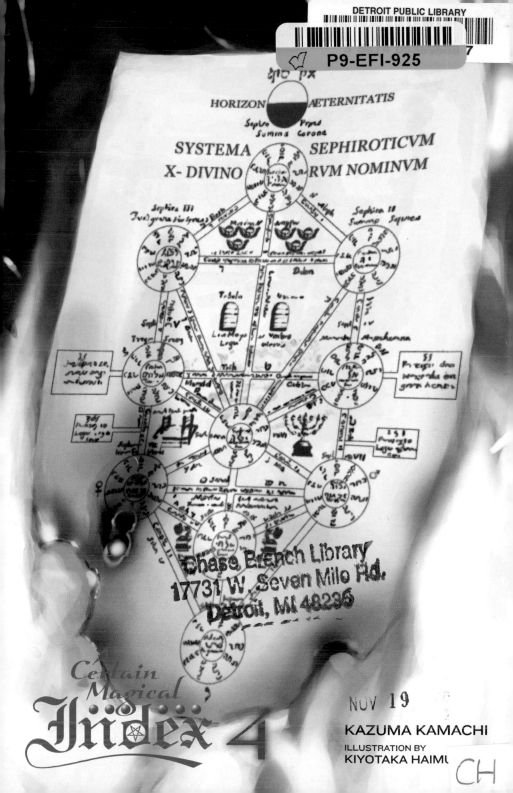

"What?!"

Academy City Tokiwadai Middle
School Student **Mikoto Misaka**

"Oh my, my. Is the little sister character a little too straightforward for you, Touma?"

Nun managing the Index of Prohibited Books **Index**

"Is it okay to be lazing around here?"
Academy City High School Student **Touma Kamijou**

Fugitive **Jinsaku Hino**

"......What?"

Touma Kamijou's neighbor **Motoharu Tsuchimikado**

"_____"

Sorcerer **Misha Kreutzev**

contents

PROLOGUE   *A PARALLEL WORLD IN THE WORLD OF REALITY*   1

CHAPTER 1   *THE HEX SUSPECT IN THE WORLD OF SORCERY*   21

CHAPTER 2   *DETECTIVES IN THE WORLD OF COMBAT*   87

CHAPTER 3   *ANGEL FALL IN THE WORLD OF INJURY*   143

CHAPTER 4   *THE LAST SORCERER IN THE SINGLE WORLD*   189

FINAL CHAPTER   *MY BETRAYER IN THE WORLD OF NORMALCY*   223

VOLUME 4

KAZUMA KAMACHI

ILLUSTRATION BY: KIYOTAKA HAIMURA

NEW YORK

A CERTAIN MAGICAL INDEX, Volume 4
KAZUMA KAMACHI

Translation by Andrew Prowse and Yoshito Hinton

This book is a work of fiction. Names, characters, places, and incidents are the product of the author's imagination or are used fictitiously. Any resemblance to actual events, locales, or persons, living or dead, is coincidental.

TOARU MAJYUTSU NO INDEX
©KAZUMA KAMACHI 2004
All rights reserved.
Edited by ASCII MEDIA WORKS
First published in Japan in 2004 by KADOKAWA CORPORATION, Tokyo.
English translation rights arranged with KADOKAWA CORPORATION, Tokyo,
through Tuttle-Mori Agency, Inc., Tokyo.

Yen On
Hachette Book Group
1290 Avenue of the Americas
New York, NY 10104

www.hachettebookgroup.com
www.yenpress.com

Yen On is an imprint of Hachette Book Group, Inc.
The Yen On name and logo are trademarks of Hachette Book Group, Inc.

The publisher is not responsible for websites (or their content) that are not owned by the publisher.

First Yen On edition: August 2015

ISBN: 978-0-316-34056-4

10 9 8 7 6 5 4 3 2 1

RRD-C

Printed in the United States of America

PROLOGUE
A Parallel World in the World of Reality

August 28. The weather was fine.

A high school student named Touma Kamijou awoke to a female's milky voice calling, "Hey, big brother!"

"…Huh? What was that hair-raising screech?"

Kamijou cracked open his eyes, still half-asleep. He saw the towel blanket that had been covering him at some point lying crumpled up in a ball next to him.

He thought he'd heard the girl's voice from the other side of the door.

Reflected in his peripheral vision was a Japanese-style room, six tatami mats in size. The floor was covered with worn-out tatami, there was a fluorescent light with an ancient-looking square cover on the ceiling, the paper sliding door for the closet was stained with something oily, and there was a wooden door with a simple keyhole that probably led to the bathroom or something. Instead of an air conditioner, there was an electric fan whose plastic body was a faded yellow color. If he lifted his nose a bit, he could smell salt.

He was not in his one-room apartment in the student dormitories. He wasn't even in Academy City.

This was a certain shore in the Kanagawa prefecture—in the ordinary world—and he was inside a guest room on the second floor of a beach house called *Wadatsumi*, Japanese for "sea god."

Kamijou's parents and Index would each be in their own rooms.

"...That's right...We came to the outside, didn't we?" mumbled Kamijou to himself, head in the clouds.

Academy City, the Supernatural Ability Development organization in which Kamijou lived, rested in the western areas of Tokyo. Because of that, there was nothing more distant for the residents of the landlocked city than the beach. (Though there were aquarium-like swimming pools if you went to a fisheries school or somewhere like that.)

Plus, in consideration of its own secrets, as well as the potential threat of student kidnappings (read: theft of test samples), Academy City stubbornly disliked allowing its students outside of its walls. Gaining permission to leave required three written applications, the implanting of microscopic devices in your bloodstream, and the arrangement of a legal guardian...

But we really did come here to the beach, huh?

Kamijou rubbed his right upper arm. He couldn't feel the traces of those painless injection needles by touching the spots where they'd been inserted. They'd been no more than mosquito bites.

His particular case was out of the ordinary. Normally, a student would fill out the applications and politely ask a teacher to let them leave the city. Kamijou's teachers, however, ordered him to "go outside, stupid."

About a week ago, he had defeated the most powerful Level Five in Academy City.

Although there isn't too much interaction among students during summer vacation, rumors of the altercation had spread across town in a heartbeat. They did not, however, result in Touma Kamijou gaining any sudden recognition.

Instead, a bunch of confident city punks had started a massive survival game with him as the prey, under the impression that if they could beat up "that Level Zero moron," then they would claim the title of Academy City's strongest.

The upper echelons of Academy City were the ones most bothered by the commotion. They said to him, "Hey, hey, Mr. Kamijou. We'll fix up this mess with our information control, so go away some-where you won't cause needless chaos, stupid." And so here he was.

Well, still. I'm sensing some pretty clear enmity in the destination they picked, though.

Kamijou gave a great yawn. There had been a huge outbreak of giant jellyfish on the Pacific coast this year, so in spite of the heat wave, there were essentially no guests at the beach. Even if that hadn't been the case, he was required to bring legal guardians along to the outside world—meaning, basically, his parents. It was one thing to be accompanied by a cute young lady or a pretty older woman. This was a little sad, though. Did he really have to play with his parents at the beach at this age?

However, if this was what it took to bring everything to a close, then he'd just have to settle.

With his victory over the best Level Five "Superpower" that Academy City had to offer, he had forced a very large project connected to many research institutes into suspension. He may have also earned animosity from some of the more important ones. They hadn't put a lot of pressure on him, but the only reason for that was probably because the gossip regarding his fight with Accelerator had placed him in the public spotlight. If the scientists were to take any drastic measures, people would know about it right away.

Even so, the bleary-eyed Kamijou lacked a certain sense of excitement.

...Ugh, so tired. Is everyone up already?

He hazily thought of the sister in white. She was probably snoring in the room across the hall by herself. If he was to categorize her, she'd technically be a "cute young lady." Unfortunately, he would have to wonder about anyone who might see her childlike body in a swimsuit and think to himself, teary eyed, that all his summer wishes had been fulfilled.

Though he had gotten a frightful surprise in the swimsuit section of the department store when she'd emerged from the changing room.

He'd gotten a similar surprise when he'd seen the number of zeroes on her bathing suit's price tag.

Incidentally, he hadn't originally planned on taking the nun in white to the beach house Wadatsumi at all. She was supposed to have stayed behind. She and the calico were going to crash at Miss Komoe's, and he'd actually purchased a swimsuit for her with the intent that she could go play in the pools in Academy City.

It seemed obvious when he thought about it, but she wasn't from the city. She had smuggled herself in, as it were. If they just nonchalantly went up to the borders, they might be caught by the Anti-Skills. She couldn't fill out an application to leave, either.

However, the sister in white had been deaf to all of these considerations. He'd commanded her to mind the place in his absence, but in the end, he couldn't tolerate that teary-eyed stare of hers anymore.

So he'd taken on the challenge of sneaking her out.

To put it simply, he'd called a taxi, forced Index to lie down in the backseat, and tried to get through the gate like that. Kamijou had been pretty worried about the chances that such a lame method would actually work, and sure enough, they'd been stopped. Apparently, the checkpoint was equipped with infrared cameras or MRI scanners or something.

When he thought about being arrested, he'd frozen like a deer in headlights. However, the Anti-Skill managing the gate hadn't been particularly angry. After referring to his computer, he said something about there being a registered temporary guest identification for her.

Of course, neither Kamijou nor Index recalled anything like that.

Who the heck did that?

Registering for an ID necessitated the input of the person's fingerprints, voiceprint, and retinal pattern into a terminal. Kamijou supposed that it was more than possible to steal someone's voice and retinal scan by using a high-resolution video camera or what have you. In addition, you could easily collect fingerprints by using aluminum or carbon dust, just like the police do for criminals.

But why would someone go through all the trouble?

Kamijou had been dubious at the time, but he didn't let it show. There was no need to give the Anti-Skill any reason to be suspicious.

Once he'd held Index still enough to get her to take the nanomachine injection (they actually used a mosquito needle, so it was painless), the pair had slipped through the gate fair and square, albeit quite confused.

Ugh, ah…I'm so sleepy…, thought Kamijou only half consciously, covering himself with the blanket from his head down and giving his body over once more to slumber. Morning was still a drowsy time of the day for him, as someone who had been doing the whole "stay up late every night" shtick for summer vacation. Like a limp, melted piece of candy, he surrendered himself to the sandman, but then he heard the lovely female voice again, seeping through the door at him, saying, "Hey, big brother, wake up!"

One of those "useless brother plus reliable sister" dynamic duos must be staying in the house, he figured. *What's the deal with that charming kind of pair, anyway? The only girls around me are the dangerous sorts, like Index and Deep Blood*, he reflected, not fully awake. *But wait, with the jellyfish outbreak, shouldn't there not be any visitors at the—*

Just as doubts began surfacing, the door flew open with a resounding *bang!*

What, what, what the hell?! Before Kamijou could poke his face out of the blanket he was wrapped in, the sound of light, girlish footsteps pattered over to him and a voice said, "Hey, how long are you gonna sleep? Big brother, wake up, wake up, wake up, wake up!"

The girl's cute, dreamy voice was coupled with the impact of a body press.

The girl's full weight slammed directly into his gut. Kamijou gave an incomprehensible yelp. This scenario was sure to happen in manga and dating sims, but more importantly, it was a pro-wrestling move.

He coughed violently underneath his blanket. *That's strange. Touma Kamijou has no sister. There's no reason this should be happening.* He vaguely got the feeling that if he began to think about what part of the girl's body this soft feeling was from, the one he was getting around his stomach from across the blanket, all the blood would go to his head and he would pass out. Right now, though, he couldn't think that far. Anyway, he was sleepy and wanted nothing more than to somehow put an end to this mistaken prank as fast as he could.

Kamijou gathered his strength.

"...Who are you? Who the hell are you, graahh!!"

Shouting, he sat up vigorously, like a jack-in-the-box. He heard the mass on top of him fall off with a shriek.

Damn it, who ruined my restful sleep time?! he thought, incensed. He looked at the girl who had rolled off of him, and—

—there was Mikoto Misaka, lying on the tatami.

"Oww. Hey, I come all the way to wake you up, and this is what I get?"

The girl, wearing a red camisole, had cutely (really, seriously unfitting for her) fallen on her butt (possibly completely shattering her identity) and was making a somewhat petulant face at him, one cheek puffed out.

"Wha—"

—t's going on here? Every trace of his exhaustion had completely evaporated.

Mikoto Misaka. The ace of Tokiwadai Middle School and an Ability Development legend. One of just seven Level Fives in Academy City. A strong lightning user, quick to anger, but actually a bit of a crybaby. Following a certain incident, she'd ended up owing him a debt. When he'd mentioned it, though, her face had gone beet red, and she'd come at him with all that *biri biri.*

It goes without saying that she wasn't his real sister, nor was she his stepsister.

He hadn't the faintest idea what was happening, so he gave talking to her a shot.

"Huh, what? Eh? Did you end up getting chased out of Academy City because of the incident with the Sisters, too? Wait, is this some kind of island where people get exiled when they're run out of the city or something?"

"Huh? What are you talking about? Why is it weird that I'm here with my big brother?"

"Gross! Why the heck are you talking to me with that sappy voice?! Your reign of terror is just about the furthest thing in the world away from that kind of impression!"

"How rude!" she retorted, clearly angry given her expression. His entire body broke out in goose bumps.

Dumbfounded, Kamijou tried to think through this.

Possibility 1: Mikoto's morning surprise, after she was also ordered to leave Academy City.

Possibility 2: Mikoto Misaka swallowing her pride and playing the little sister to pay her debt (stepsister mode set to "on").

Possibility 3: One of Mikoto's sisters has a bug.

I mean, it's #1, right? It's gotta be #1, since #3 is impossible! She seems like a little sister character at the moment, so I'd be happy if it were #3, but I feel like I, Touma Kamijou, have never raised a single of those fabulous flags in my whole life, but I guess if it were #3...if it were #3?

...

...Ooh.

Huh?! After a few seconds' silence, Kamijou finally snapped back to reality.

As if this were a summer mirage caused by primal desires that he needed to clear out, he tried yelling them away.

"Bah! Underestimate a high school student, you should not! Do you think Touma Kamijou will be swayed by some middle school kid's early-morning prank?!"

"Big brother, you seem too excited for this early in the morning."

"Damn, characterizing me as some guy who gets happy when a girl calls him 'big brother'...! In the first place, what do you mean by 'brother'? Your backstory—are you related to me by blood or not?! Ah, shit, I figured out the ending! If I go on thinking we're not blood related, then you're gonna come out and say at the very, very end that I was actually related to you and then I can't beat the game, is that where this is going?!"

"Huh? You look like you're channeling some kind of alien

language. So early, too! I can just call you whatever, right? Big brother is my big brother, after all."

"It is not good! Why are you trying to be my little sister?!"

"Hmm?" Mikoto pressed her index finger to her cheek, her expression showing that she didn't understand the question. "Do I need a reason to be my brother's sister?" She got up from the tatami with a *hup* and finished, "Okay, look, if you're so energetic, then get up and come downstairs so you can eat breakfast!"

Then, as if it was the most natural thing ever, she bounded lightly out of the room.

...Okay. So what's going on here?

Kamijou was missing something crucial. He changed his clothes and left the room.

Three doors lined either side of the short, straight hallway. Describing it that way might make it sound like a boardinghouse. However, either because of the sea breeze or the fact that many years had passed since it had originally been built, the boarded floors were blackening like an antique temple, and the minute amount of sand that had gotten inside was sucking all the moisture out of the air, making it feel kind of disgusting.

The staircase was at the end of the passage.

Just as he was heading that way, he heard a door click open behind him.

"Good morning, Touma. Hmm? Hey, you've got some pretty bad bedhead in the back."

It was his father's voice.

Touya Kamijou. A man with a stubbly beard in his midthirties whose features somehow resembled Touma's, he actually traveled overseas three times a month on business for a relatively large firm with foreign affiliations. Reflecting his lifestyle, perhaps, he gave off an intrepid yet intellectual air.

For the amnesiac Kamijou, his "father" presented a bit of an odd topic. Of course, Kamijou himself didn't remember the man. Nevertheless, his parents would encroach upon his personal space without the slightest hesitation.

As a high school student, even college students two or three years older than him represented people living in a functionally different world, one whose life and habits were completely foreign to his experience. The age difference between Touma and his father was even greater than that, which made it all the more challenging to figure out how to bridge that gap.

"Mm...mornin'—— Wait, what?" When Kamijou turned around, he gave a start.

"? What's wrong, Touma?"

His father, Touya Kamijou, frowned.

Leaving him aside for the moment...Kamijou shifted his gaze toward the cause of his discomfort—the person standing next to Touya.

"Hey, Index? What the heck are you wearing?"

Yes—next to Touya stood the silver-haired, green-eyed foreigner.

Normally, Kamijou would have described her as the "sister in white," but right now, Index wasn't wearing her customary white habit. Despite the heat, she had on a thin, long, short-sleeve one-piece that went down to her ankles, wore a cardigan on her shoulders, and even had a big, wide-brimmed white hat sitting atop her head. For someone who was, bluntly, an extremely active girl, her garments were overwhelmingly unfitting. He wanted to demand what kind of sickly character or rich summer resort lady she was pretending to be. Now that he thought of it, though, he got the feeling that his mother, Shiina Kamijou, wore this kind of clothing.

Shiina's hobby, he heard, was flying in powered paragliders. In the classes that took place at the park near their house, there may or may not have been eyewitness reports of married women dressed like rich girls sitting in a parachute that looked like swings, with fanlike propellers strapped to their backs, flying through the air.

"Where did you even get those clothes, anyway?"

In response to his question, Touya gave him an expression that said, *What are you talking about?* then asked:

"Touma, is it strange for your mother to be wearing her own clothes?"

                    *   *   *

Kamijou looked at Touya's face with a *What*?

Touya had definitely just looked at the girl next to him and called her his *mother*.

While looking at the silver-haired foreigner, who was not even fourteen years old by *anyone's* standards.

"Huh? What? Dad, are you saying you're seeing Mom when you look at her?"

"What else would I be seeing, Touma?"

"Wait, just hang on a sec. Is this some kind of body-changing technique? This is beyond a joke. You're playing the fool so seriously that you're not giving the straight man any openings to retort!"

"Touma, what about your mother isn't convincing you?"

"What about her? Everything! Look at her! She can't possibly be my mother!!"

He relentlessly pointed at the fourteen-year-old girl. She lightly grabbed her own clothing and said, "Oh my, oh my. My fashion sense just isn't okay with you, Touma, is it?"

"Now, Touma. You're making your mother sad!"

"Not that! However you look at it, you're freakin' *younger* than me! Even if this were some play in kindergarten, it would make absolutely no sense to cast you as the 'mom with a kid in high school'!"

"Oh my, oh my. I look younger than my age to you, Touma, do I?"

"Now, Touma. You're making your mother happy!"

Kamijou gave an "Enough already!" and buried his face in his hands.

He'd admit it. Back a month ago when he'd been hospitalized with a severe head wound and his mother and father had come, the "first" time he'd interacted with his parents, he was surprised when he learned that his father, Touya, and his mother, Shiina, were the same age—he'd admit that. He'd even straight up confess that Shiina's outward appearance made her look like a young lady in her late twenties. (Though of course, if she *actually* were in her late twenties, that would mean Kamijou had been born illegally.)

Nevertheless, Touma Kamijou would *not* be tricked by this body-swapping ninja technique that used Index, who was, however he looked at her, less than fourteen years of age.

"What is it, Touma? You look distressed. Are you going through those bothersome puberty feelings? Then you can have this protective talisman sort of thing I bought when I was on a business trip in India."

"What? I don't need it; I don't even believe in lucky charms, and besides, it's probably just a thing mass-produced in a factory downtown anyway— Wait, what? That looks totally like a palm-size statue of male genitalia!"

"Well, your dad doesn't understand it, either. Apparently it's a religious thing?"

"What the heck does it protect you from? It looks like a strap you'd put on a cell phone! But if you did, people would call you weird names. Never mind running the risk of getting arrested!"

"What? Touma, do overseas souvenirs not agree with your skin? Then I'll keep it domestic. This is something I bought while I was on a trip in Akita recently, see?"

"What's it this time…? Wait, it's another phallus! A wooden sculpture of one! You're acting like a six-year-old who's into dirty jokes!"

"Mgh. When I brought it to the office after the trip, it met with a whirlwind of laughter…"

"How can you tread into harassment territory so blindly, you idiot?!"

As Kamijou grew more and more befuddled, Touya made a curious face.

"By the way, Touma. Shouldn't you go and wake up the girl you brought with you?"

"I'm saying she's standing right next to you! And anyway, where did Mom go?!"

"Oh my. Someone my age should be treated as a 'girl' rather than a 'mother' in your opinion, Touma?"

"If I hear one more word out of you, I'll argue you down until the day is over!!"

Then, all of a sudden, the door next to Kamijou opened with a *click*.

Touya blamed him, saying it was his fault that he woke her up because he was being so noisy.

Kamijou turned his gaze to the side, saying, "Index?"…

…And out the door came Blue Hair, wearing a completely white nun's habit.

He was a large man, reaching 180 centimeters in height. Moreover, he hadn't forced himself into Index's habit; it appeared that he had gotten a new one from somewhere, with the exact same design, just in extra large.

The large man spoke.

He spoke heavily with a deep, manly voice that would surprise even the Three Tenors.

"Ahh, mm? Touma, you seem really excited for morning time. Did something happen?"

"…Ah—"

The large man rubbed his eyes in a very cute way indeed. "Oh, sorry, I forgot to say good morning, Touma. Anyway, the beach! Beach, beach! I always thought that Japan's beaches were covered with concrete, and there was oil and stuff floating around, but it's actually really pretty. Yeah, let's go play!"

"Ah…"

The large man abruptly peered at Kamijou's face from below. "Huh? What's the matter, Touma? You got all stiff. Ah! Could you be imagining all sorts of things about what I'm gonna look like in a bathing suit—"

"Aaaaaaaaaaaaaaaahhhhhhhhhhhhhhhhhhhhhhhhhhhhhhh-hooooooooaaaaaaaaaahhhhhhhhh!!"

Not really able to endure it any longer, Kamijou took the wooden door, which had opened to his side, and slammed it shut in Blue Hair's face. *Bang!* came a loud noise as the man was beaten back into the room.

"T-Touma! Take a seat right there, okay? Assaulting a woman should be reported to the police, you know?"

"Oh my, oh my. You have quite a ferocious liking of women, Touma, don't you?"

Putting aside his father, flustered about something or other, and Index, currently wearing her weak young lady outfit (a long one-piece dress and a cardigan plus a giant hat), Kamijou tried to make heads or tails of this whole thing.

Wait a second. Calm down. This is all some kind of massive wake-up prank, like the kind on TV where they put up hidden cameras everywhere so variety show hosts can laugh at people. Though I have no clue why Blue Hair is outside the city. The more ridiculous of a reaction I make, the more I'll be playing into their hands!

Touya and Index were worrying about Blue Hair, whom he had shut back into the room, but Kamijou ignored them and headed for the first floor. It would be dumb to entertain them any longer. Besides, he was going on an empty stomach, so he hadn't the stamina to do so.

He descended the narrow wooden stairway.

The first floor of the beach house Wadatsumi was a wide space with a boarded floor. The entrance at the roadside and the exit toward the sea were both completely open to the outside, with no walls much less doors; the salty wind was blowing straight in. A few antique arcade game cabinets were placed in one corner of the shop. By the roadside entrance, there was something like a counter cutting away the wall.

The mysterious electric girl calling herself his little sister, Mikoto Misaka, had taken up camp at one of the round coffee tables (or were they tea tables?) scattered about the center of the room, and she was disinterestedly reading a magazine. Her two thin legs extending from her short camisole waved back and forth underneath the table. She looked extremely bored. There was a television right next to her, but it was turned off.

Kamijou, fed up with it, said, "...So, Biri Biri. Why are you just sitting here like you belong?"

"How rude! Are you still in that rebellious phase, big brother? It's actually okay if I hug you, and follow you around, and loaf around with you, you know."

"…" It looked like that gross flattery character she was acting out was still in commission. "Ugh. I feel like an idiot for having a transmitter stuck in my blood vessels."

He breathed a heavy sigh, entirely exhausted by it all. Mikoto, for her part, closed the magazine tiredly, then she laid down on the floor and started rolling around from left to right.

"Oh, right, big brother. Do you think we could turn on the TV by ourselves?"

"Huh? What are you talking about all of a sudden?"

"Mgh. I mean, I can't find the remote. TVs in places like this seem like the kind that, you know, belong to everyone, so 'don't go touching it without asking, you little brat,' that sort of thing. So I can't touch it, big brother."

"…" *Still going with the little sister nonsense?* Kamijou held his head in his hands. "What the heck is this? The audacious Miss Mikoto is acting so reserved."

"Who's Mikoto?" The Level Five seemed to want to play the fool all day. "I guess I'm *reserved*, because that guy in charge of the house looks scary! Big brother, go ask if we can turn on the TV, okay?"

"…I take it back. Even if you're in character, you're still audacious."

Be that as it may, one way or another Kamijou had a habit of turning on the TV in the morning, too. It was hard for him to settle down if he didn't. He looked around, wondering where the shopkeeper was. There wasn't anyone behind the counter. He wondered whether or not that was acceptable from a service industry standpoint. Just then, though, the smell of cooking oil reached him from the exit to the sea. "?" He looked over there, and he saw the back of a tall man roasting something just outside the exit, on the sand, with some charcoal fire and wire netting.

"Oh, look, it's that guy. Go ask him about the TV! Go ask, go ask!" requested Mikoto, swinging her feet around under the table.

Suddenly he harbored doubts about all this. If he recalled correctly, the keeper of the beach house was tall, unfriendly, and a little scary when you looked at him. But had his hair been long enough to reach his shoulders, and was it always dyed bright red like that?

Nevertheless, his feet clapped along the floor planks, and he approached the shopkeeper with a short "Excuse me."

The long red-haired shopkeeper turned around.

The person, wearing a T-shirt and shorts, with a towel around his neck…

…was the sorcerer Stiyl Magnus.

"————Nabahhh???!!!"

That was when Kamijou's mind reached the pinnacle of chaos. Standing at a little more than two meters, the long red-haired Englishman was an otherworldly sorcerer who could control fire and thought nothing of killing people.

"'Ey, you're up early. Water's still cold. Or are you the type that couldn't sleep because of how hot it was out yesterday?"

Those, however, were the sorcerer's words as he fanned the corn cooking on the charcoal fire.

"Whoops, this isn't done yet, so I can't feed it to customers. Hey, Maou! Take the customer's order and give him whatever!" said the sorcerer wearing beach sandals and a towel around his neck.

Wh-what's going on? What the hell is going on here?!

For the first time since this all started, he finally began to think that something was wrong. Would that sorcerer, a combat—no, *killing*—professional, really be this cooperative for some joke or prank?

Kamijou's thoughts were about to slam into a brick wall in the face of the shocking imagery, but the sound of footsteps pattering up behind him snapped him out of it. A girl's voice called out from the rear.

"Hey, Dad! You can't just say 'give him whatever' in front of the customer!"

Who is it this time? he thought, turning around. There, wearing only an apron over a pair of navy blue swim trunks, a sunburned, simple and honest-looking Mikoto Misaka was standing.

"Huh, is she playing two roles? No, wait, this one is the mass-produced little sister, isn't it?"

"Uh, Dad? This person is a customer, so I'm not allowed to tell him off, right?"

A tight Japanese businesslike smile came across her face.

Little Misaka had retained her impassive expression even when she was on the verge of death. Now, however, the grin she gave was vague and one that was completely out of the question for her.

Wait, stop, what kind of joke is this; she's basically naked under that apron, isn't she; if you look from the side, if you look from the side, you can kind of see her chest; that's terrible; gah, is it normal to go through with a wake-up prank like this far?!

Then, next, from inside the beach house, the voice of the original Mikoto came flying at him.

"Big brother! Did you ask? Did you ask about the TV? I'm turning it on, okay!"

Kamijou took a peek inside from afar and saw her on all fours in front of the TV, hitting the power button. The volume was up really high, perhaps in consideration of a crowd of guests being present, so the voice on the TV reached all the way outside to Kamijou.

"Yes, this is Komori at the scene. Jinsaku Hino, the convict on death row who broke out of the Shinfuchuu prison in the capital early this morning, has still not been located. There's a tense atmosphere here, as schools in the vicinity, such as the middle school, have issued an emergency cancellation on all club activities."

The reporter's name was Komori, wasn't it?

Yet, for some reason, he felt like he was listening to the familiar, childishly undeveloped voice of Komoe Tsukuyomi, his homeroom teacher.

...Komoe Tsukuyomi?

"Wait, that can't be! Why is Miss Komoe on TV?!"

Kamijou rushed over to the television, and right there on the CRT screen was a 135-centimeter-tall female teacher, whose outward appearance looked twelve years old, holding a microphone and reading off of a news draft.

Why is she...? Is this all part of the prank? Then does that mean this is a recording? No, there's no tape deck or anything. Then, did they hijack the airwaves? For what? A prank? That's strange. This is way out of the realm of a wake-up prank!!

He pushed Mikoto out of the way and took up a position in front of the TV. His finger repeatedly jabbed a small button beneath the screen.

"Hey, wait. I wanted to watch *Morning Fade-in!*"

He paid no mind to Mikoto's plea for authority over station changing. As channel after channel went by, he saw an old man being treated as a sexy, appealing female newscaster and a brunette, heavily tanned high school girl as the president of a certain country giving a speech on the righteousness of war. The oddest part about it was the fact that they were all news programs being broadcast over open air, and they were all completely absurd. Behind an anchor reading off a script with a serious-looking face (this guy also looked like a factory worker or truck driver or something), there was a kindergartner with his hands on the steering wheel of a big bus, an old lady wearing a miniskirt fiddling with a cell phone, and the oft-seen-on-the-news prime minister playing a guitar in the road.

The news broadcast site seemed to be a station packed with commuters, and there were more than just a couple hundred people going back and forth behind the anchors. And every person in the throng was odd in some way.

Hey, wait, wait, wait. Is every single channel like this?!

Even if this were all one big setup, how much money would it have taken to pay all these extras? And even before that, the prime minister himself showing up for this made the possibility of a wake-up prank a bizarre one in the first place.

He got the feeling that this was not a prank.

However, if it wasn't some joke, then…what was it? Index was calling herself his mom, Blue Hair claimed to be a sister in white, and Stiyl turned into the old man in charge of the beach house.

It was as if everyone's inside and outside had been entirely swapped.

By what logic?

Kamijou had a huge, hopeless headache. It no longer made sense to consider the situation either realistically or scientifically.

CHAPTER 1
The Hex Suspect in the World of Sorcery

1

Despite the reality before him appearing to be so ludicrous, time marched on.

Touya, Index, and Mikoto immediately made plans to go to the beach, leaving behind Kamijou, who was still clueless. Confused, he'd been commanded to change into his swim trunks posthaste and come along. Then, he was ordered to go onto the beach and set up the parasol for them. He now sat underneath it, alone on a picnic sheet with his hands clasped around his knees, not altogether sure of when he had actually put it up.

Is this okay? Is it okay to be lazing around here? It really seems like the world has gotten itself into a huge mess, but I have no clue how to deal with any of it!

Thanks to the mass outbreak of giant jellyfish, there wasn't a single other beachgoer on the sands. A hit song was lonesomely crackling out of the speakers stuck on the wooden poles placed at regular intervals along the shore. When he beheld it all, the world seemed so very peaceful. Unfortunately, though, he had seen pure mayhem on TV.

No matter what channel he flipped to, all he saw were people with mixed-up clothes.

The fact that the broadcast stations were **like that** meant that the disaster didn't only encompass their beach house; the same thing was happening all over Japan. No, maybe, just maybe, it was the entire *world*.

...Hmm. Or maybe I'm just seeing some weird hallucinations?

A problem was occurring all across the planet, but its physical scale paled in comparison to the other thing: Everyone around him was forcing him to believe that this scrambled world was normal. It was toying with his emotions, even though he *knew* he was seeing clearly. He was letting himself be washed away with the current, like a truly useless Japanese person.

As he sat there in exercise position, he heard the sound of feet crunching over the sand, coming up behind him.

"Hey, Touma. Thanks for saving our spot. Though, well, since there isn't anyone else here, I guess that means you didn't do any work!" The male voice bellowed a "Wa-ha-ha."

Oh, it's just Dad, he thought, twisting his neck to look behind him——and he froze.

"Hmm. What is it, Touma? Dad's swimsuit strike your fancy?"

Kamijou ignored Touya completely and looked next to him.

He looked at Index, standing where his mother, Shiina, should have been. *W-wait. What's with that insane swimsuit?!*

Index was wearing a black bikini, unsuited to her childlike body.

However, normally bikinis are constructed from both cloth and string. In Index's case, though, the string was made out of transparent vinyl. So when you looked at her from far away, it looked like she had stuck fabric onto all the parts she needed to hide using double-sided tape.

He'd put it bluntly. No matter what, that was an utterly stupid, utterly *adult* swimsuit.

Damn! I guess this is the world of gaps and imbalance, though! No, wait, calm down—this is no time to be happy. Index has no money! Where did she get something like that?!

As Kamijou stared in stupefaction, Index pressed one hand to her cheek.

"Oh my. This outfit just isn't convincing for you, Touma, is it…?"

"No, there's a bigger problem! What's with that bathing suit? You had a different one yesterday!"

"Oh my. I brought along two or three different swimsuits, that's all."

"A-ha-ha!" laughed Touya. "Yep, your mother still has it in her, doesn't she? Swimsuits sure are expensive, but this means that your father's gift wasn't for nothing."

The moment he heard that, Kamijou's eyes flared up.

"You jerk! Did you tempt her with money and buy stupid shit for her?! And wait, where did you learn Index's sizes? Or did you go shopping for it together or something?!"

"Oh my. Touma, if you press your thumbs against his carotid artery and squeeze his neck like that, your father will pass out, all right?"

"Don't stop me, Index. This lolicon is targeting you!" Kamijou howled, looking like he was about to send flames shooting from his mouth. "Damn, I knew it. I always thought it was weird, how Mom looks so young even though she's the same age as you. I bet she's actually only twenty-eight, isn't she?! So how old was Mom when she gave birth to me?! You're a criminal!!"

"Bgh-ghgh. T-Touma, calm down! Here, I'll give you this family household protective charm I got when I went on a trip to Ireland, so, so bghghagh!"

"What the hell?! This is a figurine of a naked woman! Are you implying you know exactly what you're doing?!"

"N-no, I mean, this is apparently Sheela-na-Gig, the weather godde— Ugh! Guhghgh!"

As Kamijou was on the verge of veering permanently onto the path of demons, Mikoto Misaka came up to him.

"Huh? What are you fighting about, big brother? Is this one of those fabulous events where it turns out you weren't related by blood?"

"You…you…Don't go forcing in a 'not related by blood' option here! And what's with that getup?! This isn't some chlorine-stinking school pool, so why are you in a school bathing suit?"

"Huh? Is that weird?"

"Kuh…So you plan on playing the flattering little sister character for good, huh…?!"

What the hell is going on?! Unwilling to keep this up, he let his hands drop like an octopus's down from Touya's neck and sighed. Touya, coughing violently and holding his neck, looked at his own son's face and remarked, "H-how careless of me…I never thought that you doted on your mother this much…"

"Oh my. Freud said that boys unconsciously hate their father and love their mother. I guess it really is true, isn't it?"

"That's not good. His long, lonely dormitory life may have created an eager need for familial love."

"…Every single one of you…" Kamijou bit down on his back teeth. "Quit it with your aggressively incorrect, amateurish psychological analysis and labeling me as some guy with an Oedipus complex! Everyone sit down right there! I will dig holes for you with this toy shovel and bury you all up to your necks under this blazing sun!"

The three weirdos gave a squeal of glee and fled toward the water. Kamijou gathered up the shovel in one hand and was about to go after them with a "You shall not escape!" but then he suddenly realized he was forgetting about something.

He heard footsteps coming up behind him again, making crispy noises as they touched down on the sand.

That's right, for some reason Blue Hair was in that beach house, he thought, and then he froze.

Yesterday, Index had been wearing her tidy white one-piece bathing suit.

Today, Blue Hair was wearing a white habit of the same design as Index's for some reason.

So what would Blue Hair's outfit be here on the beach?

No, wait. Could…? Where is this syllogism going—?!

"Touma, Touma! Sorry for being late. Thanks for waiting!"

That detestable, *truly* detestable, feline, male voice.

Don't turn around, he thought to himself. *I bet Blue Hair is standing right there, and if I witness him, I'll lose something important to me.* That's what he thought, but with slow, jerky movements and much trepidation, he turned around to face reality.

The demon there in the white one-piece—

"—Huh?!"

The next thing he knew, the sun was somehow in a higher spot than before. In his hand was a sand-covered shovel, and at his feet was an unconscious Blue Hair buried up to his neck in the sand. Only his neck was visible, sprouting up out of the beach, like when they mounted heads on a pike after beheadings in the Edo period.

Did I do this? Just what was I…? And judging from his head's angle, he's buried in a vertical pit!

After thinking about it for a while, he decided not to dig his terrible friend out of the sand. If he saw his outfit right now, he'd probably lose something important to him.

Oh, right, where's Dad—damn, there he is! Look at him, playing with a beach ball by the shoreline with Index and Mikoto! And he's got those beastly eyes of his set right on the Index route, ready to challenge it! D-damn it! I finally get to the beach, and this is the kind of summer vacation I get?!

Anyway, I must destroy that lolicon not acting his age! he thought, running toward the beach in large, swaying motions, with the toy shovel in one hand. In the meantime, he internally wondered if it was all right to be worrying about something this peaceful and that maybe he was overlooking something pretty important—

"Unyaa~! Kammyyy, I finally found ya!"

Then suddenly, a strange cat voice flew at him. If you were to ask what about it was strange, it would probably be the fact that, besides of course being a cat's voice, it belonged to a male, not a female.

Wh-what,·what, what is this? Wait a minute, hey, I think I know that voice!

Kamijou stopped running and turned around, and there he saw a large man, possibly 180 centimeters in height, dashing toward him.

"T-Tsuchimikado?"

Motoharu Tsuchimikado. He was Kamijou's next-door neighbor and his classmate (...apparently—Kamijou didn't have any memory of it, so he didn't really know). He had uniquely long arms that dangled all the way down to his knees. The blond hair atop his tall stature was spiked up, and he wore shorts and a Hawaiian shirt with nothing underneath. He sported pale blue sunglasses, and with the gold chain he wore around his neck to top it all off, he gave off the impression of a wandering, ill-bred boxer has-been. However, in reality, his delinquent nature was because he wanted to at least be a little bit appealing to girls. In addition, his younger stepsister with the standard-issue maid gear, Maika Tsuchimikado, made him an indulgent older brother.

"...Hey, wait a minute. Why are you here?! How did you get outside Academy City? Is Mai with you?!"

"I wish you wouldn't give my sister a nickname so casually, but I don't even have time to mention that. Kammy, just making sure, but...do I look like Motoharu Tsuchimikado to you?"

Kamijou couldn't tell what he was getting at. "Huh? What are you talking about? More importantly, how did you get outside the—"

"But that means...nyaa, that can't..." After mumbling to himself for a moment, he said, "Well, whatever. Anyway, Kammy, we gotta get out of here. It's dangerous. What's dangerous? Well, only the part about that angry lady about to attack us, that's all!"

"Huh? Lady...attack? Hey, wait, is there still something?!"

"It doesn't matter, just listen to what your neighbor is telling you, 'kay?!"

Tsuchimikado seemed deranged, and his point wasn't quite getting across. Kamijou tilted his head in confusion, and his neighbor started waving around so frenetically that his sunglasses slid down one side of his face.

"Jeez! Haven't you realized that something weird's been going on ever since you got up this morning, nyaa?!"

"Hm? Yeah, everyone's acting kinda weird. It's like their insides and outsides got totally swapped out or something, but...Huh? How do you know that?"

Kamijou looked over toward the waves coming in. The group of weirdos was playing with the beach ball.

"What I mean is—Sis thinks that you're the criminal who used magic to make this substitution happen!"

"Huh?"

Criminal? Right as he thought about that one, puzzled—

"I have found you, Touma Kamijou...!"

He heard some sort of female voice filled with enormous animosity come at him from the side.

"Whoopsie!" Tsuchimikado looked up at the sky. Kamijou turned toward where he heard the voice. A girl was standing there. She was tall for a female, upward of 170 centimeters. Her long black hair was done up in a ponytail, but the hair it bundled reached way down to her waist. She had style, and her skin was pale enough to make him think of a princess, but strangely he didn't feel an ounce of fragility or weakness.

Her clothing was the likely reason for that. The short-sleeve white T-shirt she wore had been tied with the excess cloth around her ribs, revealing her navel, and she had worn-out jeans on...but for some reason, one of the legs was boldly cut so far up one could see the end of her thigh. Her feet were clad in the kind of boots you might see in a Wild West film. In the same genre was the thick belt wrapped diagonally around her waist. It looked like it was holding up some sort of handgun holster.

However, her waist revealed not a handgun but a katana. And it looked to be a special-order one, too, two meters in length at a glance. When combined with her long black ponytail, she looked like some sort of samurai who would appear in period films.

And, for reasons he did not understand, the Bakumatsu swordsman romanticist was staring fixedly at Kamijou's face.

She closed the distance to him directly and rudely with a face filled with ire.

The most dangerous part was that her right hand may or may not have been touching her sword's hilt this whole time.

"Touma Kamijou! We know that you caused this substitution magic—Angel Fall! Return everything to normal before I count to three!"

The Japanese sword girl seemed ready to cut him down right this moment instead of counting to three. She came within an inch of Kamijou in the blink of an eye. He flinched back. Anyone would be scared if someone came straight up to them with a vengeful look and a gigantic knife.

"Eh, what? What's this person saying? Tsuchimikado, is this girl the 'sis' you were talking about? —Hey, don't run away by yourself!"

He'd only taken his eyes off Tsuchimikado for a moment, but in that time, he'd snuck over to the sandy beach. Kamijou's yell made him stop short, and he turned back around, shivering. His pale blue lenses glinted in the sunlight like a cold sweat.

Kamijou looked over to the waterside. Index, in her bathing suit, and Mikoto were fooling around not even one hundred meters away, physically. However, it seemed to him like a paradise he would never, ever reach.

I wanna run away right now, but things are just as absurd over there, he thought. The lady in front of him seemed to cool off a little.

"Ah, yes. Yes, I see. I apologize. I was so intent on getting results that I forgot my manners. I'll ask just to make sure. Whom do I look like to you?"

Whom...?

His neck twisted at the oddness of the question. With the way she said that, one would take it to mean that "who" and "I" were different people. Well, Kamijou was an amnesiac in the first place, so he didn't know who she was. When confronted with a strange question like that, he had no choice but to return a blank stare.

Then, as if the katana girl had read something in his expression, she snapped, "...My word, your acting is awful. Didn't you just call me 'sis' before? I'm Kanzaki, Kaori Kanzaki. A sorcerer of Necessarius, of English Puritanism. Just because we've only met once doesn't mean you can say you've forgotten me in such a short time."

Kamijou was surprised on two different levels at her exasperated tone.

First was that he *knew* this weird, east-meets-west samurai girl.

Second was that she casually referred to herself as an English Puritan sorcerer.

Necessarius was something that Index and Stiyl Magnus belonged to as well. It was like an anti-sorcerer special ops team. Now that she mentioned it, her weirdo getup didn't quite blend into modern society, and it made Index's and Stiyl's own clothing make more sense (though it was rude to them to think that).

Nevertheless, there was one strange thing about this if that was the case.

With a real sorcerer here, who was Tsuchimikado, who was acting like such a good friend toward her?

Tsuchimikado saw Kamijou and sighed, then looked at Kanzaki. "Hey, hey, Zaky! You acting a little combative there, don't you think, nyaa?"

"What are you saying, Tsuchimikado? I am simply devoting all of my energy toward solving the problem in front of us. In the first place—and if you will allow me to say such a thing—*you* are the one who lacks a sense of being a sorcerer."

Kamijou couldn't let that one go.

"Wait, what did you say just now? A sorcerer?"

In utter disbelief, he turned his eyes to his neighbor. He grinned playfully.

"Yup, you got it. I'm a member of Necessarius, too."

Simply. So simply did Motoharu Tsuchimikado announce it.

So it took time for Kamijou to understand what he had just said.

Glare.

The blue-tinted sunglasses reflected the sunlight with an eerie glare.

"W-wait a minute. What? You? A sorcerer?"

"Yeppers!" Tsuchimikado nodded meekly. "Did ya think there were no sorcerers in Academy City? It's actually the opposite! The world of science is the enemy of the world of magic. So it wouldn't be weird if there were one or two spies deep in enemy territory, would it? I think there're a bunch more besides me, too."

"...But..."

What he told him did certainly have some truth to it.

However, the young man had been part of his completely normal daily life until now. The very fact that he had said something sharp and with some truth to it was already giving Kamijou an indescribably out-of-place feeling.

"I mean, really. My being *outside* Academy City in the first place is weird, don't you think? Good ol' Tsuchimikado was with Zaky inside Windsor Castle in England until two hours ago. Of course, I didn't have to fill out an application or have to get some tiny blood-borne machines inside me. I used a secret way out, nyan!"

"..."

Even coming from the man himself, Kamijou didn't feel like it was real. For him, Motoharu Tsuchimikado was this: his dorm neighbor in the realm of his ordinary life; someone who forced himself to look delinquent in order to be popular with girls; someone who, despite that, would be in a panic whenever his stepsister Maika so much as came down with a cold, then go over to Kamijou's room to ask him for advice—he couldn't see him as any more than an average guy. He could never have thought of him being related to this magical parallel universe.

Therefore, Kamijou unconsciously searched for a way to deny it. "O-oh yeah. Aren't you taking the Curricula in Academy City? If I remember right, espers aren't able to use magic, so—"

"You got it, bud. Although it might be because I've infiltrated enemy territory...Thanks to that, the highest-ranking Onmyou professor's days of magic are over. To put the icing on the cake, I'm a Level Zero who can't even use the half-assed powers he got, nyaa. I'm sick of it!" His next-door neighbor grinned at him. "But there are some spies who will stay somewhere for fifty years in order to earn people's trust. You act so surprised; you must really not know anything about the world, you catch my drift?"

"You..." Kamijou's next question vanished midway.

Tsuchimikado saw his shocked face and quirked a slightly self-deprecating smile. "Well, what I'm tryin' to say is, the one you're lookin' at right now is the real Tsuchimikado. I'm a listening device that conveys minute details of activities in Academy City to the Church of English Puritanism."

A spy.

The very word was so far out of the scope of real life for him that Kamijou almost thought they were discussing a movie or something.

Then, in spite of that, Kanzaki continued with a bored-sounding voice. "I will ask you again, Tsuchimikado, but was it okay for you to reveal yourself?"

"Who cares? The higher-ups knew about it a long time ago, nyaa. They're still lettin' me swim around, though. I'm basically dancing in the palms of their hands and waiting to see what happens at the moment." He narrowed his eyes behind his blue lenses. "Well, that just means that the information I've got isn't valuable enough for them to need to do anything about me right away, is all...But things would certainly get unmanageable the moment I discovered the truth behind the *i*th School District, the Five Elements Society. Sorry, but even though they might pay me for it—or rather, *because* this is business—I'm making a clear decision. I need to pull out for now, y'see? Any further and I'll get too deeply involved. *That* alone won't make a useful card to play against Aleister. Man, Academy City's hiding some pretty crazy darkness inside it."

"…" Kamijou shuddered at what he was saying.

Not because he had gleaned anything from it. In fact, he didn't know anything about that stuff. However, the fact was that he had revealed himself as a resident of *another world* by saying all that stuff he didn't understand. That's how he felt.

"…So, then, Tsuchimikado, you're a sorcerer, too?"

"Yeah, though I'm slightly unique and somewhat strange, nyaa."

A spy.

Even now that he knew this, the few mental images he possessed of Motoharu Tsuchimikado stayed intact. The image within him saying that he was ultimately his next-door neighbor, had a soft spot for his stepsister Maika, and sheltered her when she fled the girls' dorm from time to time—his image of him as a useless older brother hadn't been broken.

The truly terrifying part, leaving aside him revealing his identity, was the surprisingly high degree of insight he had into Academy City while still continuing to be a part of Kamijou's normal life.

"Well, enough about me," dismissed Tsuchimikado too quickly. "Right now we gotta do something about *that*. The body swapping, the substitution! Kammy, you've caught on to something, too, yeah?"

"Wait a second. 'Too'? Does that mean *you're* in the know?"

"Ah, yeah, reasonably. What I know is that the substitution *isn't* the real issue. I just know that this substitution is just a side effect, nyaa."

"A side effect…of the real issue?"

Kamijou frowned. The term *substitution* struck a chord, given how everyone was this morning when he got up, not to mention the crazy scenes on TV. But what was this about a side effect? And what would the real issue be? This was starting to sound like someone had started another *incident*.

Kanzaki saw his dubious face and sighed. "Tsuchimikado, it is cruel to expect a comprehension of the truth out of one who does not even understand the tree of Kabbalah."

"I got it. But doesn't that mean your own hypothesis was wrong, nyaa?" Tsuchimikado grinned. "This swapping of outsides and insides, the grand sorcery Angel Fall...You really think a magic amateur like Touma Kamijou could have caused this?"

Kamijou looked at him. He couldn't let that slide. "What? What do you mean by my being related?" he asked, but the one who answered was Kanzaki, with a dissatisfied expression.

"...Once upon a time there was a young man. For some reason, incidents would occur around this young man quite often. Another incident has broken out this time. A single problem arose around this young man. Everybody under the world was affected. However, there was just one person who evaded difficulty. That young man had evaded difficulty and was at the center of the commotion. Is it so strange to think that this young man is suspicious?"

"Hey, hey, hey, hey, wait a minute, stupid! This is messed up! What do you mean 'a single problem arose'?! Are you trying to tell me this craziness is some man-made incident?!"

"Well. Does *that* look like a natural disaster to you?"

Kamijou grunted in spite of himself and fell silent. Tsuchimikado gave a wry grin. "Don't clam up, Kammy! You'll get false charges pressed on ya."

"Who is pressing false charges, Tsuchimikado? In reality, he is the only one in the world not under the effects of Angel Fa—"

"Wait. Angel Fall? You mentioned that before," he interjected, picking up on a term Kanzaki had said. The two sorcerers turned back to him.

"Uhh, Angel Fall is, well...It's hard to explain. Kanzaki, go for it, nya!"

"Tsuchimikado, would you please stop saying 'nya' all the time?" Kanzaki exhaled in exasperation. "Putting it simply, this whole substitution was set up by somebody using magic. It's a man-made incident."

"...Incident?"

"Yes," she nodded quietly.

Kamijou's face betrayed his lack of comprehension for the situation, so she continued. "There is currently a **certain magic** unfolding on a global scale. The case files in the British Library have nothing to say about the phenomenon, and the particular techniques involved and composition thereof are unknown. Because of its particular effects, we have opted to call it Angel Fall for convenience."

"...You know what's gonna happen even though you don't know how it works?"

Far away...

...by the seashore, he heard the merry voices of Index and the others. It sounded so, so very far away.

"It's simple. Just imagine a giant, unidentified sea monster attacking a city." Tsuchimikado smirked. "The SDF investigates all sorts of things about the monster, but in the end it's still *unidentified*. What they do know is they need to stop the monster before it causes a lot of casualties. I suppose it's like that, nya? Well, for you, it'll be A-OK if you just put aside your preconceptions of common sense and listen to us like we're telling you the rules to a video game."

"??? I haven't the foggiest what your example means." Kanzaki's petite neck bent in confusion at Tsuchimikado's explanation.

I'm a little surprised that Kanzaki can make such a girlie gesture, thought Kamijou rudely.

"Let us continue. Angel Fall is related to a concept in Kabbalah of something called the Sephirothic Tree. Have you heard of it?"

"...I don't think so?" Kamijou actually thought he might have heard it somewhere, but it was only a vague recollection, so he denied it. He had a feeling the sorcerer Stiyl had mentioned it during their fight with the alchemist, but...

"The Sephirothic Tree is basically a ranking chart. It has the ranking of the souls of God, angels, and humans graded on a ten-step pyramid. Just think of it like that.

"To put it bluntly, it's like a map of God's absolute reign that basically says that this territory is for humans and this territory is for God—so don't go coming in all willy-nilly.

"The number of people and the number of angels are all decided beforehand, so normally, a human cannot climb to the status of angel. It goes both ways; an angel also cannot fall to the level of a human.

"Basically, all the ranks are filled to capacity."

"By the way," Kanzaki continued after Tsuchimikado's comment, "what we call Angel Fall is referring to an angel of a heavenly rank being forced down to the rank of humans. Like a cup that was already filled, if you pour in one more drop, if an angel falls to the rank of humans, then— I-is something the matter?"

"Er, well..." Kamijou gave an extremely apologetic face. "Umm... *angels*?"

"Yes. Specifically, not envoys of the heavens but envoys of a master. What about them?" Kanzaki answered with a serious look.

Hmmm?...And there his thought processes came to a halt.

The voices of Mikoto and the others playing with the beach ball reached the ears of the silent Kamijou. They were the only ones on the excessively spacious shoreline, so their delighted voices sounded a bit lonely to him.

Well, he *got* it and everything. He understood that his scientific common sense wouldn't work on Kanzaki and Tsuchimikado, who lived in a world of magic. Really, he nearly died one time in a certain incident involving a vampire, after all.

But these were *angels* they were talking about.

If some problem were to occur throughout the world, and he suddenly told a person that "It's the fault of an angel!"...And if they reacted like, "That's terrible news!" then that person would seriously seem to him like they were just tired of life in general.

"...Well, you're just throwing the word *angel* all over the place. I mean, it's not like you can see heaven if you go through the atmosphere in a space shuttle or anything."

"Mm. Heaven and hell aren't a matter of altitude, of 'up' or 'down,' you know."

"Then what are they?"

"Well, for example, people can't see infrared rays or hear really high-pitched sounds. You understand that, right, Kammy?"

"Huh? Well, yeah."

"The whole 'high' and 'low' here is like that. It's the high or low of the *range that humans are able to sense*. If it's too high, then you can't detect it. Same if it's too low. Like, if God were right next to you, Kammy, you'd never be able to notice it."

Tsuchimikado grinned happily. "Incidentally, when we say low, we mean things like hell or demons. It's the ultraviolet rays in comparison to infrared light, and low-frequency waves compared to high-frequency ones. They're of opposite phases. They just have different wavelengths, but they're all the same *waves*. So normally, if an angel were standing next to a demon, neither of them would realize it. They would have to interfere with the wavelength in between heaven and hell, or *Earth*."

"Tsuchimikado," objected Kanzaki, astonished.

It seemed like she didn't appreciate the analogy to infrared and ultraviolet rays.

"On the other hand, if you shoot infrared rays into an object, it'll heat up, and if you shoot high-frequency waves at glass, it'll smash all over the place, right? To put it really roughly, divine punishment and miracles and stuff correspond to that, nya. Heaven may not seem to the untrained eye to have any point of contact with Earth, but depending on the time and place, it can still have effects on Earth. Even the opposite is possible."

Kamijou still didn't understand anything. Tsuchimikado continued further. "And so, Kammy, in religions that worship an idol like Buddhism or Crossism, the power of God or angels is actually pretty close at hand, ya know."

"..." He gave a disbelieving grunt.

"I'm not lying, 'kay? Like you know how there's never *not* a cross on top of churches? Crosses have special power. But if you ask if one is the cross of Golgotha used for the saint's execution, the answer would be 'Absolutely not!'" Tsuchimikado waved his hands dismissively. "The ones on churches are obviously fakes. Fakes can have power, too, though. As long as its form and function are similar, it can contain a certain percentage of the real thing's power. It's a fundamental idea of religious worship.

"To put it simply, it's like how *iron sword* plus *light magic* gives you a *magic sword of light*," he added.

"The rules of religious worship apply to angels, too, nya. If you use some tricks, you can stuff angelic power, or *Telesma*, into various objects. For example, if you engrave the carving of an angel into a sword's hilt, the blade will have its power, and if you inscribe the name of an angel into a protective magic circle, you can borrow the angel's strength. Stuff like that...Although borrowed power can only be a certain percentage. A natural, pure one hundred percent angel falling is unheard of aside from in the Old Testament, nya."

"If you do not assume that angels exist from the outset, we can't go on."

"...I know, but still..."

Kamijou, though forever ignorant of it all, hesitated to reject it outright. After all, they were professionals. They weren't joking or fooling around—they were speaking seriously. It was all the more serious for Kamijou, who had only listened to *half* of Stiyl's explanations back when they fought the alchemist and had ended up having a damn difficult time.

"Um, just a question. All of this...It's not just some kind of wake-up prank, is it?"

"I'm not sure what you mean by that question. Anyway." Kanzaki gave a cough. "Because an angel has been forcibly moved from a higher sefira to a lower one via Angel Fall, because of the fluctuations it has caused, the four worlds creating the form of the ten sefira—specifically, Olam Atzilut (the shaping world), Olam Beriah (the creating world), Olam Yetzira (the formative world), and Olam Asiyah (the physical world)—are being affected."

"...Mr. Tsuchimikado, what on earth is this person saying?"

"Hmm, how would you put it simply, nya? Like you said, everyone's insides and outsides got swapped out. It's essentially a game of musical chairs. At the start of the game, all the chairs and people who need to sit are scattered around, right? But there isn't a chair for every single participant in the game. The one who gets bounced out would end up in heaven, sitting on the angel's chair."

Substitution.

Like the shore over there and what he saw on TV.

Kamijou scooped out only that part, and Tsuchimikado grinned in a carefree way. "But really, the logic isn't that important. Anyway, you just gotta know that something strange is happening, and we need to stop it."

"...Stop it? You can do that?"

"You got it. Seems Angel Fall is still incomplete. If we're gonna stop it, it's gotta be now. Even with your right hand, Kammy, you obviously can't take the ashes of people roasted with magic and return them to normal. It's the same thing. If it's completed, it'll probably be too late."

"..."

Kammy's right hand.

It's not like it really mattered, but how did Tsuchimikado know about the Imagine Breaker?

Seeing his mystified expression, Tsuchimikado explained, surprised, "Hey, man, we went over this already. The Index Struggle, the Misawa Cram School Takedown, the Level Six Experiment Prevention. That's all stuff that was easily leaked. Actually, I was the one who collected information on the Index and Misawa ones, ya hear?"

He brought the conversation back to its main course as naturally as he had said such outrageous things. "And the exact technique is unknown, but Angel Fall is a global-scale sorcery. It's too much load for a single sorcerer to handle, so they've probably set up a ritual site that's using a barrier or a magic circle or something," he explained, amused. "Therefore, there are two options for stopping Angel Fall. One is to take down the caster. The other is to wreck the ritual site. We do have a time limit at the moment, but we don't know when it'll run out, so it's quite the heart-pounding situation we're in!"

In the end, Kamijou didn't really understand any of this, but the important thing was that someone made everyone's insides get swapped out...right?

At this point he might have just thrown it out as unrealistic, but unfortunately, Kamijou was a resident of a city with 2.3 million espers. On top of that, he already had connections with these *sorcerer* people. He had learned that there are problems one can't just discard as "impossible" or "freaking stupid."

So he did his own thing and gave a long groan.

The reason everyone was acting so strangely was apparently because of that substitution. He thought back to this morning. Ever since he'd woken up he'd had a terrible time. *I mean, that Mikoto Misaka was calling herself my little sister and...* "—Hey, wait a minute. That's weird. She was saying she was my little sister. But I don't have a little sister in the first place."

Even if this absurd "substitution panic" situation were real (which was extremely doubtful in itself), he never had a sister to begin with, so Mikoto substituting in for one would be strange.

But then Kanzaki replied nonchalantly, "Who knows? However, since she is in actuality substituted, there would have needed to be a seat for her to begin with. Couldn't it be that you have a little sister somewhere in the world and didn't know about it?"

"Eh?! What kind of place is this to unearth some kind of family tree mystery?!"

Kamijou was in shock at this. However, the fact that he said something like that in such a carefree way could be viewed as evidence that he didn't really believe it in the first place.

"But, man, what could our enemy be thinking, pulling some crazy stunt like this, nya?"

"There are two main groups we can separate predicted reasons into. One is to capture an angel fallen to the rank of human and place a collar on it to use as a familiar. Or perhaps they plan to usurp the now-empty heavenly rank."

"Either way, if it succeeds, the Kabbalah world will be in an uproar. Stella Matutina would go mad."

"Angelic power…With it, one would have enough power to destroy the Vatican alone, depending on how they used it. I certainly cannot think they carried this out to show off or on a whim. They may have some kind of overzealous plans."

"Umm…" Kamijou, left behind, timidly tried to ask a question. "I'd like to get back to the topic. So, what will happen to me now? What did you want from me? You came all this way, after all."

"Ah, right, that, nya," answered Tsuchimikado in a tone that suggested it wasn't important at all. "Like we mentioned before, when we investigated this event, we found that in every way, the 'distortions' had their epicenter right on you, Kammy. It's spreading out from you, nya. But despite that, for some reason, you stand at the center, alone and unharmed."

"…Yes?"

Kamijou's pupils became tiny dots.

"So obviously we'd suspect you, Kammy! I mean, look at computer hackers spreading viruses throughout the world. Their own computer would be the one thing they wouldn't infect with it."

"Yes? Hey, wait a minute. You say that, but you two haven't changed at all, either!"

"In all fairness, Kanzaki and I got lucky. I told you that Angel Fall is centered on you and is emanating out. However, Zaky and I were both in London at the time the magic was activated, nyaa~."

"…So what. Europeans are fine?"

"Not at all. Angel Fall isn't that nice. We were attending Windsor Castle. It's got a fortress-level barrier about as strong as that white Walking Church or higher than that. Other than us, it looks like people in Westminster Abbey and the Southwark Cathedral made it out better than we did." He grinned. "Well, it's the *distance* and the *barrier*. With both of them, we avoided the beginning difficulties. Most sorcerers were engulfed by Angel Fall. Only a very select handful even realizes something has happened."

"Huh. I don't really get it, but in other words, I guess it was a blessing in disguise."

"Well, maybe not. Sis here aside, I wasn't in the deepest levels. As the outer wall of the castle was holding off Angel Fall for around three hundred seconds, I somehow got up a barrier."

"…? Huh? But I thought you couldn't use magic."

Kamijou still didn't really have a realistic grasp on this whole magic thing.

However, the very moment the student espers in Misawa School being manipulated by the alchemist used magic, it would cause their bodies to explode like a strong allergic reaction. Espers cannot use magic.

Then, as if reading Kamijou's intentions, Tsuchimikado pulled up the ends of his mouth and told him…

"Yeah, well, I'm pretty wrecked in places you can't see, you know? If I use magic one more time, I'll die for sure!"

The wind teased the front of Tsuchimikado's Hawaiian shirt.

Within its fluttering, expanding shape, there were dark blue bruises covering his left side caused by internal bleeding. It looked as if some unknown *thing* were corroding his body.

"Well, I did all of that, but I still couldn't avoid Angel Fall entirely!" Still, he laughed. "We're all exceptions here. When others see me, I do look substituted. Incidentally, people think I'm the idol Hajime Hitotsui. Apparently a magazine disclosed him making a move on some famous actress, so I'm in the middle of quite a pleasant vicarious life experience. Whenever my eyes meet with a passionate dreaming lady idol fan, I get chased all over the place with a metal baseball bat.

"Check it out, I'm in disguise," he added, indicating his sunglasses with a finger.

"So, in other words…" Kamijou looked at him once again. "When substituted people look at you, they see the face of a super-sexy idol?"

"Yep, that's about it, nya~," he replied, boundlessly jovial.

"The hell?! I'm going through all this trouble, but what, are you just enjoying the popularity?!"

"Kuh. This is a pretty harsh life, you know, nya~. We've gotta settle things with Angel Fall as soon as we can, but if a mountain of people cluster around me, I don't stand a chance, nya~."

"...I guess you have *some* professionalism," Kamijou muttered, looking back at Kanzaki. "Umm, so let me get this straight. This lady here looks like someone else when a substituted person sees her, too?"

"..." Kanzaki, who had been silent until now, gave a slight twitch of her shoulders.

What? Did I accidentally hit a nerve that I shouldn't have touched? he thought uneasily.

"......————gnus."

"Huh?"

Kamijou's eyes became pinpoints, and Kanzaki explained in a resolved monotone:

"I appear as the sorcerer Stiyl Magnus. Yes, apparently when people see me, they see a two-meter-tall, long red-haired man. So I get the police called on me whenever I so much as step inside a bathroom or changing room; I get mislabeled as a molester every time a train so much as wobbles; yes, it was extremely surprising; at first it looked like the entire world was trying to pick a fight with me, so I didn't have any idea what to do."

Human emotions can be better understood through the presence or absence of facial expressions and the strength or weakness of their tone of voice. *Then what is this?!* wondered Kamijou. He never thought a flat voice and an impassive face could be this scary.

It was clear to him.

This lady was, for some reason, absolutely livid.

Maintaining her cool, puppetlike expression, Kanzaki shot her hands up to grab Kamijou's shoulders. "By the way, you really aren't doing anything, right? You really haven't done anything, right? Just confess honestly; I won't be mad. Handing an angel over to a sorcerer is unprecedented. Do you understand the extent of the danger implied by that? I am done with this. I would like to resolve this right now. I am telling you that it is *difficult* to endure being called a 'giant Englishman walking with an oddly girlish gait' by people passing by."

"Ughghgh! D-do-do-do-do-do-do-don't shake me around like that!"

Kanzaki didn't move so much as an eyebrow as she used an inhuman strength to jerk him back and forth pretty hard. His sense of self-preservation politely informed him that this could be all it took to snap his neck.

"Anyway, Kammy, you're here in the middle of the distortion. You're pretty much the criminal in the minds of the sorcerers throughout the world who escaped hardship. They want you dead or, well, dead. You catch my drift?"

"Quit acting so carefree and get this shaking demon offa me!!" he shouted, rapidly growing sick to his stomach. "Uugh...! W-wait, Angel Fall is sorcery, right?! Then how could an esper like me be using it?!"

Kanzaki's hands stopped abruptly.

She stared into his eyes for a moment, frozen. Then her face gradually turned into a worried scowl, like ice melting inside a glass.

"Then we are up a river without a paddle. We do not know what the criminal is trying to use the angel for, and yet we must check Angel Fall's progress as soon as possible. Must I go on living the rest of my life as a 'giant Englishman fluent in Japanese except he talks like a girl...'?"

Urk. He hadn't done anything wrong, but nonetheless, Kamijou couldn't help but feel a guilt-like sentiment for some reason.

What could this be? This sensation, where I feel like I'm seeing the weak, unexpected tears of the usually perfect-acting girl next door? Something's telling me she's different from a full-on caretaking girl like Index.

"Now, now. This only means we have to start over from square one," soothed Tsuchimikado in a catlike voice, perhaps harboring the same kind of feelings.

"...Now that I think of it—" noted Kanzaki, looking at him, "—Tsuchimikado, you used magic even though you are an esper, right? Then..."

Her voice, despite its quietness, froze his spine. Kamijou replied in a panic, "Wait, wait, wait just a minute! I don't even know the *M* in magic!!"

"Yes. However, you have Index by your side, do you not?"

"Oh, that's right," Tsuchimikado responded in an easygoing way, with a bit of admiration thrown in. He sent a stabbing glare at Kamijou. Then, with a somehow insincere smile, he followed up. "But Zaky, when an esper uses magic, somewhere on their body must overload. Internal bleeding if it's minor and visible destruction of the body's makeup if it's major—it was written in the Misawa battle report, too. See? Kammy seems totally healthy, doesn't he, nya~?"

"Hmm. Then I will check and make sure."

No sooner had she said that than she casually reached her hands out and lightly touched Kamijou's sides.

"Eehihaah! Wh-what are you doing?!"

"Why did you jump? I am only confirming the presence of internal bleeding via palpation. However, you did respond in an overly nervous manner. As I thought. Is there not some wound within your body I just cannot see?"

"A high school kid would jump at that by default! That's how we're built, so don't touch me!"

"Suspicious indeed. Are you afraid of being examined? If you are innocent, then you should not care about any kind of questioning, correct?"

Kamijou looked back over at the seashore. He would definitely not want Index and the others seeing him be tickled to death by an older lady. He'd never be able to get off the ground again if such a thing were witnessed.

"...(If he refuses, it'll imply he's the criminal right there, eh? I suppose I should have expected it from one of Necessarius's Inquisitors, nya~.)"

Tsuchimikado, who had knowledge of the inner workings of the occult world, was impressed, but Kamijou of course had no inkling of those house rules.

"Guh…kuh…fine, okay? In exchange, if you don't find any wounds or internal bleeding, you'll let me off the hook for real this time— Hey, owaoah! D-don't touch me so weirdly!"

"??? Just hold still."

Kanzaki's long, slender fingers ran slowly across his chest and armpits. Despite her icy impression, her touch was gentle and warm. Perhaps it was because some sort of emergency sweat breaking out on his body was wetting her fingertips—he was attacked by an extremely unfamiliar sensation, like a small tongue was licking his body.

Hey, wa…! Bad, whoaa! At this rate…at this rate, my summer will awaken some kind of perverted hobbies within me!

"…" Then, after Kanzaki's hands had examined him all over, they suddenly stopped.

Her gaze turned down.

She silently focused on Touma Kamijou's swim trunks.

Umm. Well, various places on the healthy high school student Touma Kamijou's body were unconsciously reacting to Kaori Kanzaki's completely unreserved physical exam, you see. And, you see, the epicenter of these reactions was, of course, inside his bathing suit.

"W-wait a minute, Kanzaki! It was inevitable! This was an inevitable accident! An accident! I'm sorry, I really do apologize, so please spare me the katana!" shouted the startled Kamijou frantically. However, it seemed Kanzaki was thinking about something else.

For a few seconds, her hands stayed still as a statue, and finally she said one thing.

"…You are right. If I am going to do this, I should do so aggressively. I must examine inside here as well."

"The fu— Who the hell would let you do that?! Ah, but if I tell her not to do it, then I'll be treated as a criminal! But no shit, I don't want her to do it! Can't a healthy young man get in one word of objection here?!"

"Hmm." Kanzaki raised her eyes from his trunks. "I see. I was somewhat impertinent as well. It would be obvious that you would feel pain when examined that far by someone of the opposite sex."

"Y-yeah, that's right! Yeah, see? When we talk things out calmly, we can come to an understanding!"

"Therefore, I will leave this in Tsuchimikado's hands, as he is of the same sex."

"Wha———! By Tsuchimikado? Touching me like you did?? Inside my bathing suit??? N-no way! That's even worse than before!!"

"I see. Then, I will carry it out after all."

"Well, no. This isn't one of those things where A is bad so B is okay. I mean, aren't there any choices besides A and B?! Uh, excuse me, Kanzaki? What are those thin rubber surgical gloves for— Hey, wait! Wait, ah————————???!!!"

Option C. He brandished the toy shovel in the air and shouted in rage that he would kill them.

The angered, half-crying Kamijou distanced himself from his suspicious neighbor and the katana lady. Holding down and protecting his swim trunks for dear life, he looked at Tsuchimikado and Kanzaki like a wounded animal.

There stood a pair of sorcerers who had gotten a little uncomfortable to be around.

"S-see, it's like I said after all, isn't it, nya~? Kammy didn't get substituted because he's the criminal, it's just because his Imagine Breaker canceled out the effects of Angel Fall."

"Hmm. That is problematic. This means we really are up the river without any paddles. If Angel Fall is completed, there is a possibility for a calamity of mythical proportions to befall us...If only we had some clues."

"Oh, but we do. At the very least, Angel Fall *is* happening around Kammy, you know? There's a high probability the criminal is someone close to him, nya~."

"Even still, it is not a requirement that the criminal come into contact with Touma Kamijou."

"What a conundrum, eh? There's always the bit about if I use magic one more time, my coronary artery will rupture and I'll die. Oh, that's right! What about putting Kammy to work in my place?"

"What are you talking about? That's ridiculous. You would make residents construct a house for lack of carpenters?"

"Huh, but still. We can protect Kammy from the criminal, and we can have Kammy come with us when we go to destroy the ritual site where the magic circle is. I think it's a wonderful give-and-take deal, you know, nya~? What do you think of that, Kammy?"

No response.

Kamijou just continued to draw in the sand, with his index finger, the words I'LL SUE YOU.

2

At eight PM, the summer night finally arrived.

The members of the Kamijou family—well, all the weirdo *substituted* members, anyway—were all sitting around a circular table on the first floor of the beach house.

Among these weirdo members was Kaori Kanzaki, here as Kamijou's friend, quite naturally taking her seat at the table. Though, of course, she apparently looked to others like an "unkempt, red-haired Englishman punk friend."

He didn't know whether they should be leaving Angel Fall aside when they weren't even sure when it would be completed, but as long as all the commotion was centered on him, Kanzaki seemed to want to be his personal bodyguard, too.

Parenthetically, Tsuchimikado wasn't here. Maybe he was out playing with the wharf roaches behind the tetrapods or something—he *did* appear to the world as a problematic male idol, after all. It didn't seem to be his forte as a professional spy to let a mountain of people besiege him and make it difficult to move.

One way or another, there was a bunch of real characters at the table (on the surface, anyway).

He wanted to get dinner over with quickly, but for some reason the shopkeeper was nowhere in sight.

Melancholy news stories were being read off in Miss Komoe's voice, like a death-row prisoner named Jinsaku Hino or something having broken out and yet to be found. They were the only things on TV, so that wouldn't make for good conversation, either.

Without a particular topic to broach one way or another, Touya addressed Kanzaki. "It's nice to meet you. I'm Touma's father. To think we live in an age where Touma can be friends with foreigners—internationalization definitely at work! Oh, as a symbol of our acquaintanceship, here, have this Egyptian protective souvenir. It's a scarab. They said something about never losing your way with it, even in a desert!"

Touya brought out a container about the size of a saltshaker, and Kamijou looked at it aghast and shouted.

There was some kind of clattering, dry bug inside it.

"Wait, that's a dung beetle in there, isn't it?! Don't take stuff like that out at the dinner table, stupid!!"

"No, not at all." Kanzaki, however, replied coolly. "In Egypt, scarabs are depicted as a 'spiral image'—a symbol of samsara. I have heard that it is a favored souvenir from the country, along with the Eye of Horus and ankhs."

"??? O-oh, by the way, Touma. Though I don't understand the specifics one bit, you still shouldn't reject other cultures just out of your own prejudices."

"Wha...? Why only me?! Am I the only one who thinks taking out a dried-up dung beetle corpse at the dinner table isn't okay?!"

Kamijou slumped down in shock. Mikoto, next to him, pulled on his clothes a couple of times.

"...No, you're right! I'd be scared if someone used something like that as a cell phone charm. It would clatter around when you have your phone on silent!"

"I would *like* to thank you for your decent comment, but that flattering voice you keep giving me is forever a pain in the ass."

"What?!" retorted Mikoto with indignation. Kamijou smoothly ignored her.

Then, he suddenly thought of something.

There was no little sister in his family. Who did that Mikoto look like to everyone else?

He moved his seat over to Index, playing the part of his mother, and whispered...

"(Hey, can I ask you something? This has been bothering me. Who the heck is this little sister character?)"

"Oh my, my. Is the little sister character a little too straightforward for you, Touma?"

Kamijou gave her a light smack on the head, considering his mother's bugged-out thought processes ought to be fixed. It was the sort of smack you might give a broken TV.

"My, that one was a bit lacking in compassion. She's your little cousin, Otohime."

"(...Cous—?)"

"My, oh my, Touma, have you forgotten? Did you forget about your aunt and uncle Tatsugami, too? You haven't seen them since coming to Academy City right after you graduated from kindergarten, but still, my, my. You used to sleep on the same futon as Otohime, too."

"B-but she wasn't here yesterday."

"She came late and got here this morning, remember?"

Meanwhile, heavy footsteps came thudding through the house and the shopkeeper arrived through the entrance facing the sea.

"Hey, sorry for leavin' the shop open like that. The cable broadcast on the beach broke, and fixing it ate up a lot of time."

Kanzaki, the closest to him, turned around at the voice and said, "Do not worry about it. It's likely in place for tsunami information and disaster relief. People's lives depend on it, so it should be prioriti— Wait, Stiyl? Wha...? That's impossible!"

"Stiyl? That some kind've new lingo?" The large man with the long red hair looked confused. "Havin' dinner, I see. The menu ain't much, but we can have it ready for you at light speed, so let us off the hook, eh?"

"I mean, er...(Gah, how careless of me. Stiyl had been here in Japan hunting for some time.)"

It seemed that Stiyl was completely and totally under the effects of Angel Fall. It was more than likely that *most* sorcerers were in the same situation and that those like Tsuchimikado and Kanzaki who had noticed something was wrong were in the minority.

Kanzaki grumbled something to herself, but nobody noticed. Everyone went on deciding what they'd get from the menu, which contained only ramen, yakisoba, and curry.

The footsteps thudded away again into the back after the giant shopkeeper took orders, and Index put her hand on her cheek and looked at Kanzaki.

"My, oh my. You sure are skilled at Japanese. I'm beside myself in admiration!"

"Eh?" Kanzaki's shoulders twitched for a moment. "Oh no. Yes. Please, don't worry yourself over it."

While Kanzaki was someone from English Puritanism like Index, a certain incident had caused them to break off relations, so she wasn't sure how to deal with her addressing her so suddenly.

However, nobody knew about her circumstances (including Kamijou, who had lost his memories).

"My, oh my. And your demeanor is so polite, too. You have **such a large and firm build**, so I must admit I had a different impression of you at first."

Twitch. Kanzaki's shoulders moved slightly. She was taller than the average Japanese person.

Nobody around noticed, though. This time, Mikoto said something.

"But you've got the nuance a little wrong in your word choice, though. I mean, those are words girls use! You have **such a sturdy body**, so you've gotta fix your talking to sound more manly. You're acting **just a little** girlie, you know?"

Twitch-twitch. Kanzaki's cheek muscles pulled back slightly. She was more sturdily built than an average girl.

Oops, that's bad, thought Kamijou, catching on to something. Before he could do anything, Touya continued.

"Hey, now, give it a rest, you two. In language, all that matters is that the proper meanings come across. He probably just speaks this way because a Japanese woman taught him. **His looks are one thing, but they're not important.**"

Twitch-twitch! Various places on Kanzaki's body were trembling.

Kamijou frantically covered for her using body language.

"(Miss Kanzaki! Miss Kanzaki! That's not it! Everyone sees you as Stiyl Magnus, that's all! So they're not saying your body is large, or that you have a good build, or that you're a guy no matter how you look at it, or anything————!!)"

That moment, Kanzaki wobbled up to her feet.

She grabbed Kamijou's collar, who didn't realize he was saying the worst thing of all.

"… (Oh. I get it. So that is your opinion. I see.)"

As she whispered in his ear, she dragged him across the floor and away from the round table.

"(Hey, wait…Where are we going?! Are you going to strangle me? Wait, that way is the bath…Wait! I've heard stories about an old form of torture in U.S. prisons where they give you a steady cold-water shower and take away your body temperature; is that what this is?!)"

No response.

She dragged Kamijou on like a body bag.

3

When he asked where they were going, her answer was the back of the shop.

It didn't seem like Kanzaki had a destination in mind as she dragged Kamijou there, complaining and objecting to him the whole time. After getting to a place away from the eyes of others for the moment, Kanzaki suddenly seemed to discover the frosted glass sliding door nearby.

"Now that I think of it, this beach house has a bathroom, doesn't it? I find it hard to admit, but with all the trouble that has been going on, I haven't been able to take an actual shower."

Yes, the beach house had a bathroom. It was for the same purpose as the simple showers built on the beach—to wash the saltwater off one's skin.

Kamijou slightly turned back to where they came from. "But a bath...You're pretty laid-back about this. What about Angel Fall? I thought you said there wouldn't be any going back if that thing gets finished."

"Yes, well..." She hesitated at something there. "...I understand that personal feelings don't enter into this situation, but I can't do it. I simply cannot get used to that girl smiling at me. I haven't the right."

Said she, as if reflecting on something.

Said she, averting her eyes from something.

"..." He fell silent. Back when they had invaded the alchemist's fortress, Misawa Cram School, Stiyl, too, had made that kind of face when speaking about Index.

It was probably a deep wound, and one he shouldn't dig up.

Kamijou decided to therefore not say any more.

"Hmm. So why did you drag me to the baths? Is this a strategy meeting for what to do from here on out?"

"..." She lightly shook her head. "No, the favor I'd like to ask of you is, frankly, to keep a lookout. That bath is for communal use, like hot springs and bathhouses are, right?"

"Mm." He stopped again.

In such a small beach house, there was no distinction between a men's bath and a women's bath—there was only one bathroom.

Kanzaki looked to everyone else like Stiyl Magnus. Therefore, even if someone were to know from a silhouette that she was on the other side of the frosted glass, they'd think, *Oh, a guy is in there*, and there was a possibility that other guys wouldn't hesitate to barge on in. Yes—for example, the guy running the beach house.

"...I am sure you did not just think it seemed fun, correct?"

"Don't be absurd! Not a hair on my head is planning to make any jokes to a Japanese katana when my life is on the line, ma'am!"

After giving him a slightly dubious glance, she left him with a "Then I'll leave it to you," and entered the changing room beyond the frosted glass.

Even through it, one could see a silhouette. The half-baked silhouette was actually more vivid than the real thing would have been. *Whoa, whoa,* thought Kamijou, turning his head around. He rested his back against the frosted glass door and sighed.

"Heya, Kammy. Whatcha doin' here?"

Suddenly Tsuchimikado came walking right down the hallway. He didn't seem to want to take off his blue sunglasses, whether he was inside or it was night out, to keep his disguise.

"Wait, don't people see you as an asshole idol in a lot of trouble?"

"What? As long as I'm not found out, I'm fine. I mean, that's good ol' Tsuchimikado's fundamental motto," he answered, the same as always.

Kamijou saw everything about him the same as always.

"...Sorry, Kammy."

"About what?" he asked. Tsuchimikado showed him a slightly lonely grin.

"I've actually known that you've been in a lot of trouble until now, like with the alchemist's stronghold or with the twenty thousand doll-murdering experiment. All sorts of stuff. I knew about it and let you alone, without helping. So I'm saying sorry, nya~."

"..."

"I guess there's a huge difference between not being able to do anything because you have no power and not doing anything even though you have power. I may look like this, but I'm actually pretty sorry for a bunch of stuff."

"Hey, it's whatever."

Tsuchimikado looked somehow tired, but Kamijou replied in exactly the way he always would.

Tsuchimikado looked a little bit surprised, but Kamijou didn't say anything else. He didn't think there was a need to get all panicked and explain something to try and keep up appearances.

However "far" Tsuchimikado went, he was still Tsuchimikado, and that wouldn't change. In the end, to Kamijou, he was still the same dorm neighbor and classmate as always.

"I see." He grinned. "Well, then let's quit it with this gloomy appetizer, nya~. Let's get to the main course."

"Main course?"

"Ta-daa! It's the summertime, heart-pounding Kanzaki clothes-changing peeking event!"

"Wh...? Are you insane?!"

"...Look here, Kammy. Lately cell phones have been shipping with cameras in 'em."

"Listen to me! Wait, that's terrible! That Bakumatsu swordsman romanticist absolutely hates jokes! If you get caught, she'll definitely cut you in half with some kind of secret technique passed down from her master or something!"

"...How paradoxical. So you'd peek on her if there was no risk, nya~?"

"..."

"...Kanzaki's probably pretty amazing naked, you know."

Ama—?! Kamijou caught his breath but shook his head hurriedly. "B-but...we can't! Besides, you're Kanzaki's comrade, aren't you? You can't betray her like that!" he cried desperately. However, Tsuchimikado's blue sunglasses lit up.

"Hah, what is this man saying? When the Church of English Puritanism talks about the Necessarius's infiltration expert, when they refer to the 'backstabbing blade' or the 'villager from the village of liars,' they're talking about me, Tsuchimikado!"

"Whoa! Remind me not to cross any dangerous-looking bridges with you!" While Kamijou stubbornly maintained his stance of denial, Tsuchimikado said in a bored tone:

"Pfft, you're so boring. Well, you did almost get killed by her one time, so I guess there's no helping you being a scaredy-cat. Zaky isn't a scary girl, you know. She's actually pretty cute."

"C-cu...?"

"Yeppers. As you know, I came to Academy City after entering middle school. So before that, I was in London, nya~. At the time, I was one of only a few who could speak both English and Japanese, see? Then Zaky, a Japanese native, arrives at the Church. So whenever an English person would start rattling on about something or other, she'd have to resort to all this crazy body language, and man!" Tsuchimikado hit the wall lightly. "Back then I was the only Japanese person in Necessarius. When Zaky would come to me all worried, looking for help, with an English textbook in her hands, wow, did she score high with me."

"…I can't believe it. I can't believe there would be a situation where someone'd rely on you."

"Stop worryin' about it already, and let's get to the peeking. ♪ Let's go get that cute lady!"

"I told you, don't use your cell-phone camera!"

"Kammy, you should be more honest with yourself, you know?"

"Why are you totally willing to do this?! Besides, I thought your fielding range was a lot smaller and younger, Sergeant Sister-Complex!"

"You take that back! Do not call me by that name! Besides, what grounds do you have for saying that?!"

"Well, loving a real stepsister like that isn't normal, stupid!"

"Bghah! I'm not *in love* (please note the difference) with her; who said anything like that, nya~?!"

"I mean, it's not like you can *do anything* just because it's legal, right?"

"Do?! D-d-d-d-d-d-d-do, do what? Do what?!"

"What was that? Why are you so agitated? Hold on a second. Tsuchimikado, I was just joking, but could you be for real…?!"

"Stop it, don't pry any further, one more word out of you and I'll kill you and put you on display!!"

Tsuchimikado was forcefully pulling on Kamijou's collar to get him to be quiet, but the moment they heard a new *step-step* in the planked hallway, Tsuchimikado darted from shadow to shadow like a ninja and disappeared somewhere.

Ah, I guess if someone were to see that situation, they'd have perfect pictures for an article about a performer grabbing a boy's collar, huh?

As he thought about it in a relatively calm way, he turned around to where the footfalls emanated.

"Hey, 'sup, big brother! Whatcha doin' here?"

It was Index and Mikoto.

Or should he switch that to "my mother and cousin walked toward me"?

"Huh? Wait, are you already done with dinner?"

"My, oh my. Not at all, Touma. It seems that it'll be a little bit until things are cooked, so we just thought we'd come take a bath in the meantime."

Then, Mikoto turned her eyes to the frosted glass door and said, "...Big brother, is there somebody in there?"

"Ah, well, yeah. I'm here on lookout duty."

"Lookout? I don't get it. You don't need something like that. It's probably just your friend in there anyway. So you should go in there with him."

"Eh?" Kamijou was without a clue what to say back.

It easily took five full seconds for the meaning of those words to fully sink into his mind.

Oh, that's right, **Kaori Kanzaki looks like Stiyl Magnus to other people***.*

"W-wait, hold on! I didn't say anyone was in the bath! In addition, there is no rule stating that I must take a bath with my friends! It'll be okay if I just wait for him to get out—!!"

"Ehh? If we start waiting for every single person, dinner will be ready in the meantime. **You're both boys, so get in there!**"

"Nabhah?! Hey, wait! Wait, seriously, wai—— AAAAHH!!"

"Yeah, yeah, sorry, sorry!"

They unhesitatingly threw open the sliding door and mercilessly threw Touma Kamijou into the changing room.

There,

before his eyes,

Kanzaki was standing there in such a way unbefitting of description in prose.

Had she been the type to take long baths, this tragedy likely wouldn't have happened with this timing. There was a second door barring the way to the bathroom on the other side of the changing room, after all.

But it seemed that Kanzaki had just gotten out of the bath. There was nothing in particular on her body; her hands were, anyway, around the back of her head to tie her wet hair. As she stood there with her ponytail string in her mouth, it seemed like time had stopped for her.

Directly behind Kamijou, the sliding door slammed shut.

"..."

"..."

A silent, heavy pressure fell over the secret room. If she broke out in tears or flew into a rage, Kamijou would have also been able to offer several different reactions, but there was not a shard of an expression on her face at all, nor was she concealing anything. All she did was reach her hand, swaying, toward the long black sheath standing up against the wall.

Her eyes, however, spoke volumes. Her eyes, sparkling black like obsidian, were speaking for her.

They asked him: *Do you have any last words?*

"Ne—"

Kamijou figured an apology or excuse would doubtlessly send him to the grave. His mind now in a state of extreme chaos, he cried without thinking:

"New, sensational katana-thrusting action?!"

Directly after came a single, unremitting glint from the black sheath.

4

Ten o'clock PM.

Kanzaki was standing on the beach house's second-floor balcony. Despite it being the middle of summer, it was a fairly chilly night, perhaps because the sandy beach has difficulty retaining heat during the nighttime, like in a desert.

Then Tsuchimikado arrived, having wriggled his way up one of the balcony's support pillars. Because everyone around him would see an oft-talked-about performer, he couldn't adopt a normal route to get there.

He looked at the quiet Kanzaki, her hair being whipped by the night wind, and asked, "What's wrong, nya~? Your face is all red. Still bothered by it, nya~?"

"...It would be strange if I wasn't."

"Ack. Smokin' hot body *and* happy you got seen—that was a joke, okay? Zaky, you seem pretty quick to anger despite all the responsibilities that come with wearing a sword at your side, you know?"

Kanzaki replied with a dismissive "I understand that" and, heaving just one sigh, continued, "However, well...It certainly seems he hasn't much to do with Angel Fall. How do I put it? He doesn't have the proper personality to be a sorcerer."

"And he doesn't have a motive for putting this in motion, either, nya~. Ditto for everyone around Kammy, too, though, eh? Even if one of them *was* able to capture an angel alive, I can't see them knowing how to use it."

They weren't looking down their noses at them or anything. It was a simple matter of differing classifications. An angel, possessing vast power indeed (supposedly, anyway), would be as pearls before swine if the holder were to harness one without knowing anything about sorcery. It's very much like saying Japanese appliances are excellent, but they can't be used overseas because the outlets are different. The outlets certainly aren't a determining factor in which of them was "superior."

Unfortunately, when it came right down to it, they had no other potential suspects.

They didn't know what steps should be taken next.

Their indecisive line of thought was at a standstill, and the topic slid to something else before they knew it.

"At any rate, I wonder if it is really all right to leave Touma Kamijou at *her* side. In a day—no, in just half a day—we've already had that unexpected situation. In this age not even an eight-year-old would laugh at charging into the women's bath. There might be a situation occurring between the two of them that is also unexpected, maybe even more so..."

"Hmm. I think Kammy is doing his best, though. I mean, he's not the type to go charging in on someone sleeping." Tsuchimikado folded his arms. "For certain, he's no professional. You understand? He's not a professional. He has a reason to fight, like we do, and he doesn't try and falsify the sin of killing an enemy. He doesn't place his own blame on anybody else. He accepts it, and still he advances toward you. Can't you see the value in that, nya~?"

"...Well, that is..."

"In the first place, Kammy is the one who saved the archive's life. You're getting furious at him, to say nothing of the fact you haven't thanked him. Seems to me like you're barking up the wrong tree."

"I understand that much, at least. I do."

Yes—it was Touma Kamijou who once saved Index's life as she was on the verge of death.

It was not Kaori Kanzaki, nor was it Stiyl Magnus—it was Touma Kamijou.

By all rights, it was an act worthy of gratitude. No, simple words of thanks would be too petty. The logical thing to do would be to repay the debt with an equal act by her own action. Even cranes and turtles can repay their obligations, after all.

"...However, well. The timing is just so poor."

Admittedly, although it had been difficult because of her job and position, she hadn't been able to properly thank him ever since the Index incident had been resolved. It was enough for Kanzaki to feel a sense of indebtedness.

"And despite that, right as I was about to...My word, I can't even bring up the suggestion of having to repay the debt—"

"What? Kanzaki, you'd forget your debts just because he saw you naked, nya~?"

Kanzaki grunted and fell silent.

"Wait, what? Kanzaki, is that all the debt you carry *counts* for, nya~?"

Kanzaki groaned and looked at Tsuchimikado, biting down on her teeth.

At around that time, Touma Kamijou was alone on the first floor of the beach house Wadatsumi, getting some thinking done.

The lights were on, but no one was here anymore. From what he could hear of the girlish laughter coming from upstairs, Index and the others might be playing cards or something up there.

The nightly news was streaming by on the TV, which was still on. Nightly news is basically just a rerun of daytime news with some needlessly detailed sentences thrown in to pad it out.

"The inmate who broke out of Shinfuchuu prison, Jinsaku Hino, has still not been located. Hino has spawned many enthusiasts and copycats because of his unique, ritualistic killing style, and the police have reported that it is possible they were involved in the breakout as well..."

Kamijou stared lazily at Miss Komoe, reading off the script on the other side of the CRT screen.

"...In addition, there are records of Jinsaku Hino's stay at a mental hospital, and even during the last hearing, they judged him to have multiple personality disorder. The question of whether or not he should be held accountable created much uproar, but..."

Jinsaku Hino.

Without any memories, he didn't know anything about the time when the murderer was actually active. However, his name tended to get dropped whenever any kind of atrocious incident happened. Talk shows and magazines would still occasionally show a mug shot, too, so he could guess that what the murderer had done had been proportionately shocking.

Watching this wasn't doing much for his mood, so he changed the channel. As he stared at a variety show introducing surprising weight-loss methods hidden in health foods, his mind clung to the news he had just seen.

Split personality, huh? Part of my summer makeup lessons was on this, wasn't it? Something about split personality espers or something.

Kamijou thought about it, still watching the television with glazed eyes. Even if the term *multiple personality disorder* sounds fairly specific, it doesn't always manifest itself in a situation where personality A and personality B would cleanly swap out. Other patterns of "coexistence" have been reported, such as a different personality controlling each hand, or personality B moving both hands while personality A was busy thinking.

—And that was all something he'd learned during the summer classes he'd taken about a week ago. He'd heard that for a while, there was research being performed regarding whether someone with multiple personalities would have multiple abilities. *There is a wealth of data regarding things of this nature!* went Miss Komoe's explanation.

"...Blech." He dropped his head to the table, remembering how much he hated his studies.

There sure has been a lot that's happened today, he thought, mentally organizing everything that had happened thus far.

A sorcery called Angel Fall had activated.

It was apparently a technique through which one could obtain an angel possessing enormous power.

As a side effect, everyone in the world had swapped outside appearances.

Its effective range was large enough to cover the whole world.

Angel Fall was in an incomplete, temporarily active state, and the commotion might still be fixable.

However, he was given to think that when Angel Fall completed, there would be no repairing it.

In order to stop Angel Fall, they apparently either needed to take down the practitioner or destroy the ritual site.

The distortion's epicenter was apparently Kamijou, and it seemed he was being mistaken for said practitioner.

Because of that, the handful of sorcerers who understood Kamijou's situation might come for his life.

Therefore, Kamijou needed to uncover the true criminal before Angel Fall was completed, and either take down the practitioner or disrupt the magic circle at the ritual site.

"...Hmm."

Kamijou, still flopped down on the table, considered it alone.

It was quite a defenseless act for somebody whose life was under threat.

But still, there's not quite the same sense of tension, huh?

Yes—this time, he wasn't leaping into a building where the killer was hiding, like Misawa Cram School last time. He also wasn't trying to settle a situation as fast as he could lest twenty thousand people be killed. The problem occurring across the planet was certainly preposterous, but what was with the dumb, comical vibe he was getting from all of it?

And besides, there're two magic pros with me this time.

He still strongly saw Tsuchimikado as his neighbor, but the two of them were professionals of their trade (apparently). The fact that he had specialists on his side for some reason caused him to feel an unconditional sense of security.

In actuality, he, the amateur, was only shoving responsibility for the problem into the hands of Kanzaki and Tsuchimikado, the experts—he did not realize this, the small, small high school student that he was.

——The "watchful eyes" stared fixedly at that defenseless boy.

Those "watchful eyes" were hidden underneath the floor of the beach house Wadatsumi. In order to prevent sand and moisture from trespassing into the house, there were approximately seventy centimeters of empty space below the floorboards.

From between the tiny gaps between each board, the "watchful eyes" watched the boy.

"...My Angel, my precious Angel."

The mouth from which those words came belonged to an unhealthily skinny middle-aged man, and yet his voice was as high as a prepubescent boy.

"...Oh, my precious Angel. Please hear me."

Scritch-scratch. A faint sound, like a nail clawing at a wooden board.

These "watchful eyes" had, in reality, been driven into a corner. Even *he* didn't want to be hiding himself in a place like this. His actual plan had been to visit his former associates, but his movements had been restricted because the police had moved more quickly than he had anticipated.

"My Angel, please listen, my precious Angel."

However, on the face of those "watchful eyes," there was none of the unease, none of the terror that should have accompanied somebody on the lam.

In his right hand was an oddly shaped knife. In his left was a notebook-size wooden plank, upon which were many cuts.

Scritch-scratch. He gazed in jubilation as the knife's tip flew across the plank.

"My precious Angel. How can I hide from the police and arrive safely where my friends are?"

Scritch-scratch. The "watchful eyes" followed the fingertips of his right hand, which, as if in response to his voice, were moving of their own accord. All those cuts were engraved letters. It was a message from his Angel.

"My precious Angel, **again**? If I offer a sacrifice, I will be saved again?"

Scritch-scratch. The "watchful eyes" always obeyed the carved-out letters. *Angel is always correct. If I do as Angel says, I can't go wrong. Angel sometimes orders me to do things I don't want to do, though. I killed twenty-eight people because of it.*

"My precious Angel. Then would that boy make a good sacrifice?"

Scritch-scratch. Three letters carved out the word *YES*. The face of the "watchful eyes" clouded over. *Will I kill another? I don't want to. I don't, but…I suppose there is no choice, because that's what my precious Angel told me. It isn't my fault anyway.*

"My precious Angel. I will have faith in you this time as well."

So saying, the owner of the "watchful eyes" stuck out his fat, short tongue and slid it across the oddly shaped knife.

Then, the "watchful eyes," which belonged to the escaped death-row prisoner Jinsaku Hino, stabbed the knife into the thick electric cable running under the floorboards.

Click-bzt. Suddenly, all the power went out.

A blackout? Kamijou thought, frowning in the dark. The entrances to the beach house were wide open, so enough moonlight was shining inside to make it not pitch-black…

When the power goes out, perhaps you have a habit of unconsciously turning to look at the silenced appliances. Kamijou casually directed his eyes up to the fluorescent lamp on the ceiling that had abruptly lost its light—

—scratch.

He heard a sound from underneath the floor, beneath his feet, like something lightly scratching its wooden planks.

What's that? He stood up in spite of himself and immediately looked down at the floorboards underfoot—

—craaack! The blade of a crescent-shaped knife pierced up through the floor under his feet.

"…!!"

Kamijou's throat dried up. There was a knife sticking out of the tiny space between his two feet. If his attention had been on the dead lights above for just two more seconds…If he had ignored the noise and stayed sitting down…Just the thought of it caused a gross sweat to break out all over his skin.

A knife blade.

It was long and thin, the shape of a crescent moon, and about thirty centimeters long. However, the blade itself was not on the outside of the crescent but on the inside. It seemed more like a claw or a sickle rather than a knife.

Scritch-scritch. The blade wiggled back and forth a little, then finally, slowly, disappeared back underneath the floor.

Kamijou knew he needed to get out of here right away, but he couldn't move. The back of his head was sizzling like a suspicious drug had been poured into his veins. Shaking, his heart about to beat out of his chest, he stared in stupefaction at the hole in the floorboards created by the crescent knife.

Then he saw something.

From inside that slight hole in the floor…as if peering inside a room through a keyhole…down in that damp pit of darkness… bloodshot, muddied—

—eyes filled with madness.

"Hee…"

Kamijou let out a pathetic yelp and backed up. A moment later, as if following him, the knife stabbed up from the floor, just grazing past his foot. His feet tangled. He fell to the floor. The knife blade disappeared into the crawl space once again, taking aim for yet another strike.

Calm down, calm down!! he repeated like a mantra, but it only caused his body to lock up even worse. He tried to think; his head was numb. In any case, it was way too dangerous to fall on the floor. *I only need to jump up on the table to get away from the attacks coming from the floor.* So he thought, but as he tried to stand up—

—*Criick!!*

The floorboards burst open and an arm thrust upward, grabbing onto Kamijou's ankle.

"Hee…eee?!"

The strange shock caused Kamijou's heart to leap into his mouth.

He tried as hard as he could to move his leg, but he couldn't remove his ankle from the iron grip. It wasn't as if his foot were being held down by capstan-like, superhuman strength. It just wouldn't move for him, as if it were numb.

Calm down; don't panic. Don't be afraid. I don't know who this guy is, but he's not some unidentified being. Sticking a knife through the floor or punching through it with your fist is definitely not something impossible for a human to do, so calm dow—

—then, after he thought that far, he suddenly saw it.

The hand grabbing his ankle.

Some nails were split, some were torn off, and some were blotted by hardened black blood. The fingers were turned the bluish-brown indicating internal bleeding, and on the back of the hand, large dried-up scabs had been ripped open, exposing the mushy, flesh-covered black wound beneath.

It looked like a rotten fruit, covered with a translucent mucus.

It looked like the hand of a corpse, eaten away at by queer, human-devouring bacteria.

"Ah, wha—! Ee, hee, ah...!!"

His breath twisted within him. His heart moved in strange ways.

Each of his assailant's actions was, individually, well within the realm of possibility for humans. It wasn't anything to write home about compared to the "One-Way Road" Accelerator or the alchemist Aureolus. If he took a step away, he might even get a sense that the commotion, this confusion, wasn't worth his breathing difficulties and heartbeat irregularities.

But consider this example.

Say a person has a live cockroach inside a clear vinyl bag. Even though they know they won't be directly touching the cockroach because of the vinyl separation, would they be able to bite the bag and crush the cockroach inside with their teeth?

It was the same thing.

He knew all of these things logically, but this chill, this trembling—they weren't something he could deny.

His assailant used physiological revulsion and discomfort to bind his prey.

"Ha, ahi, a, egh, ugh…!"

Kamijou desperately worked his legs and attempted to pry his foot free from the assailant's arms. However, he couldn't put any strength into it. It was like it had been numbed with anesthetics. He couldn't get rid of the black revulsion that had seeped into his mind.

As he lay on the floor, his foot confined, he began to hear the *scritch-scratch* of a knife tip shaving away at a wooden board from the planks near his chest.

And then.

Another set of watchful eyes, lying flat on the dark, dark beach 150 meters away, observed the situation in the beach house Wadatsumi.

It was a red nun.

She was a girl, thirteen years old. Her long, wavy blond hair and white skin seemed to reflect the moonlight. Her appearance was cute, but everything on her body was out of the ordinary. She wore only an overcoat slung over the underclothing normally worn beneath a religious habit. It was, however, essentially one-piece underwear, even appearing to show off her delicate body lines. To add to that, there were black belts and metal fixtures in various places. It looked like something created to serve the same purpose as a straitjacket. To top it off, reins extended from her thick choker, and many things stuck out of the belt on her waist, such as metal pliers, a hammer, an L-shaped nail puller, and a saw.

They definitely weren't for crafting. They were torture instruments used in witch trials, meant to crush human flesh, grind human bones, and cleave human bodies. At a closer look, one could discern that they had slight modifications from the normal implements.

The girl was decorated with countless of the torture instruments, but her face was absolutely impassive.

Her head was down, so her bangs covered most of her face, but her small mouth, the only thing visible, gave a sigh.

She searched for signs of life.

There were multiple people present on the second floor of the beach house Wadatsumi. They seemed to have realized something was going on, but it would likely take six seconds for them to descend to the first floor.

Given that much time, the assailant under the floor would easily be able to pierce through the floor and through his victim's heart.

Beneath her face hidden by bangs, the girl sighed once more.

Slowly and dully, she rose.

Without any preparatory motions, her petite shadow closed the 150-meter distance in far less than six seconds.

Fifty meters per second.

Her speed was the same as a crossbow bolt, possibly even faster.

That moment...

With alarming speed, the sister in red burst into Kamijou's vision suddenly from the side.

She went so fast that he couldn't even see that it was a human girl.

The figure in red ran so low to the floor she could touch it with her tongue. She took out the L-shaped nail pullers on her waist and drove them with all her strength like a bat into his assailant's wrist, which was sticking out of the floor.

Crunch!

With an amazingly dull sound, the assailant's wrist twisted around in an unnatural direction.

It wasn't just broken. It was nearly torn asunder.

"Gi, bih! Gigah!!"

With a shout, the hand gripping Kamijou's ankle fled back under the floor. *Rustle-rustle.* He heard the sound of rubbing against wood, the noise of his assailant trying to move away.

"..." The nun in red tossed her nail pullers aside and removed her hammer this time. Then, she slammed it down hard into the floor underfoot. The wooden planks broke, making way for a large hole about seventy centimeters across.

The girl with the gently waving blond hair dropped the hammer, took her pliers, and leaped into the hole.

One second of silence, then...

A great *thump-thump* sound roared up from under the floor. Something was raging down there. It felt kind of like a beast stuck in a cramped cage struggling to break free.

Kamijou let the sounds of battle underneath him slip into his ears, dazed, but...

Crash! Suddenly, a floorboard five meters in front of him shot up into the air like a geyser. It jumped like a dolphin leaping above the water, and a black shadow burst out from underneath.

A black shadow.

It wasn't the sister in red.

It tumbled onto the floor, then rose—the shadow was a skinny, middle-aged man.

He could tell at a glance from his unhealthy skin that his organs were in a bad state. He wore beige work clothes stained with sweat, mud, blood, and oil. In his right hand was a crescent-shaped knife reminiscent of an iron claw. His left wrist was broken, his blood congested in blue. A line of redder blood hung from his lips. A front tooth and a canine had been pulled out of his mouth.

"Gebeh, gah!!"

The injured beast brandished the knife and attempted to fall on top of Kamijou, who was still sitting there.

Kuh...!!

Kamijou reflexively examined his surroundings, but there were no weapons in sight that could stop the blade. Backed into a corner, he dove into his pocket and there his fingertips touched upon something solid. He brought it out—it was his cell phone. He swore. It wouldn't be of any use against a knife...but then it hit him. After flipping open the phone with his thumb, he aimed its camera lens at the enemy figure running at him.

Pshee! went the camera's intense flash through the darkness.

"Bweeeh!!"

The crescent knife in the blinded man's hand stopped. Kamijou didn't waste any time trying to get away, but he couldn't get his leg to work. He managed to roll across the floor and put distance between him and his assailant.

The middle-aged man readied his knife but didn't follow up with an attack.

He swayed. His body relaxed and he muttered something to himself.

"My precious Angel..."

Something around the chest of the work uniform glinted in the moonlight.

It was a name tag.

"My Angel, my precious Angel!"

The plastic name tag, sewn firmly onto his clothing, had this written in inorganic letters:

Prisoner Number 7-0687, Jinsaku Hino

"My Angel, what's happening? My precious Angel, I listened to what you said, so you can't be wrong! What's going on, my precious Angel? **I've faithfully offered up twenty-eight to you!**" the man in the prisoner's clothes screamed. He screamed like he was broken, like he had gone mad, like it was all over.

At long last, Kamijou remembered the news being run the entire day.

"Yes, this is Komori at the scene. Jinsaku Hino, the convict on death row who broke out of the Shinfuchuu prison in the capital early this morning, has still not been located. There's a tense atmosphere here, as schools in the vicinity, such as the middle school, have issued an emergency cancellation on all club activities."

But...

He looked at the confused, screaming man. He could tell he was a criminal. And from the clothes he wore, he could figure out that he was Jinsaku Hino, broken out of prison.

But if that was the case, then why wasn't Jinsaku Hino swapped with somebody?

————It was so odd that not everyone had swapped because of Angel Fall.

And who is the "Angel" he's been yelling about this whole time?

————What was the Angel Fall sorcery ultimately trying to achieve?

This guy...Could he be...?

The moment he was about to forget himself and ask, Jinsaku Hino waved his knife in the air and screamed:

"Answer me, my precious Angel! What do I do? What should I do from now on?! My Angel, you'd better take responsibility for this! Answer meeeeeeeeeeeeeeeeeeeee!!"

He brought it down.

But not toward Kamijou. He stabbed his own chest with the crescent knife. *Scratch-scratch.* The blade's tip moved all over the place. The knife he was so absurdly wielding sliced through his work outfit, cut into his sweat-soaked shirt, and immediately began to draw blood.

At a glance, the countless wounds seemed random, but they were in the form of letters, like scribbles carved into a desk.

GO ESCAPE

There was no grammar to be seen, just two English terms next to each other. However, when Jinsaku Hino saw those words, his blood-covered face turned into a grand smile.

In the next moment, the floorboards between Kamijou and Hino shattered all over and the nun in red jumped out. The pliers she held in her hand were gripping something small and white. It looked like human teeth even. She gripped the pliers and smashed them to bits with ease.

Jinsaku Hino, who happened to be without his front teeth, took one step back, then another, without paying any mind to what the red sister had done. Then, he took out a moist leather cloth, wiped the blood from the blade, and hurled it at the nun.

The red sister smoothly moved her head out of the way to avoid it—so smoothly that the word *whoosh* would be appropriate.

Having lost its target, the hurled weapon came straight for Kamijou's face.

"Eh?" he grunted in spite of himself, then realized how utterly idiotic he sounded. While he was doing that, the crescent knife was flying toward his eyes with the force of a hammer about to drive in a nail.

"Uwah!!" He attempted to roll to the side right away, but the knife grazed his cheek.

That was all.

Even so, however, in the next moment, his sense of balance got muddled. He was lying down, and now he wasn't able to get up. An unpleasant sweat broke out all over him, and a seasickness-like urge to vomit came upon him.

Poi...son? Damn, he put something on that knife...!

He had wiped the knife's blade with that leather cloth in order to paint it with toxins.

A small handful of tribes around Africa apparently hunted wild beasts with wooden spears covered in the juices of crushed venomous insects. Was it like that? He should have a certain amount of resistance to drugs because of Academy City's Curricula, but none of that seemed to make a bit of difference.

His vision blurred and darkness began to creep in.

Along with an unbelievably happy voice, Jinsaku Hino ran out of the beach house—that much he could understand.

The sister in red hesitated for a moment on whether to follow, but then ran over to Kamijou.

That's when he blacked out.

5

Had it been one minute or one hour?

Kamijou awoke to a dry throat, like he had come down with a fever. He was resting on a hard floor. As he lay there, he looked around and saw various pieces of the floorboards blown out.

This was the first floor of the beach house Wadatsumi. It seemed he hadn't been carried off anywhere, so maybe it hadn't actually been that long since he passed out.

Tsuchimikado and Kanzaki were crouching near him.

Despite all the commotion, Mikoto and Index hadn't come down. Ordinarily they would have noticed something even if they were asleep. *That means that maybe Kanzaki used some magic like the one Stiyl uses to keep people away?* Kamijou thought, his mind hazy.

As he thought that, though, he saw Little Misaka in a T-shirt, shorts, and an apron among the sorcerers. She was looking around the destroyed shop quite nervously.

Of course, she was an employee here at the moment.

"I set up Opila on the second story, but…Apparently the employees sleep on the first floor, so…you were witnessed. Fortunately, the shopkeeper was doing some work upstairs," Kanzaki said, causing Little Misaka's shoulders to jolt.

After all, she had witnessed a criminal organization's crime scene. Her expression was waiting for what kind of "punishment" awaited her.

In any case, Kanzaki touched the hilt of her ridiculously long katana and said, "I will caution you just in case for now. Please do not tell anyone what you saw today. If this katana doesn't look like the real thing, you may ignore it at your own peril."

Her voice was terrifyingly sharp, but Kamijou noticed that Tsuchimikado, next to her, was trying to hold in laughter…Were they not being serious?

On the other hand, the sister in red was hiding herself in the shadows a bit away from them.

Who is that? he thought. He thought about it more carefully. She intervened with *extremely* good timing, but who on earth *was* she?

"Oh, that's not an enemy," Kanzaki said, realizing where he was looking. "She says she's a member of Annihilatus, of the Russian Orthodox Church."

There were some indecipherable foreign words mixed in there, and Kamijou didn't really understand. Tsuchimikado read him there as well and said:

"Well, if you take the English Puritan Church to specialize in witch-hunting, then the Russian Orthodox Church specializes in ghost-hunting. Whether it's jack-o'-lantern, Ustocc, Shinnaterao… They're basically ghostbusters, experts in all sorts of nonexistent things."

Kamijou looked again at the blond-haired girl blending in with the darkness.

She didn't move a muscle, despite the conversation turning to her. Kanzaki continued to speak, as if that lack of social-interaction ability wasn't too unusual in the occult business world.

"She says her name is Misha Kreutzev. She is apparently the one who sucked the poison out of your wound, so how about thanking her?"

She sucked the poison from my wound. He calmly listened to those words, but then suddenly flushed red. The wound was on his cheek. It was excusable as an appropriate act of medical care, but he still got this weird sweaty feeling.

"I-I see," he offered, the sides of his throat feeling like they were stuck together. "Thanks. If you hadn't jumped in right then, I'd probably be dead right—"

The smile he managed to put on his face suddenly froze.

He thought Misha was standing a way off, but she had instantly stepped right up next to him. Her right hand went to her belt and took off a tool—the saw. Before he could blink, she was standing over the top of him with that jagged blade pressed against his neck.

Nobody reacted. Kamijou was still, of course, but even Tsuchimikado and Kanzaki, whom he thought were beside him, didn't move. The sensation of the cold blade coiled around the skin on his neck.

He looked up at Misha Kreutzev, who was holding the saw. Her eyes were absolutely steady as they peered at him from the gaps in her long bangs. They only contained exceptionally cold emotion even chillier than the blade.

"Question one. Are you the one who caused Angel Fall?" she asked in a machinelike, level voice.

Kamijou was at a loss. Tsuchimikado and Kanzaki looked at Misha with confusion in their faces, too.

"W-wait a moment. Misha Kreutzev, did you not defend Kamijou from the assailant and suck the blood from his wound based on the fact that you thought he was *not* the one behind Angel Fall?"

Misha rolled her eyes straight to Kanzaki when she heard that and stared at her face.

"Answer one. I came here to prevent Angel Fall. I withheld judgment because I was not able to ask for an explanation on whether this boy was the criminal or not. That's why I'm questioning him now."

Kamijou, saw blade still up against his neck muscles, looked at her. She took her gaze off Kanzaki and brought it back to him, and stared like she was observing his eyeballs.

"Question one, once more. Are you the one who caused Angel Fall?"

"...No."

"Question two. Do you have any way to prove that?"

Misha shot another question at him as if she had predicted his answer from the outset. She was probably thinking something like...he was lying for the moment to distance himself from harm.

"I don't...have any proof. Besides, I don't even know anything about magic anyway."

She tilted her head slightly as if to give voice to her internal doubts.

Kanzaki sighed. "If you need, I can answer as to Necessarius's official stance."

So saying, she began her explanation to Misha. About how Kamijou wasn't a sorcerer, and how they didn't believe that he brought about Angel Fall. That espers using magic put a load on their bodies, but that they found no signs of it. That the reason Kamijou wasn't under the influence of Angel Fall was likely because of the effect of his right hand, the Imagine Breaker, which could erase anything occult just by touching it, and so on.

Misha nodded shortly with an "uh-huh" many times, as if checking off items on a list one by one. Then, at the end, her eyes rolled back to Kamijou—to be more specific, her gaze fell to his right hand. It seemed that she was stuck on the phrase "Imagine Breaker" from Kanzaki's explanation.

"Valence. Forty, nine, thirty, seven. Eighty-six in all."

Crash! came the sound of a water stream erupting through the floor behind Misha. It looked like an underground water pipe had burst.

"MEM TETH LAMEDH ZAYIN (Correspondence. Water, assume the form of a snake and lunge like a sword.)"

Misha continued to move her mouth, and like a snake, the spray raised its sickle-shaped neck. It was a watery serpent split into many branches, like a hydra or a *Yamata no Orochi*. Before the back of his mind had time to put up warning flags, the flows of water turned into spears and powerfully shot straight for him.

Gush-gush!! The liquid lances pierced through the floor near Kamijou one after the other.

One of the streams, without hesitation, came right for his face.

"Whoa?!"

He immediately used his right hand to block it, and the javelin burst in every direction like a water balloon. As if safeguarded by an invisible shield, not a single drop of it hit him.

Misha, very carefully observing the water that had scattered onto the floor, said, "Correct answer. The opinion of the English Puritan Church matches the results of this experiment. I will acknowledge this explanation as a method of proof for revocation of suspicion. Young man, I apologize now for having pointed my weapon at you due to a mistaken explanation."

"Pointed your weapon? You nearly stabbed me with it! Also, look at the person's eyes when you're apologizing to them!"

"Question three. If you are not the criminal, then who is the one who executed Angel Fall? The epicenter of this havoc should indeed be here. Do you have any ideas?"

"Listen to me, you...! Wait, you're not sorry in the slightest, are you?!"

Kamijou looked at the big hole in the floorboards from his laying position.

Then, Little Misaka, who had been trembling the whole time without a clue what was happening, fearfully addressed him. Perhaps she was regaining some presence of mind.

"Hey, is this…is this filming for some kind of *tokusatsu* hero TV show? And that guy who ran away before, wasn't that the Jinsaku Hino guy who escaped from prison? Could you all be one of those police bait teams they show on TV all the time?"

"It would be for your own benefit not to investigate us any further." Kanzaki flat out refused her question.

However, something about what she said bothered Kamijou. "Hey…wait. Did that look like Jinsaku Hino to you?"

"Who else would it look like? Anyway, who's gonna reimburse the shop? Hino? The police? The TV station?"

Kamijou was speechless.

Take Blue Hair in the nun outfit, for example.

He looks to everyone like Index, and Kamijou sees him as Blue Hair.

If his inward and outward appearances were the same, then…

"He's…not substituted?"

He explained his thought process to the sorcerers, and their faces all stiffened very quickly.

"Question four…You mean the person who escaped before?" Misha stared in the direction that Jinsaku Hino had fled in. She was about to run off that way, but Kanzaki grabbed her shoulder and stopped her.

"Wait. If we follow the same prey, why not act in concert?"

"Question five. What merit would that have for me?"

"I'll answer your question with another. Are you practiced in hunting humans? Those weapons are the Seven Implements from the Tower of London, aren't they? Someone local wouldn't be using brand-name goods like that. A normal ax is more practical than a golden ax or a silver ax, after all," alluded Kanzaki smoothly. "The Russian Catholic Church's specialty would be spectral extermination. If you are to go man-hunting, with which you are unfamiliar, I don't think having an expert English Puritan guide with you would be a bad idea."

"…Wise answer. I thank you for your question." Misha abruptly held out her small hand to Kanzaki. The latter looked taken aback at first, but then, when she realized Misha wanted to shake hands, smiled a little and took it in hers.

Kamijou, watching this, asked, "So what do we do? Should we go chase him down right away?"

"Your enthusiasm is splendid, and Tsuchimikado could learn a thing or two from you, but in your case, regaining your strength takes priority, I think. It may be safer if we protect you while you recover. We do not know Hino's objective, but there is a nonzero possibility he could come back later tonight and attack you in your sleep."

When she heard that, Misha asked:

"Question six. There is little necessity for us all to protect him. Am I able to pursue the suspect alone?"

"Without knowing the enemy's forces, splitting up does not seem like a good plan. In the worst case, he may be in possession of an angel, right?"

Misha fell silent, looking unsatisfied with the answer. Maybe she was already regretting having made an agreement with them. However, Kanzaki didn't stop to think about it, and continued.

"In accordance, we should have a discussion about our next move with you, Kreutzev. We must next somehow repair this disaster. Once that is over, we will return to our positions as bodyguards… Tsuchimikado, you're making a disagreeable face."

Kamijou thought, *I'd like it if you waited a moment.*

If they went ahead and did that, they wouldn't get an ounce of sleep. He didn't want to indulge himself in indolent sleep by himself as the others whittled away at their energy and morale. Whether he was injured or not, it was his own fault for not being cautious, so that was no reason.

That's what he was thinking, but he didn't give voice to his concerns. A burning pain developed in his dry throat.

Kanzaki looked at him with uncharacteristically pained eyes. "We'll explain the results of our discussion with Kreutzev afterward. You really should go to your room and get some rest. Letting an amateur suffer any more grave wounds would put our own positions at risk, too."

"Well, we're not wretchedly *professional* enough to live while letting an amateur die," Tsuchimikado said in an unusually distant tone of voice.

They have their own obligations. Kamijou sighed shallowly—
Hm? Go back to my room?

Then, he felt himself get caught up on the voice of his own mind.

"Ah, aaaaaaaaahhhhhhhhhh! Wait, Index?!"

He flashed up and sprang to his feet as if the damage he'd taken was nothing.

Leaving the flabbergasted group behind, he hurried up the stairs and burst out onto the second floor.

Strange symbols were engraved on the railing that looked like they were from a sword. As soon as Kamijou grabbed it with his right hand, he heard a sound like glass breaking. *Was that the human ward or something?* he thought, but this was no time to be paying attention to that.

His destination was not his own room, nor was it Mikoto's.

The door he suddenly pulled open was the one to Touya Kamijou's room, with the intent to bust the thing down if it had been locked.

He threw open the door with a *bang*, and there was a double futon laid out on the floor in a room with the lights out.

And was that Touya Kamijou, about to dive straight into the futon in which Index was currently sleeping?

Of course, from Touya's point of view, she was his wife, Shiina, so there was nothing shameful about it.

However, the vision of his own father in his midthirties about to charge in on Index, who he was doubtful *didn't* look to him to be fourteen years old, could only appear to Kamijou to go beyond the surreal and into a nightmare.

"Stop, stop, stop, stooopp! Wait a minute, you bastard!"

So Kamijou ignored the dizziness from the poison remaining in his body and hurled himself right into it, diving straight into the middle of the futon.

Touya was the one who was surprised.

Incidentally, his mother, or Index, was tough enough to keep on talking in her sleep despite the ruckus.

"...(Wha—! T-Touma! Don't barge in like that at such an embarrassing time!)"

"Be quiet, be quiet, be quiet! We're sleeping like this tonight, with me in the middle! Special technique: special operation 'family bonds'!"

Thus began their battle in the dead of night.

Without any regard for Kanzaki's consideration toward him, a sick person, Touma Kamijou did not get a wink of sleep that night.

CHAPTER 2
Detectives in the World of Combat

1

The next day...

It was an early summer's morning permeated with an aura of relaxation. Index, playing the part of mother, opened her eyes a little, and she looked at the quarreling father and son, each with black rings under his eyes.

"Good morning, you two. Oh my, male bonding? Were you up all night trading stories? How nice. It's kind of like we're at an outdoors school or a field trip."

The anguished, cheerless negative energy swirling through the room certainly rivaled that of when boys in their room on field trips tell late-night love stories (about 80 percent of which are ostentation and falsehood). However, Kamijou couldn't get a handle on that idea, given his unrevealed amnesia.

In any case, given all the additional exhaustion from yesterday, Kamijou was completely beat and couldn't even answer her. He thought, *Ha...ha-ha. Damn it. I managed to protect her. It'll be fine now that it's morning.*

Immediately afterward, drowsiness took him and he dropped right down onto the futon.

He was about to fall asleep with a reassuring, victorious feeling, but…

"See, now, Touma has fallen asleep and isn't looking, so we should at least give each other a *morning greeting*."

"Oh my, how troubling. What could you have been discussing the whole night for you to feel that way now?"

Touya seemed to want a wake-up kiss as if she were Snow White.

Just before the couple's lips met, Kamijou's eyes shot open with a *bam!!*

"Behold…my Guillotine Upper!!"

Right before their lips touched, his fist sent Touya flying directly upward, and Kamijou fell back down into the futon, faceup. He didn't think he hit him too hard, so Touya was probably staggering from his own sleep deprivation. *This time it's fine for sure*, he thought, also falling back onto the futon.

However…

Touya certainly wasn't the *only* formidable opponent Kamijou had to deal with.

"Big brother, brother, bro, dear brother, my brother, lord brother, brother dear, ABCDEFG! Daybreak Wake-up Flying Body Attack!!"

Mikoto, in an incredibly cheerful mood, suddenly came in and attacked him, delivering a pressing attack with all her weight behind it directly to Kamijou's solar plexus. He bent over his stomach and awoke (total sleep time: fifteen minutes).

"Mgah! Gah, gahagebekobuh! W-wah! What?!"

"Aha-ha-ha-ha-ha!!"

"Quit climbing on me and laughing about it! Could I have a *convincing* explanation for this?!"

"Alarm clock functionality via weird pro-wrestling moves comes standard issue on little sisters, Captain!"

"Shut up! So you're trying to act like the flattering character, are you?! I won't allow it! I'll tie you up with a jump rope and leave you to rot in the gym warehouse!!"

Then, Blue Hair, playing the part of Index, overheard their commotion and came romping into the room.

"Aah! Touma, you're having such a fun time waking up! Me too, me too! I wanna do that to Touma, too!"

"Wait, I— Hold on, you giant! Your body presses are no joke!"

"Why?! Why do you have to keep leaving me out?! I want to, too, I wanna do that, too, that's what I said, so I just decided I'll definitely do it!"

"Eh, what? Hold on! I'm sorry! Here, I'll give you two thousand yen, so please forgive me, *bgah!*" Kamijou's organs took such an impact he thought they would burst. "Uh, uh. Ugh. Uhu-hu. I'll kill you. I'll take those happy little heads of yours and slice them in half like a watermelon in summer!!"

This was how the second day of Angel Fall began—with much noise.

2

Twelve o'clock noon. The sun was at its peak.

I have summer heat fatigue; please, leave little old me here and go have fun, Kamijou had said to his family, who (along with the freeloading nun from the Kamijou residence) rushed toward the beach. Then, as if they had chosen the exact time, Kanzaki, Tsuchimikado, and Misha arrived at the beach house Wadatsumi.

If Tsuchimikado, whose appearance was a male idol in a lot of trouble, was found out by the guy in charge of the beach house, things could go south pretty fast. They decided to hold their war council in Kamijou's own guest room.

Incidentally, the fact was that time had elapsed and it was already noon. Kamijou really *had* been collapsed with summer heat fatigue until just a little while ago. It was a disaster when he awoke, sleep-deprived and dehydrated.

Misha had apparently been searching for Hino by herself since morning, but she had turned up nothing. The fact that Kamijou was only dragging them down filled him with regret.

"My word. What do you mean you didn't get a wink of sleep? What could you have been doing?" asked Kanzaki of him in a voice colored with both exasperation and worry. He was sagging like a plant its owner had neglected to give water to for a long time. Her words caused him to start slumping down even farther.

Then, Tsuchimikado's eyes smiled wryly behind his blue sunglasses. "Now, now, Zaky. There's nothing in it to humiliate a sick person even more now."

"What are you saying, Tsuchimikado? If you do not scold someone when they need to be scolded, they will repeat the same mistake. There's no telling whether we will be able to rescue him for sure next time."

Those words sounded like she was reprimanding a child for playing with fire too much, and they stabbed right into Kamijou's vital spots. Tsuchimikado, unable to let them pass, brought his mouth to Kanzaki's ear and whispered into it like a lover sharing a secret.

"...(Hmm? You okay with this, nya~? That's a pretty oppressive attitude. Kammy wanted to protect your precious, precious Index even while he was being violated with poison.)"

Her breath froze.

"...(You okay with getting mad like that even though you're grateful to him? I mean, sis, you haven't even thanked him or apologized for **the incident before this**. What'll ya do, hmm?)"

Her movements froze.

Misha, watching the two of them from a step away, breathed a soft sigh, softly but certainly making fun of them. Her bangs hid her face because she was always looking down.

Kamijou didn't really get it, but he got the feeling that if he left them alone, then at this rate, their temporary party would break apart midflight. Now a little bit worried, he decided to place himself in the chairman's seat and move the conversation along.

"So, should I take this to mean Jinsaku Hino is the criminal behind Angel Fall?"

Jinsaku Hino—the assailant who had attacked him from beneath the floor last night.

"Judging by Little Misaka's and my eyewitness information from yesterday, he definitely doesn't seem to be substituted, does he?"

Kanzaki looked at Kamijou and responded, "I have not personally seen Jinsaku Hino, so I cannot say for sure. If that is the case, however, then he is very likely our criminal."

"...Which would mean that we need to get our hands on the guy... But, nya~." Tsuchimikado made a difficult face and fiddled with his sunglasses.

Yes—to even catch Jinsaku Hino, they first needed to know where he went, and they had no hints of that nature.

"If Hino is a sorcerer, then can we not track him via his mana residue?"

"Answer one. Did not find any traces of Hino using magic last night. I conjecture that he is likely using some trick to throw off pursuit."

"And the biggest bottleneck is that we can't sense the angel, nya~. But we're talking about something on the level of an angel here. If we left it be, it would distort the very land by itself. I don't think there's much doubt that he's using some method to conceal it."

"Conceal...Is it that easy to do?" Kamijou asked. Kanzaki, after thinking for a moment, replied:

"Though solely in the Old Testament, there *are* descriptions of angels hiding their identity and going into human towns, into people's houses, and eating with them. There was one archangel who rescued a drowning child in the same way. We may want to consider that this kind of concealment technique has been around from the outset."

Misha offered a small nod to Kanzaki's viewpoint.

He couldn't read her expression because it was hidden behind her bangs, but this seemed to be her specialty. It was for Index as well— did nuns like talking about the Bible?

"Whatever the case may be, we gotta get some info first. Hi-ya!" Tsuchimikado flicked on the old-fashioned TV sitting in the corner of the guest room.

As usual, Miss Komoe was on the news program, holding a mic in her hand and talking about something.

"An entire day has gone by since Jinsaku Hino broke out of the Shinfuchuu prison. Here with me in the studio today is Raizen Oono, a criminal psychology professor at Miwa University. Professor Oono, how are you today?"

"Doing well, thanks," responded the person in a weighty tone, though he looked like a third grader. With Miss Komoe alongside him, it looked like some kind of educational show.

Professor Oono spoke. "Historically, Jinsaku Hino's behavioral patterns are extremely rare for a criminal. He has murdered twenty-eight innocent people, and yet he insists that he did not kill any of them under his own volition. He seems to be saying that a presence named 'Angel' has been guiding him, so perhaps this should be classified under the header of ritualistic murder, which can be seen in cult crimes in Europe..."

Kamijou nodded lightly as he listened to the elementary school student wearing a suit and talking like an old man. "That's right, 'Angel.' Hino said that yesterday. If this commentator is talking about Hino before he was substituted, then it matches up with him after the fact."

"Question one. I'll confirm this once. Does this mean that Jinsaku Hino is the perpetrator of Angel Fall after all?"

He nodded at her.

Hino by no means possessed the Imagine Breaker like Kamijou did. In spite of that, he hadn't undergone any sort of substitution, so it wasn't a problem to consider Jinsaku Hino the most suspicious person at present.

"But what is this 'Angel'?"

"About that—while we were repairing the floor last night, this thing popped up."

Tsuchimikado took out a thin wooden plank about the size of a notebook. Its surface had been marked up into a mess by something like a nail. There wasn't anywhere on it that wasn't cut up.

"It looks like there's some English letters carved on here. It's been overwritten again and again, though, which is why it looks like such a wreck now, nya~." Tsuchimikado sighed. "This is a kind of oracle, or Automatic Clerk. It's more than possible that Hino was moving in accordance with the orders written by his right hand under its own power. The nuance here is kind of like 'divination by planchette,' like Ouija, I guess?"

...*Ouija?* Something bothered Kamijou about it, but he stayed silent. This was their field—occult territory.

"So then, a ritualistic killer of twenty-eight people, just from the confirmation that it was done on the orders of this 'precious Angel.' **What kind of ritual** could that be indicative of?"

"...Are you saying it could be Angel Fall?"

They'd mentioned planet-wide grand sorceries and ritual sites before, but he shuddered anew at the fact that twenty-eight people had been killed for it. It was like the devil-worshipping black mages in picture books.

"But if that's the case, things get pretty complicated. If we assume that Jinsaku Hino did bring about Angel Fall, then the one who commanded him to do so would have been *his* 'Angel,' right? If it's an *actual* angel, then why would he be causing Angel Fall at all?"

Tsuchimikado groaned and folded his arms. Without thinking, Kamijou asked, "...Maybe because, like, it wanted to come down to earth? Just straight-out?"

"Mgh. Kammy, this will sound contradictory when I say it, but angels don't have a personality. Angels are God's errand people. They're actually closer to fleshy puppets filled with vast preternatural power. The concept is in the same vein as how fake crosses in idol-worshipping religions hold a portion of power, so from a purely theoretical point of view, you could even separate an angel's 'substance' into one hundred parts and put it into swords and armor and stuff. So fundamentally, angels don't actually create miracles, or save people, or fight against evil unless God orders them to do so. They're basically just radio-controlled cars."

"...That's all angels are?"

"That's all they are. In the New Testament there's something called the Last Judgment, and it's God's job to judge the righteous and the sinners, then send them to heaven or hell at the end of the world. In other words, an angel changing history by going off by himself and saving people or killing people would be terrible.

"Incidentally," he added, "like I said before, angels are pretty much remote controlled by God, but they don't run out of batteries and stop taking orders or get their wires crossed or anything. Those would be demons."

Kamijou was a little surprised at that. The angels and devils that appeared in video games were a completely different story. He had this image of angels as these blond-haired, winged people who looked down arrogantly on humans from above. Of course, that was just what he got from movies and manga.

"..." Once again, he said without thinking, "Then maybe it wanted a mind?"

"**It doesn't actually have a mind to *think* that it wants a mind.** Even if an angel looks like it's thinking on its own, it only *looks* like that. Even if it seems like it's moving by itself, it only *seems* like that. In reality, though, if a puppet's strings are cut, it loses all ability to move around freely."

Having thought through it, Tsuchimikado scratched his head. "Well, I suppose we'll just have to rein him in and make him cough it up. Let's think a little about what the enemy might actually have on his side in the way of *concrete* forces."

All Misha did in response was glance at him. It seemed like she was bad at voluntary conversation and only spoke when spoken to. So Kanzaki answered him instead. "First off, whether or not Jinsaku Hino has acquired the angel."

"Having heard all that before, it's pretty dubious. I mean, if Hino had completely seized an angel, he would have already been using it during the pinch we were in last night." Tsuchimikado thought for a moment. "I've got the feeling that Hino's commands aren't being completely conveyed to the angel, like there's some radio interference. Quite the contrary, it's looking like Hino is the one taking orders from this *angel*. So even if he had delivered a command in an important situation, it's not a given that the angel would even listen."

Now that he mentioned it, after Hino was cornered last night at the end, Kamijou thought he remembered him voicing displeasure toward his "Angel." Like, "Why aren't you helping me?" or something.

"Then on the contrary…we can't ignore the possibility that when the live angel does arrive, it would be under the desperate Hino's control, correct?" asked Kanzaki to Tsuchimikado, whose eyes smiled ferociously back from beyond his blue shades.

"I mean, there's no harm in always keeping the worst-case scenario in mind, right? Though if I'm going that far…heh-heh. The *worst* case would be having the angel as an enemy, I guess. All of human history could end here, nya~."

So he said, but it wouldn't sink in for Kamijou.

He couldn't come to grips with these *angels* or one wiping out the entire human race thoroughly and completely.

"Moving on. About the enemy's strength in terms of his *human* relations…What is the probability that Hino belongs to some sort of organization or collective?"

"Low, it seems like. If his 'Angel' commanded yesterday's attack, then Jinsaku Hino coming *by himself* seems somehow pathetic. Though that theory wouldn't hold up if they were working on other projects simultaneously, nya~."

"Hmm. The collaborator theory doesn't hold much weight. Then, where do you think Hino went to receive treatment for his injuries? According to Kreutzev, she pulled two of his teeth and broke his left wrist."

"If he just straight up went to a hospital, they'd notify the authorities immediately. He couldn't go to a back-alley doctor, either, since he just broke outta prison—he's got no cash. All that's really left is to rob an armored money truck to get that money or to start making preparations for a recovery spell, I guess."

"The only thing we know is that nothing is for certain. I'm worried about where he obtained that knife and the poison. He may have hidden them along with other equipment somewhere before being arrested, or they may have been weapons that somebody else supplied to him. He may have the money, and he may have given weapons to his comrades. I'm no psychological analyst, though. Speculating any further on his criminal profile might only serve us with mistaken information." She sighed.

When she stopped, the conversation came to a halt as well. Only the voice on the television resounded inorganically amid the somewhat oppressive air.

Then, all of a sudden, the robotic TV voice livened up.

Kamijou looked over to see a "breaking news" caption on the screen. Whoever that commentator was, he was chased off to the side, and in bewilderment, Miss Komoe looked over a news bulletin that someone had abruptly handed to her.

"We have just received a follow-up on the Jinsaku Hino incident! Hino has fled into a residence in the Kanagawa prefecture, and the riot police have arrived and surrounded his location! Here's— Can you hear me? Here's Miss Kugimiya, on the scene."

The eyes of everyone present reflexively locked on to the TV. Even Misha leaned in silently, a step away from them, and looked at the picture.

The screen cut to a new one.

It was an average residential area, the kind one could find anywhere. The quiet neighborhood was lined with ready-made two-story houses. In it, there were curious onlookers, police officers holding them off, and the riot police clad in dress that made it seem like a war was about to break out, all causing a commotion. However, the members of the police and riot squad were all substituted with old men, kindergartners, and the like, giving Kamijou a pointed sense of unease.

A guy who looked like he might be a produce seller was holding the microphone. "As you can see, all civilians, including reporters, are being barred from getting any closer than six hundred meters to the house in which Jinsaku Hino is holed up. Those around me appear to be evacuated residents. According to the authorities, Jinsaku Hino has fled inside a home and shut himself in, closing all the curtains and storm doors, making it impossible to see inside."

Tsuchimikado swore under his breath.

His eyes, buried behind his sunglasses, showed flickers of what looked like irritation.

Was the vexation because he had made a huge scene of everything or because of the house's residents?

"We do not know what's going on inside. The riot police seem to be avoiding a frontal assault, as they cannot judge whether Hino has any hostages nor what kind of weapons he may possess— Wait, what might that be? A single passenger vehicle has crossed into the off-limits area. Could it be a police negotiator?"

The screen cut to another picture again, this time showing an aerial view taken by a helicopter. Was the red-roofed house being displayed the hideout location in question? "Idiots," Kamijou muttered, unable to help himself. Bringing a helicopter over the house Jinsaku Hino was shut up inside would needlessly provoke him. And Hino could be watching TV right now, too. The image was still zoomed in, so that wasn't a problem, but if they broadcast video from higher up, it would tell him where the riot officers were located.

...Wait...huh?

Kamijou got a weird feeling from the video, but with abrupt and unnatural timing, as if something had intervened, the broadcast snapped back to the studio. Miss Komoe was in dire distress reading a manuscript describing Hino's crimes thus far and urging nearby residents not to leave their homes.

"Well, well, what a pain. If Hino gets handed over to the police, it'll be a disaster for us to get him to undo Angel Fall himself. I'd like to grab the guy before they butt in, if possible. What should we do, nya~?"

"Tsuchimikado! Do you have any idea what sort of result that would incur if he *did* have hostages?!"

Kanzaki was unusually enraged, but Tsuchimikado turned her ire aside easily. "Nyaan~ Well, regardless of whether we are going to capture Hino or rescue his hostages, we have to actually go there first. Where's the scene, though? Kanagawa prefecture's a pretty big place, you know."

"Umm," uttered Kamijou, timidly raising a hand.

Kanzaki, in an annoyed voice, said, "What is it? If you wish us to bring you there, we refuse. I don't know about Stiyl, but I haven't the slightest intention of dragging you into a battlefield."

"Not that. There was something about that aerial image that's bothering me."

"What?"

"Well, I mean…But still, I guess…I might be mistaken, but even so…"

"Explain yourself this instant."

"Yeah…My mom has this paragliding hobby…Oh, there're a lot of kinds, I think. Was it the motorized kind? I don't know. Anyway, you sit in this harness with a parachute on it, and you wear this huge propeller on your back and fly through the air. When I first enrolled, and I didn't know the neighborhood at all, she brought me a whole pile of photographs she took from the sky."

"Aerial photographs? What do they—" —*have to do with anything*, Kanzaki was about to say before she caught on.

"Yeah." Kamijou nodded.

"I'm pretty sure I've seen that red roof before…in aerial photographs of my house."

3

The intense pain had stolen away his calm judgment.

The death-row prisoner Jinsaku Hino held onto his left wrist, which looked like a rotten fruit, and spat into the darkness. It was still before noon, but light was prevented from entering because he had closed all of the windows, sliding doors, and curtains.

It seemed like the riot police had cut off the electricity here. Even the lingering summer heat of late August was harsh, and without an air conditioner or any open windows, this building was hot as a greenhouse. The temperature in the room was so disgustingly high that he even began to worry that it could be causing his wound to fester, though he was pretty sure that was impossible.

He had tended to his broken wrist using some wire and timber he found on the way here to make a cast. He couldn't do anything about his extracted teeth. Strange pains quickened inside the heated openings of those wounds.

Jinsaku Hino, entire face dripping with sweat from the heat and the pain, said alone into the darkness:

"My Angel, my precious Angel…"

As he spoke, he considered the situation.

When he first became known as the "mysterious ritual killer who murdered twenty-eight people," it had spawned numerous enthusiasts and copycats with the Internet at their core. The university student who built a website in support of the serial murderer, Hino, lived in an apartment near here. He had originally planned to go there after breaking out in order to ask for a place to hide and funds to run away, but…

The room was powerless, and the TV was no exception. He didn't know what was happening outside. It did seem like the nearby residents had been ordered to leave, though. That meant that his "collaborator," who would have been living nearby, had also been chased outside their encirclement.

"My Angel, my precious Angel…"

What should I do now? Hino thought. There were no signs of the riot police rampaging in for the time being, probably because they didn't know what it was like inside. If they knew he had no hostages, though, they'd come to attack immediately.

Unfortunately, a careless bluff could end up backfiring and informing the riot police of his combat strength anyway. The important thing was to maintain their ignorance. Hino specialized in psychological attacks; he knew that the most troublesome thing was not a raging thug but a ghastly, silent figure.

What should he do? How would he escape?

He had reserves in the form of that crescent-shaped knife, but a single knife wouldn't be enough to cut through their siege.

"My Angel, my precious Angel…"

Then, his right hand, holding the knife, began to move of its own accord.

The knife's tip immediately lightly pierced into Hino's gut and ran around it, engraving more letters. The red oracle carving his flesh quietly showed him the answer.

CALL AN AMBULANCE

I see! I could do that! thought Hino, impressed. *I knew there was no mistake in my precious Angel's solutions. I was caught by the police once and sentenced to death, but I didn't want to die—and my precious Angel granted me that wish. My precious Angel really will lead me to a happy future.*

With that out of the way, things were simple. Hino began his preparations, without even tending to the wounds on his stomach.

The flashier his entrance, the better.

4

Touma Kamijou was an amnesiac.

Therefore, he didn't actually *know* where his house was. After he parted with Tsuchimikado and the others under the pretense that he was going to the bathroom, he recalled the aerial image he'd seen on TV. He punched some coordinates into his GPS-enabled cell phone and examined the general area.

Fortunately, there had been a large shopping center in the image on the broadcast. Based mainly in the Kyushu region, there was only one establishment in the Kanagawa prefecture, so he pinpointed it right away.

Nonetheless, even a cell-phone GPS couldn't cover the names of every single residence, of course.

They'd have to go to the general area and then figure out where all the commotion was centered around.

After finding the spot, he left the bathroom and headed toward the beach this time. Ignoring the faces playing by the shore, he came to their parasol, a little apart from them. In a careless act, the bags with their stuff in them had just been left there. Kamijou felt himself momentarily stricken by guilt, but he sniffed out his father's wallet, took the key to their house from it, and returned to the beach house Wadatsumi.

On the first floor, he found Kanzaki waiting for him. "So, where is your home?"

"Mm. It's about twenty minutes away by car. It'd probably be safest to call a taxi."

"...I'll say this again, but there's absolutely no need for you to come along."

"...I'll answer again, but that's *my house*. I'm scared it'll be wiped off the map if I leave it to all of you," he insisted, though he was actually worried about *them*, too. Misha had repelled Jinsaku Hino with an overwhelming display of force last night, but that wasn't enough to set him at ease.

"If Hino's a sorcerer, then my right hand can at least do *something*. We decided that yesterday, right? You know, when you tried to drag down my swim trunks?"

"Wha..." Kanzaki didn't know what to say to that, and Tsuchimikado and Misha came back. Kamijou couldn't tell who Misha was substituted with at a glance, but Tsuchimikado was a performer with a shady history, wasn't he? It should be on his mind what would happen should he run into the man in charge of the house.

"Yo! So, Kammy, if you're ready for this, then let's get going. You're the only one who knows your house, so you're in the lead, 'kay?"

Misha, as usual, didn't say anything. And she didn't have a drop of sweat on her despite this damn heat.

"Ah, about that. It'll take, like, twenty minutes from here by car. So it might be easiest to call a taxi."

"Ehh." Tsuchimikado grunted in dissatisfaction. "All right, then until it comes, we'll go hide somewhere, nya~. I'd be rolling on the floor laughing if the beach house guy who looks like Stiyl started makin' noise."

No sooner had he said that than he disappeared out of the house with ninja-like agility. "Tsuchimikado!" shouted Kanzaki, running after him. Perhaps she wasn't okay with him trying to get Kamijou involved so easily.

Kamijou was startled, but for now, he decided to use his cell phone and call the taxi. After hanging up, he thought, *Oh, right, who's gonna pay the fare, I don't really wanna, but even if I say we should decide with rock-paper-scissors, I'd lose right off the bat...* Then, suddenly, he felt a presence at his back—

—and there he saw Misha Kreutzev still just standing there.

"Whoa?!" Kamijou cried out unthinkingly, totally having thought she'd gone somewhere.

"Question one. What surprises you so?"

"Well, nothing, really...," attempted Kamijou, words caught in his throat.

Misha's unique, inquisitive way of speaking was superb at transmitting information, but it didn't seem too suited for small talk.

It would probably take five or ten minutes for the taxi to arrive. He couldn't talk to Tsuchimikado or Kanzaki, since they'd vanished somewhere, but it would also be kind of awkward to just leave Misha here at this point. In the end, he was stuck with her, and an elevator-like silence descended upon them.

Misha only had on a mantle atop her inner uniform, which looked like a one-piece swimsuit. Somehow, reminded that it was only the two of them, he couldn't look at her face directly.

Th-this pressure...This is awkward; I can't manage a smile...!

After just thirty seconds of silence, Kamijou gave up. His favorite expression was "lively dinner table." His eyes darted here and there in search of some topic they could talk about. When he reached into his pocket, he got hold of something solid. He took it out to see that it was chewing gum.

"Y-you want one of these?" he hazarded timidly. Misha didn't move a muscle, though.

"Question two. I assume from your question that this is something to eat?"

"It's something to eat, but you're not supposed to swallow it."

"?" Misha tilted her small neck. He held the gum out to her again, and her hand moved without a sound. She took the chewing gum by its edge so that she wouldn't touch his fingers. It was an act not wholly unlike the courtesy offered to customers by a convenience-store clerk as he hands over change.

As if she'd never heard of chewing gum before, she stared intently at the foil-wrapped object for a while. At last, she hesitantly began to unwrap it. She put the gum to her nose and sniffed it a few times like a squirrel, then touched it to the very tip of her only slightly stuck-out tongue and licked it.

Ugh...She doesn't trust me. She's totally trying to make sure it's not poisonous.

Kamijou may have been all smiles, but his heart was in tears. Finally, she tossed the gum into her mouth. As she bit it once, she froze. Maybe its texture was unfamiliar to her. She stood at attention for a moment, but before long, she started working her mouth again. It looked like she liked it.

"Opinion one. Yes, this sweet taste is nice. A type of sugar is said to be the source of longevity—I am reminded of the blessing of God."

He couldn't see her expression behind her bangs, but her mouth quirked into a tiny smile...or so he thought.

At long last, he felt like he'd finally broken free of the heavy air between them.

Kamijou gave a sigh of relief as he watched her, looking like a young child eating candy, but...

Gulp. Her throat made a move.

"Ubah?! What did you swallow it for?!"

"Answer three. What's with your reaction? Should I not have swallowed this? Is this a variety of chewing tobacco?"

Misha just bent her head a little at Kamijou's mostly reflexive cry. As if it was only natural, she abruptly held out her small hand. She was asking for another one.

Is it all right? he wondered to himself as he explained the proper gum-chewing protocol to her. *Well, I mean, you do put it in your* *mouth, so I'm sure it's not toxic...*He handed over another piece of gum. Again, she grabbed it by the tip.

Incidentally, though he had no way of knowing, gum's main ingredient is plastic.

5

The taxi arrived after a little while, and Kamijou and the others headed for the encirclement. The cabdriver (well, there was a substituted high school girl holding the handle) told them she could only bring them part of the way because of the police blockading the road, but they replied that they didn't mind.

Kanzaki's katana was close to two meters long, so in order to fit it in the cramped vehicle, they had to place it through the middle, from the backseat to in front of the passenger seat. The driver made a bothered face at it, but the fact that it was a katana must have been scaring her too much to complain.

They decided to alight from the taxi a little ways from all the bystanders.

As her guests got off, the driver looked at Tsuchimikado. "Yer that idol, Hajime Hitotsui, right? My daughter is a big fan o' yours," she said with a pleased expression, bringing out a notebook. Tsuchimikado smiled and signed it in big, blocky letters.

The taxi drove off. The huge siege would be placed at a radius of six hundred meters from the scene, if they took the TV info on faith.

"An encirclement with a six-hundred-meter radius is fairly overblown, though. If the police force wasn't able to maintain one at such a scale, they should have just made it tighter. I wonder why they are going through such lengths."

Kamijou's answer in reply was matter-of-fact, though it didn't feel too good to say it aloud. "They've probably got permission to fire. They're taking care so that stray bullets won't hit any civilians."

Nevertheless, even a thief hiding out in a bank during a robbery likely wouldn't call for this enormous road blockage. This wasn't in preparation for just one or two shots but for a chaotic, extensive battle involving automatic weapons and explosives. Leaving Europe's EOD incident aside, this level of caution was unprecedented in Japan, and for a single criminal, at that. Was Jinsaku Hino really that special a crook to the police?

Ignoring Kamijou's thoughts, Kanzaki and Tsuchimikado continued with the conversation by themselves.

"Hmm. The TV helicopter is gone as well. Perhaps it was warned off by the police."

"It looks like the mass media on the ground is all being stopped by the blockade. It's weird that those hyenas are listening so patiently for once. They might be under some pleasant pressure from this whole thing," Tsuchimikado suggested, adjusting his blue sunglasses. He seemed to be bothered by the term *mass media* that had come out of his own mouth.

"Are you suggesting that someone in Japan's police force knows about Jinsaku Hino's Angel Fall? Wasn't the existence of a Spiritual Ability Investigative Division Number Zero debunked as a baseless rumor in the report of the first half of the year?"

"Unyaa. I don't mean anything like that, just that maybe they simply don't want to broadcast the riot police blowing Hino's brains out with their .22s? There could be all sorts of reasons. Politicians have to value their image even more than idols do, after all."

"Hmm." Kanzaki groaned, making an unpleasant face. She stared at the no-entrance zone. Misha remained silent, chomping on gum. Kamijou looked at the three professionals in sequence and said…

"So what do we do? Aside from the strict police officers, there're a lot of bystanders around. How do we get to my house? Pop open a manhole and go through the sewers?"

"I have a feeling that the police would have thought of any sewer routes as potential escape paths for Hino. Well, whatever. In any case, let's get over to Kammy's house," suggested Tsuchimikado incredibly plainly. Now Kamijou was flabbergasted.

"How?"

"What do you mean how? We'll go through there, of course," he said, pointing out the concrete wall around a nearby residence.

*   *   *

The police force was blocking all roads in the vicinity.

However, put another way, there were no policemen in places where there were no roads. The yards of the houses under mandatory evacuation—those spaces could not be seen from the road due to shrubbery and concrete walls.

Kamijou followed after Tsuchimikado and the others, who were running from yard to yard quite naturally. They jumped fences, scaled walls, and ran from house to house.

Of course, just that shouldn't have been enough to escape the police force's prying eyes.

They had been assigned to the roads, certainly, but that didn't mean that they were completely ignoring the house yards and the shadows cast by cars. If the police officers, by some chance, saw Kamijou and the others, they'd be in for a chase.

Yes, if they were seen.

By some chance—for example, adjacent officers talking to one another, one concentrating on his walkie-talkie, one looking at a stray cat that jumped out of an alley, one casually looking up at the sky. The group ran straight by the officers by taking advantage of those sorts of miniscule lapses. Moreover, they weren't huddling in the shadows to wait for openings to appear. Those inattentive moments oddly all came one after the other and the very second the group ran past, as if it were all planned.

As a result, the sorcerers ran at full speed through the encirclement without stopping for very much.

And on top of that, they did so while dragging the amateur Kamijou along with them.

Kamijou imagined video games, like the spy ones where you have to infiltrate a terrorist hideout without being found by enemy soldiers or the ninja action games in samurai mansions chock-full of bodyguards. He felt like they were going through a speed run of a game like that.

However, there was one difference between real life and video games...

...*Stages* that, from the start, were constructed with the player being able to clear it in mind...

...and *battlefields* that, from the start, were designed not to let anyone break through.

This may not sound like a huge difference, but the gap between them is virtually impassable.

Kamijou again fully grasped the fact that Tsuchimikado was a professional after witnessing this kind of inhuman technique, even though he had felt so close to him before. It was a bitter sensation for him. As he penetrated the siege, humming a tune to himself all the while, Tsuchimikado felt somehow *distant*.

After making it past the police force's six-hundred-meter encirclement, they didn't see anyone for a time. After running farther, however, a lot of people wearing body armor and hoisting polycarbonate shields started to show up. They were the riot police. Some of it seemed a little bit unreliable, though, given the old men and old ladies substituted in there.

Tsuchimikado stopped and hid himself in the shadow of a parked car. Everyone else followed suit.

"Let's see here. Getting any farther in secret's definitely gonna be tough. All of the riot police surrounding Kammy's house have their eyes glued to it with binoculars. Looks pretty much impossible to make it there and take down Hino without anyone noticing."

"Impossible...Then what do we do?" pried Kamijou, who had never considered they might get stranded out here.

"Well, it would be possible to use a technique to intrude on their consciousness—say, to put them to sleep or have them stand there in a daze. But if we do that, the police force outside could pick up on it because of their radio silence and think something was odd," explained Kanzaki, falling silent afterward.

She seemed to be carefully choosing her next words.

"Instead, why don't we go with shifting their focus?"

Kamijou didn't understand what that meant at all. Misha looked at Kanzaki without a word.

"In other words, we could force the riot police to think a completely different house was actually Touma Kamijou's. That way, no matter what happens at his house, the riot police would only report that there was nothing going on."

Shoo came the noise of something cutting through air.

Around Kanzaki appeared metal wires, slender enough to be invisible without the sunlight glinting off of them.

"A prohibition barrier—from that old summoning rite for house-protecting gods coming out of southeast Asia?"

"Tsuchimikado, why must you reveal the trick in front of the audience?" She sighed. "In order to place the entire riot-police siege under the effect...With the way they are, it looks like I will need to construct the spiderweb with a one-hundred-meter radius. It will take me approximately twenty minutes to hang all of the *string*, so please conceal yourselves somewhere in the meantime."

"Aye-aye, sir!" answered Tsuchimikado reasonably, putting his fingers to the frames of his blue sunglasses.

"In addition, Touma Kamijou, please do not touch the wires. Rather than a two-dimensional magic ring drawn on the ground, the prohibition barrier is a three-dimensional magic circle spread using wires. They're the barrier's core, so if your right hand touches it, the spell could be undone."

"Well, I mean, I don't know why I'd go and touch one. They look like they'd cut my finger clean off if I tried. And besides, I just had my whole *right arm* cut off, so there's no way I'm letting it get wrecked again so easily. I wouldn't be able to blame that on pure **bad luck**, you know?"

The emotion suddenly drained from Kanzaki's face.

"Unya~ But Kammy, didn't that turn out to be **fortune in the midst of misfortune** during the Misawa battle?"

Neither Tsuchimikado nor Kamijou noticed Kanzaki's sudden change.

"It's not like it got cut off because I wanted it to. Jeez, that damn lolicon alchemist. Meeting someone like that was **rotten luck** in the first place, you know!"

Click went the heels of boots. Kanzaki turned her back to Kamijou.

Kamijou followed Kanzaki's back with his eyes and felt a chill creep up his spine. She hadn't done it with any particular intent. It was more like...her body moved out of some reflexive danger sense.

Her back said nothing.

"Wh-what's up? You feeling sick or something?'

"Nothing," came the reply.

Without turning around, Kanzaki left them and went to spread the barrier.

Kanzaki ran through the deserted residential area building up the barrier, pulling the wires around.

Unlike Academy City, normal towns have telephone poles. They were suitable "fulcrums" for hanging the invisible cords over a large area. Using the poles and wires, she created a three-dimensional magic circle about two hundred meters across from a position slightly away from the riot police. By using this barrier, she could throw magic of a particular wavelength at them in order to blur their awareness. The shape of the prohibition barrier was akin to that of a wok, though Kamijou might call it a parabolic antenna.

Kamijou.

She scowled, recalling his usage of the words *bad luck*.

He's not to blame. Taking out my anger on him would be unreasonable.

She understood this logically, but another part of her would never, ever allow things to be settled just like that.

Kanzaki had bitter memories of the words *bad luck*.

Bitter enough that she would choose never to hear those words again if she could.

She ran on, in fear that it would pry open the sealed door to her memories. She ran farther, she ran stronger, she ran with more focus—as if absorbing herself in her work to try and turn her thoughts away from that which she feared the most.

After Kanzaki ran off, Kamijou, hidden behind a parked car, breathed a sigh.

He was surprised. At the sorcerers' skill level, of course, but even more so at their quite haphazard movements. Putting it bluntly: What would they have done if Kanzaki couldn't use that whatever barrier? Would they have been stranded here? That would have been the most boneheaded thing ever.

There were scenes in action movies where even the cannon fodder "special ops" team would look at some maps and come up with a detailed plan before diving into a terrorist hideout.

Now that he thought of it, back when he and the rune sorcerer took on the alchemist at Misawa Cram School, he felt like he didn't have any kind of in-depth plans, either.

When he voiced these concerns, mixed in with a bit of whining and complaining, Tsuchimikado answered as if it were so obvious even he should know.

"Kammy, we sorcerers may call ourselves professionals, but we're not some special-forces team with textbooks programmed into our heads, nya~. We don't get any of that 'organizational murder training' or 'collective educational ideologies' beaten into us like they do in some countries. We're amateurs when it comes to combat."

"What?" Kamijou frowned. What he said seemed like it had absolutely nothing to do with the sorcerers he'd met until now.

"You're kidding, right? I mean, Stiyl and Aureolus are the kind of people who could, like, take down a Type-90 tank head-on and smile while they were doing it. Those battle-crazed demons can't possibly be *amateurs*."

Misha held out her hand to him wordlessly, and he handed over another piece of gum. Once again, she didn't attempt to touch his hand, and she took the stick of gum like a convenience-store clerk handles change.

Tsuchimikado looked at the two of them from his blue lenses. "I mean, it's like this. Envision a middle school student holding the launch button for a nuclear missile. Those guys've got some exceptional magical skills, but that's not because they went through military training or anything." He grinned. "Haven't ya ever thought it was strange, Kammy? How sorcerers, who should be trained as *professionals*, get caught up with personal feelings during battle? Like, the enemy telling them some shocking truth and they freeze in place on the spot, or sincerely lending an ear to what the enemy has to say, or sympathizing with the enemy, or insisting on honorable, one-on-one combat? There are all sorts of **unnecessary** things going on in sorcerer battles."

It was true that cold "human weapons" indoctrinated with military training would never listen to the words of an enemy or sympathize with them. They wouldn't even let themselves be seen, much less fight face-to-face. Even if they'd just learned some kind of shocking truth, they'd shoot first and ask questions later. If they were told to kill the criminal, they'd shoot straight through the heart of the child he was holding hostage. That's what it meant to be professional combat personnel.

"Sorcerers are children in those terms. We're kids holding knives. In fact, we're crying, trembling brats complaining that the world has betrayed us."

Tsuchimikado exhaled slightly.

"That's what sorcerers are. Their wishes won't be granted, and their God won't save them even if they pray—the last thing those wayward people cling to is the ultimate dirty trick: *sorcery*."

"..." Kamijou didn't respond. Tsuchimikado himself was a sorcerer. However cheerful he may act, he was still a sorcerer. There had to be a dried-up void inside the heart of this grinning young man.

That applied to Misha, who was silently chewing gum, as well.

"Sorcerers—particularly the kind who assumed a foothold in the nineteenth century, or 'advanced sorcerers'—engrave our own desire upon our souls. I'm talking about our magic names. We carve into our hearts the Latin for the reason we study magic, the one wish we have that we would give our lives for. For me, it's Fallere825, and Kanzaki's is Salvere000, nya~. The numbers afterward are in case there're doubles of the same term. It's kinda like an email domain in that respect."

"...How—"

—*much resolution must they need for that?* Kamijou thought. He only had vague goals at best, and even he was embarrassed to talk about his dreams in front of others. There's always the fear that one's dreams will be rejected, too. There are plenty of people who dream of being actors or professional athletes and then are always rejected as foolish by their parents or teachers and just give it all up. That's how damaging it can be to a person to be denied a dream.

Aren't sorcerers afraid?

Just how hard must they steel their souls to stick to their dreams without giving up, even when others deny them?

"For people like them, it doesn't mean much to belong to an organization. You just stick together because you have similar goals is all. Kanzaki and Stiyl would both leave the organization if it were getting in the way of their lives, no questions asked. Of course, now that they've got a *hostage* situation on their hands, I don't think they'll be leaving."

Dumbfounded by the word *hostage*, Kamijou sighed.

The meaning of *professional* in terms of sorcerers was the complete reverse of the *professional* in terms of special forces. That much he understood. They were the polar opposites of special forces, who, with a simple order, would commit murder against those who disobeyed. Sorcerers didn't listen to orders, they didn't want money, but they still didn't want to bend their own feelings, no matter what. *Those* were the concepts that these "professionals" stood at the pinnacle of.

...Then that means...

Kamijou looked off in the direction Kanzaki had gone.

There was nobody there. Only the empty silence of the now-vacant residential streets prevailed.

Had he thoughtlessly said something to damage her principles as a professional to her back, which looked somehow irritated as she left them?

Perhaps Tsuchimikado caught on to his slightly anxious expression. He grinned and said:

"Ah, I wonder if Zaky didn't quite like how you used the words *bad luck*, nya~."

"Bad luck?...Did I say something like that?" Kamijou wondered, tilting his head. He looked at Misha, but she didn't answer. She just kept chewing her gum.

"Well, that's because it's basically a habit for you, nya~. You know, saying 'rotten luck.' Well, Zaky's got it bad, too—she's got her own 'devil's luck' to deal with."

"...The devil's luck?"

"Yeah. You can take it to mean 'good luck.' What I mean is, Zaky can't forgive herself for having such good fortune."

"She...worries about being lucky?" Kamijou's face showed a complete lack of understanding. Tsuchimikado nodded and continued.

"There's this hidden Christian organization in Japan called Amakusa-Style, see. Before Zaky was born, it was decided she would rise to the top of their group and be their priestess. And that she was one of God's chosen ones, a stigmata-using saint, of whom there are less than twenty in the world."

Tsuchimikado was smiling.

However, it was a different kind of smile than his usual easygoing one.

"She had the talent to succeed without effort. She had the popularity to stand at the center of people without doing anything. Everything she desired would be fulfilled, and unpredicted, happy miscalculations would happen every day before breakfast. She would somehow survive if her life were threatened. She would avoid bullets for no reason, and she would miraculously emerge unscathed even if a bomb went off right next to her," Tsuchimikado went on, as if singing a lullaby. "...That's why Zaky can't forgive herself for being lucky. Perhaps she's *cursed* by her devilish fortune."

"...I don't get it. Why would you worry over something like that?" For someone who struggled with his own misfortune on a daily basis, it was quite the enviable position.

"Who knows? Only someone used to it would understand."

Tsuchimikado smiled.

But his face didn't look the slightest bit happy.

"But, Kammy, what must it feel like to be one of the lucky ones? You'd buy one lottery ticket, and you'd always, definitely win with it. Which means that **you would be forcing those around you to pick the nonwinning ones, no matter what**."

"...Oh."

"She was promised the position of priestess at her birth, but because of that, the people who wanted to be the priestess had *their* dreams shattered. She had the talent to succeed without effort, but it made *those who worked their asses off* fall into despair. She had the popularity to stand at the center of people without doing anything, but it pushed *others* outside the circle. Everything she desired would be fulfilled, and unpredicted, happy miscalculations would happen every day before breakfast. But on the flip side, those who had one single, unfulfilled wish—*they'd* be stricken with disaster. She would somehow survive if her life was threatened, but it made the weak fall before her in an attempt to save her. They became her shields for bullets and her armor for explosions, and thus many who adored and believed in her died."

"..."

"If Zaky was a heretic, she probably wouldn't have needed to worry. But she just couldn't bring herself to forgive her own fortune. She couldn't forgive it for making those around her unlucky, precisely because those around her *were* precious to her."

Tsuchimikado sighed.

Then, looking up at the distant sky, he continued.

"Eventually, Zaky couldn't stand it anymore. She made everyone around her unlucky, and yet they would smile and tell her that fortune brought them together as they died. She couldn't bear to watch it."

Kamijou was at a loss for words.

If he recalled correctly, Kanzaki was from the English Puritan Church. That would mean she left Amakusa-Style behind. She was promised a high position at birth and was adored by all those around her. In spite of that, she wanted to stop making the people who believed in her unlucky, so she abandoned her position. She had people she truly wanted to protect, and she chose isolation in exchange for being with them forever, like she wanted.

In the end, the only people who could stand side by side with her...

...was a special group like Necessarius, which was so strong that luck had nothing to do with it.

What must that feel like? wondered Kamijou.

And he'd made her remember that. He'd said he had rotten luck, then laughed it off like it didn't matter at all, like it was obvious.

Tsuchimikado looked at his worry but grinned brightly. "But you don't need to worry about it, Kammy. It's Zaky's own fault for remembering it, that's all. Sinking into her own traumatic experiences on her own is pretty egocentric, nya~." He waved his hands dismissively. "She's just acting like a kid throwing a tantrum. There's nothing really to worry about."

So he said, simply and smiling, but it did nothing to get rid of Kamijou's blues.

The conversation stopped for a bit.

There were no particular sounds to be heard in the residential area, only dogs left behind here and there, howling as if it were the middle of the night. From very far away he heard the sound of a train running.

After a while, Kamijou looked around the deserted neighborhood.

"But still, isn't she running late? She couldn't have been caught by the police, right?"

"That's not gonna happen. Even if a squadron of tanks found Kanzaki, she could cut through them all just like that. She's one of the top ten sorcerers in London, but the techniques she uses are kinda whimsical. Drawing barriers like this isn't her forte, so it's just taking her a while."

"...Yeah, you said you were a sorcerer, too. I still can't quite believe it. Does that mean you wear priest robes like an occupational pastor or something?"

"Hey, an undercover agent wouldn't wear a uniform. That's outside my area of expertise anyway. I got a Bible once, but it's in a closet somewhere. My fundamental techniques aren't based on Kabbalah, either—they're Onmyoudou, a Japanese remix of Taoism."

"...Onmyou, you mean like yin-yangs? That's pretty Japanese sounding."

"That's right. But Kabbalah and Onmyou are actually pretty similar." Tsuchimikado nodded twice, agreeing with himself. "For example, both western and eastern arts use a pentagram as a symbol to display the five elements. They split each attribute into a color and a direction, too, and when drawing a circle, they both place guardians in all four compass directions. Though, in the west they use the Four Archangels, whereas in the east we use the Four Shikigami, nya~."

"Huh." This was all Greek to Kamijou, so he responded with a noncommittal "How mysterious."

"It might sound mysterious, but it's no coincidence, nya~. It was the Heian era when Onmyou first originated and was mastered by the old man Seimei. At the time, after all, there were a lot of foreign products coming in from the Silk Road. That's only my personal opinion, but it seems natural to think that he got some hints from there. The original idea for Onmyou came from the *Kin'u-Gyokutoku-Shuu*, which was a fortune-telling book that arrived from the mainland, nya~. If you're interested, you can just get the Index to pull it out of her head for you.

"Of course," Tsuchimikado added, as if laughing at himself, "my expertise *is* feng shui, nya~. The techniques of looking at the land do differ greatly between the east and the west."

"Feng shui? You mean like Doctor XXX?"

I feel like I've heard the term 'feng shui master' in an RPG as the name of a job or something. Geomancer, was it? Does that mean it's a side job?

"Ah, Kammy, just so you know, feng shui wasn't an actual profession in this world originally. It was originally a job for Taoists in China and Onmyouji, or practitioners of Onmyou, in Japan."

Tsuchimikado counted off on his fingers. "Feng shui was one of their responsibilities. Feng shui masters, fortune-tellers, apothe-caries, hexers, worshippers, calendar makers, water clock users, et cetera. Those are all separate occupations that split off from Taoism and Onmyou and became specialized in their own right."

"Huh. Is that like how part of Shaolin Kung Fu made its way to Okinawa and became karate?"

"Yeah, sorta. It's similar. The 'tao' in Taoism refers to a technique to hit people with your 'qi.' But if you apply that concept to the land or the world, you get feng shui. To put it more in your scientific terms, you can think of it like the Gaea theory, where the world is one single life-form," he explained, remembering something. "Of them, I'm of the Black Style—specifically, I specialize in the creation of waterways."

"Waterway creation?"

"Just as it sounds, I make waterways. The main goal of it is to protect castles and towns by drawing a huge magic circle using the flow of water. Using waterways as a circle isn't really unusual, globally speaking. I mean, just look at Venice—the City of Water—though it's not quite feng shui. Near the end of World War II, the old Japanese army apparently tried to build an enormous magic water-way circle connecting the underground bomb shelters, but it looks like that ended in failure," Tsuchimikado mused, as if remembering the distant past.

"My specialty is using waterways to make traps...or at least, it was. Well, I mean, that's what Onmyouji are. They quietly hit you with shikigami from an unseen, faraway place and draw a circle around them to conceal themselves. In Heian-kyou, ancient Kyoto, its power wasn't the reason Onmyou was feared. It was their coward-ice, their underhanded tactics, their guile, their assassinations, and their taboo foul play."

As they were talking about all these things, Kanzaki returned, as if stepping from shadow to shadow.

Her face was calm, and there was no longer any trace of agitation.

"The prohibition barrier is active. The riot police surrounding the Kamijou residence have mistaken it for another unoccupied house three hundred meters away, and they should be breaking their formation."

"Well, then, Kammy's house is deserted, so let's go let ourselves in, nya~," said Tsuchimikado awfully plainly, advancing forward at once. Misha and Kanzaki followed suit. Kamijou was left behind by himself, and Kanzaki suddenly turned around.

"Why aren't you coming? Or are you going to remain there until we've dealt with Hino?"

"O-oh yeah," said Kamijou, getting his butt in gear. He came up next to Kanzaki, who had waited faithfully for him, and followed after Tsuchimikado. As he ran, he thought about apologizing for resurrecting bitter memories for her, but...

...No, if I apologize, it'll just remind her of it again.

If they were such painful memories, then it was better not to bring it up so carelessly. Kamijou shook his head and sped up to break free of Kanzaki's somewhat mystified gaze.

6

A nameplate with KAMIJOU written on it was affixed to the end of the concrete wall, near the porch entrance and the doorbell.

Kamijou and the others hid themselves in the trees at the house across the street and scoped out the Kamijou residence.

No matter how they looked at it, it was an average, two-story, pre-built house constructed from wood.

But in the broad daylight of this scorching midsummer's heat, all of the shutters on the windows were closed, or else the thick curtains were drawn. That sight was unusual in and of itself. Despite having no memories, Kamijou wouldn't have minded a bit of nostalgia for this place. Unfortunately, the building he was looking at was radiating gloomy malice that smelled of an incident, like a case of domestic violence or the kidnapping of a young girl.

And in reality, that odd sense of his was not far from the truth.

Inside that house, shut up as if to oppose the sunlight, was an escaped prisoner who had not only butchered twenty-eight people and offered them as sacrifices for devil worship–like reasons but had also caused Angel Fall and engulfed the whole world with it.

Peeking through the windows blocked by curtains on the second floor from the shadow of a tree, Kanzaki quietly said, "Hmm. I cannot judge from here where Hino is. Perhaps Stiyl would have been able to locate his position via heat source detection," she said with just a twinge of chagrin. "However, given that the house is locked up so tightly, I believe that Hino is unaware of our approach as well. If we are to begin our raid, then let us do so quickly. Where is the key to the house?"

"Right here, nya~."

For some reason, it was Tsuchimikado who pulled a silver key out of his pocket. *Huh?* thought Kamijou, groping around in his own pockets frantically. It wasn't there. He didn't know how or when he did it, but the key had been stolen.

Kanzaki, too, sighed in exasperation at Tsuchimikado's pointless parading of his sticky fingers.

"All right. Tsuchimikado, you'll be the decoy. Break in through the front door and make as much noise as you can. When we hear you do so, Kreutzev and I will infiltrate secretly from another route."

"Aye, sir. Does li'l Misha have any objections?" Tsuchimikado asked Misha, and she responded with a brief, "Answer one, affirmative." She removed the saw from her belt and, without a running start, leaped onto the first-floor roof in a single jump. She pressed herself beside a small window on the second floor.

Kamijou had no time to be flabbergasted—next, Kanzaki bounded up. Again, without getting a running start, she just flew Straight up there, surpassed the head of Misha who was on the first-floor roof, and touched down on the second-floor roof without a sound. Then, she continued to run to the other side of the roof, toward where the backyard-facing porch was.

This was ridiculous. Unreasonable even. It was like a child had asked, "What should I do so I can run really fast?" and the completely serious answer had been, "Graft an engine onto your body." Some basic fundamental thing was totally out of whack.

Seeing the two of them off as if their actions were totally natural was Tsuchimikado, who came out from the shadows of the plants. Kamijou, left behind, hurried and asked him, "H-hey. What am I supposed to do?"

"Seeing as how Zaky totally ignored ya, I guess the best answer is for you to stay put, nya~?" He turned around. "You saw that, right, Kammy? There're three of us inhuman sorcerers all packed into one place. You've got nothin' to worry about."

"B-but…two of them are just girls, aren't they?"

Tsuchimikado turned his gaze to him, amazed, from out of his blue sunglasses. "Listen here. Zaky is a stigmata user, got it? She's a human weapon—no, a weaponized *saint*. Can you really classify her as *just a girl*?"

"…What did you say? Weaponized…saint?"

"It's just how it sounds. Kammy, I explained about idol-worshipping religions yesterday, right? The stuff about even if the cross on a church roof is a replica, it's still got a degree of power as long as its shape and role are the same."

Tsuchimikado spoke quickly, in consideration for Kanzaki and Misha, who had gone on ahead. "That applies to 'replicas of God,' too. Humans were designed in the form of God, so a human 'replica' having the power of the original God is possible. Of course, that only applies to a select few people who are like God. Such as her, who was proclaimed at birth to be a saint within whom would reside godlike power. While her stigmata, her proof of sainthood, are unleashed, she can temporarily use superhuman power. Don't you think she could take out an entire castle by herself right now?"

Tsuchimikado left him with a "See ya," as if to push him away, then sidled up to the front door. The silver key in his hand was quietly inserted into the keyhole.

Left alone in the shadows of the foliage, Kamijou pondered over this to himself.

Is it okay to leave everything to them? Sorcerers are definitely combat professionals. Misha did corner him last night, and it wasn't even a contest. So maybe it's no big deal.

But...

Do they really understand...how difficult it is to fight in the dark like that?

During enclosed battles in the darkness, the most dangerous thing is not an enemy's attacks but friendly fire. Two silhouettes appear, struggling with each other in the pitch-black, and suddenly another appears from the shadows. The scariest thing is if the one mistakes the other for an invisible enemy and shoots them. Kamijou was by no means a pro at night combat, but when he resolved himself to fight rather than run during squabbles in the city, he always tried his best to choose an open spot for it. He was always wary of ambushes.

And in all likelihood, Jinsaku Hino knew.

He knew how to fight in the dark. He knew what to do to set ally upon ally. He might be overestimating Hino because of last night's attack, but he'd gone through all the trouble of closing the curtains and shutters to create a dark zone. If he didn't think he was going for pitting allies against one another, he'd probably regret it.

Damn...That means the stronger the ally is, the more dangerous it becomes!

Kamijou chased after Tsuchimikado and ran to the porch in front of the house, nearly hitting his head on a birdhouse on a low-hanging branch of a tree next to the front door. He caught up and came beside him.

"Wait, Tsuchimikado."

Tsuchimikado swore under his breath, but as they were right about to invade, he had no time to spare having a leisurely argument with him. He said this to Kamijou in a voice that didn't make much noise but somehow oddly stuck in his head: "...I'm gonna break in, so you hide yourself behind me. But don't think you're safe just by doing that. Be extra careful to watch your back, aight?"

Kamijou more than understood that there were no "safe zones" where they were going. He nearly retorted like a child, but Tsuchimikado inserted the key into the keyhole and turned it.

He quickly inhaled once, then flung open the front door.

Bang! The drumfire of the door slamming echoed throughout the vacant neighborhood.

Uh...?!

Kamijou nearly said something as he peered past the door.

A lukewarm air came dribbling out from the inside, where it looked like someone had poured darkness in. It was the heat of a sealed-up building. What's more, there was an odd smell to it. It stung his nose and eyes, like there was a tank of rotten crayfish that had been left alone until the water inside got cloudy.

Hisssss came a strange noise from the darkness that sounded like the air being let out of a tire.

Though the opened front entrance was square, it felt more like the mouth of a giant, bizarre creature.

"..." Tsuchimikado didn't exchange any careless words with him at this point, of course. He silently moved forward. Kamijou followed after him, setting foot into the artificial darkness. Behind him, the front door closed automatically with its springs.

The stuffy, hot air wrapped itself around Kamijou. It felt like the lair of a beast.

The curtains and shutters had been closed in order to block light from entering, but the dark it created wasn't perfect. There was light leaking through the gap between the thick, opaque curtains and the windows. If Hino had taped the curtains to the window frame, he might have made it completely dark, but it looked like he hadn't.

But...

It was *because* it wasn't pitch-black, *because* it was dimly lit with light only creeping in, that it caused needlessly unpleasant ideas to come to mind. It was *because* they could see the outline of objects that the totally normal umbrella stand looked like a crouching figure. If silhouettes were to appear in the shadows of the walls, they might raise a hand against them no matter who they were. The stuffed tanuki atop the shoebox and the red mailbox ornament cast eerie shadows, too, and the souvenir wooden sword against the umbrella stand looked like a human's severed arm or something. It seemed like if they pulled up the floorboards in the hallway there'd be a corpse there, and if they ripped off the wallpaper over there it seemed like they could find an old wooden door nailed shut to keep it closed.

There were a lot of souvenirs about that looked somehow religious, like a big mask from South America and a small *moai* ornament. They were probably things Touya had bought on overseas business trips.

After coming through the front door, there was a single glass door to the right, the stairs to the second story in front of them, and two doors beside the staircase. One of them had a lock on it. Was it the bathroom?

What about Kanzaki and Misha...?

Kamijou looked above him but didn't hear anything. Of course, if he could hear them from here, there wouldn't be any point to their sneaking around.

Tsuchimikado began to walk.

He headed for the bathroom door, opened it without a sound, and checked inside. Judging by how he closed the door again, Hino must not have been in there. Kamijou came up behind him as he was about to open the door next to it.

When they opened the door, the sound of hissing, like air escaping a balloon, grew stronger. He didn't know what it was, but the sharp scent that seemed to stab into his skin intensified as well.

The door led into a changing room.

He saw the silhouettes of a washer, dryer, and counter. To the side was a sliding door of frosted glass, and he imagined it led to the bath.

Tsuchimikado opened it slowly and took a gander.

The room with the bath in it had transformed into a dark space filled with moisture. There was a urethane turtle figure, maybe a bath toy, lying on the floor. It looked less like a bathroom and more like a basement with a kidnapped child in it.

Tsuchimikado was peeking inside the empty tub.

Kamijou returned his gaze to the changing area. In the mirror on the counter was vast, clouded darkness. It was like an ocean at night. On the counter were hair spray and a T-shaped razor next to each other, and next to those was a chess piece, or a little vial made of glass cuttings, or something. Was that one of Touya's hobby souvenirs he picked up overseas, too?

Tsuchimikado nudged him to the side and started for the back of the changing room. There looked to be a kitchen beyond it.

...*Wait.*

A terrible premonition jolted through him. The weird scent, the sound of air leaking, the kitchen, the smell that got stronger as they got closer, that odd smell coming out of the kitchen stinging his nose, it was...

"...(Tsuchimikado, come back!)"

Kamijou had tried to whisper this, but it sounded to him like his voice made a huge noise within the darkness. His heart skipped a beat at its unexpected volume.

However, Tsuchimikado said nothing. He looked at him, his eyes asking, *What?*

"...(It's gas. That smell is probably propane gas. The gas main is open!)" he explained.

Tsuchimikado's shoulders jerked; he was startled as well.

Hino just might have seen them coming to invade and gotten out of the house one step ahead of them. He might have been planning to spray fire into the building and blow them all up at once (though he might have thought they were the riot police). Kamijou slowly stepped back from the kitchen, trying to get farther away from it. Tsuchimikado took a step out as well, probably having finally decided staying here was a bad idea, and—

—*sway.*

Behind Tsuchimikado—from the kitchen—without a sound, a thin silhouette appeared.

"Tsu—!!"

—*chimikado*, Kamijou tried to shout, but the silhouette had already raised its crescent-shaped knife up in an arc above the young man's head.

Who could have anticipated it?

In this situation, when the building was brimming with propane gas and the whole thing could combust at any moment. The very person who had opened the gas stop had hidden himself in the most dangerous place—the kitchen.

He had slipped into a psychological blind spot for Tsuchimikado, who still hadn't noticed that death was approaching his back.

Without a sound, the knife came down on Tsuchimikado's head—

"!"

—but right before it got there, Kamijou rammed into his body, pushing him to the side. The changing room was narrow, so the latter collided with a wall before going even one meter. However, it was enough distance for him to avoid the knife descending on him.

As the blade split through the dark, the arm Kamijou had used to shove Tsuchimikado was racked with a scorching pain.

He'd been cut. But it was shallow. He disregarded it and stared straight ahead. The silhouette—or rather, Jinsaku Hino—whipped the knife back up at him, going for his face from directly below.

As the silvery edge threatened him, Kamijou grabbed whatever his hand could find nearby and tried to stop the strike. However, before his right hand could take hold of anything, a sudden, nightmarish thought came over him.

Despite this area not being fully saturated with it, propane gas *was* floating around in here.

If he were to use a hard object to block the knife, the sparks it would create would blow up the entire changing room!

"You…fucking psycho!!"

Then, at that exact moment, Tsuchimikado, who was beside him, kicked away the knife about to stab Kamijou in the neck—or, more accurately, the right hand holding the knife. It slipped out of Hino's hand and fell onto the washing machine. It immediately put Kamijou on edge, but no sparks flew from it.

Now was their chance. Kamijou would try and tackle Hino in the stomach to take away his freedom of movement.

However, Hino opened wide his slimy, spittle-filled mouth…

"Ghee! Ghbee!!"

…and cried out like an animal. When Kamijou looked at the glutinous inside of his mouth, seething disgust caused his body to lock up for a moment. Hino didn't let that go and ran past Kamijou fiercely, grabbing his knife from the washing machine and bursting out of the changing room toward the entrance.

"You won't get away!!" shouted Tsuchimikado, giving chase. Kamijou at last broke free of his paralysis, which hadn't lasted even a second. He wondered whether to follow him, but instead he rushed into the kitchen.

The smell of gas in there was terrible. Just a bit of static electricity from his clothing might set the whole thing off. There were all sorts of metal and electrical appliances that could trigger an explosion, like the microwave, upon which three cereal-box-prize-looking tiger toys were stationed; the refrigerator, on which magnets in the shape of wooden amulets were hung; and the stainless steel sink, in which seven small glasses each in a different color were sitting. Kamijou shivered.

Anyway…anyway, I need to close the gas main! I'll pass on my life's story involving my dying in an explosion in my own house!

Kamijou felt around in the near darkness and found the gas burner covered by an aluminum oil guard. He nervously looked behind it and saw the stopcock loosened from the gas hose. He twisted the stopper with the care of someone cutting the red cord on a time bomb.

The eerie *hissss* stopped then.

No explosion happened. Kamijou sighed in relief, then flung open the back door. The direct, blazing sunlight scorched his eyes, which had gotten used to the dark. He felt the toxic gas slowly start to flow out. The boiling midsummer's air outside, which he had thought to be deathly, felt extremely refreshing.

Just then...

...he heard a deep, male shout and the sound of violent footsteps.

Kamijou looked around. It was probably connected to the living room; he heard the sounds of struggling from beyond the dim light. It was Hino and Tsuchimikado. He also heard the pattering of feet from the second floor. He supposed Kanzaki and Misha had decided it wasn't necessary to conceal their footfalls any longer.

Kamijou ran through the kitchen and burst into the living room.

It was a wide room. There was a large TV in one corner and a sitting table a measured distance away from it. The floor was covered with a low carpet. On the wall opposite the television was a cabinet, and in the open space next to that was a component stereo that looked less than current.

Tsuchimikado and Hino were between the TV and the table. Hino was flailing his knife around thoughtlessly, but Tsuchimikado didn't defend; he dedicated his energy to evasion and awaited an opportunity to counterattack. There were various objects here and there that would be able to stop the knife blade, like an ashtray and a shelf clock, but he didn't seem to want to make sparks and ignite the propane gas floating around.

Could he be thinking that far ahead...?

Kamijou was again struck by just how terrifying Hino was. By always shouldering the risk of certain death, he psychologically bound and restricted his opponent's movements. He had never seen a fighting style like that before.

He didn't think he could offer any assistance here. Carelessly exchanging blows with a weapon carried the possibility of making the propane gas catch fire, and he didn't have enough confidence in his agility to plainly dodge the phantasmagorical knife work of someone well versed in murder.

He couldn't come up with any ideas, and maybe Tsuchimikado realized it.

"Kammy, stay away!!"

As soon as he gave that loud shout, Hino's focus strayed ever so slightly toward Kamijou.

But in that moment...

Amazingly, **having used the unmoving Kamijou as bait**, Tsuchimikado took a big step up to Hino, whose attention had wavered, and drew into close range.

"?!"

Hino, speechless, hurriedly attempted to swing his knife around, but he was too late. Tsuchimikado had tread to practically zero distance, and he turned his waist to swing his arm around with all his body weight. Rather than a thrown fist like a brawl, he brought his elbow out and unleashed an elbow strike at Hino's chest. With one full-power attack, he could even crush his ribs and pierce his lungs. It appeared to Kamijou as nothing less than a technique meant to kill.

Jinsaku Hino...

...as Tsuchimikado's hammer-like elbow strike approached his defenseless breast...

...in an unbelievable twist, brought up his crushed left wrist to block Tsuchimikado's heavy attack.

Squish **came a sound like someone chewing up rotten fruit.**

Kamijou's eyes snapped shut. Despite turning his face away out of reflex, a splash of some kind of lukewarm fluid flew onto his cheek.

Once again, he came to doubt Jinsaku Hino's sanity.

The pure revulsion caused his feet to quiver. An unpleasant sensation swept through all ten of his fingertips. "Ghee-hee!" came Hino's delightful laugh, and that was when Kamijou realized this was a psychological tactic as well. He had presented Tsuchimikado with a scene that he would reflexively avert his eyes from even though he knew he shouldn't, and he had made him stop moving.

Whoosh! sliced the crescent knife through the air not a moment later.

"Tsuchimikado!" shouted Kamijou, unable to return his face to the horrifying scene—

*   *   *

—*crunch!*

The sound was not the slash of a knife but the impact of an elbow strike.

"Ah?" Kamijou accidentally made a stupid-sounding grunt and opened his eyes.

Tsuchimikado hadn't flinched at all. He hadn't averted his eyes. He hadn't let his body lock up. He stared squarely and honestly at the enemy right in front of them and without hesitation had rammed his hammer-like elbow into the man's face.

"So what?" he taunted on top of all that.

He grinned. It wasn't an insane smile, or a broken smile, or a relieved smile. He asked this with only his usual, ordinary, normal, everyday smile.

It hadn't affected him.

It hadn't affected him in even the slightest, most minuscule way.

After Hino's body took the brunt of the sublime elbow strike, it flew backward like it had been hit by the full swing of a metal bat. He flew two meters without bouncing. His body, now a wreck, rolled across the floor, slammed into the cabinet, and finally came to a stop.

"Now, then! Let's ask him what we need quick, nya~."

Tsuchimikado bared his front teeth ferociously.

A bestial glint was in those eyes behind those blue sunglasses.

Hino appeared to be conscious, but it also didn't look like he could counterattack. He had lost his sense of balance, and he could only just barely manage to move his limbs. His figure looked like an insect on the verge of death.

Most of Kamijou's thought processes came to a halt presented with such an extreme situation.

Finally, Kanzaki and Misha made it down from the second floor.

"Are you okay, Tsuchimikado?!" Kanzaki cried, then scowled. "...What is this stench?"

Kamijou's absentminded thoughts began to move again. Propane is heavier than air, so the two of them must not have noticed it on the second floor.

Misha, as soon as she saw Hino's face, tried to draw the L-shaped nail pullers from her belt. Tsuchimikado grabbed her hand before she did. If she caused any sparks while swinging them around, they'd all be in huge trouble.

Kamijou informed them about the gas. Kanzaki stiffened a little and said, "We will carry out Jinsaku Hino's interrogation. Would you mind going to open the windows to get some ventilation right away?"

Her point didn't seem to be mistaken at first, but he asked anyway.

"Hey, then, wouldn't it be safer just to take him outside the house?"

"We will interrogate him in here until we have the necessary information. We do not want to give Hino an opportunity to escape after we've come this far."

"I see," replied Kamijou, convinced, nodding for the moment.

In that case, it would be best to get all of the gas out of the house as soon as possible. If a desperate Hino had planned to blow himself up, that would cause some problems. Kamijou visited the important places on the first floor, opening the windows and doors. Everywhere he went, he saw tons of ethnic souvenirs from overseas. Kamijou was utterly amazed at how bad a hobby it was, but now wasn't the time to be thinking about it.

After he had opened every window as far as possible, he returned to the living room. The shutters and curtains had all been thrown open, so it was no longer a dimly lit haunt. It was just a living room, like one you'd see anywhere.

"...I don't know."

When he returned to the living room, that's what he heard Hino say from his limp position up against the cabinet.

"What? What is that? Angel Fall? I don't know. My precious Angel, what are these people saying? I don't know. Please answer me, this is strange, it's really strange, why is this happening?"

Mumble, mumble. Mumble, mumble, mumble. He muttered at length in a low voice like an old, heat-stretched tape replaying over and over. It sounded like he was talking to himself, but it also sounded like he was trying to get his hooks into his sorcerer interrogators.

Tsuchimikado smirked, gave a broad grin, and smiled quite pleasurably before beginning. "Now then, let's start your *hearing*. The condition for your surrender is for you to spit up the ritual site of Angel Fall, so remember that. Let's begin. First, I guess we'll dislocate your elbow. A dislocated arm actually stretches out farther than you'd think, but let's try doing it one centimeter at a time, nyan~?"

His happy tone of voice instead sent a chill up their spines. Beside him stood Misha, silently, with a screwdriver in her right hand and the saw in her left. Just by changing the time of place, those do-it-yourselfer tools had changed into heart-stopping, brutal weapons.

However, even that didn't alter Hino's attitude.

He continued to mutter to himself, drained of strength, his limbs sprawled and unmoving.

"I don't know, I don't know, I don't know, I don't know, I don't know, I don't know, I don't know, I don't know, I don't know, I don't know, I don't know, I don't know, I don't know, I don't know, I don't know, I don't know."

His voice, completely flat, without any sort of modulation, sent a chilling surge through Kamijou's spine.

The index finger on Hino's outstretched hand twitched like a caterpillar.

It moved on its own, almost as if there were electrodes stuck into the muscles of his arm. It looked like it was drawing some kind of letters on the low carpet, but without ink or anything, they didn't stick.

However, Hino looked at the carpet his finger was running across with somewhat satisfied eyes.

"Ah, my precious Angel, my Angel…"

An uncanny incantation spilling out of his saliva-filled mouth.

Kamijou put in his own question without thinking.

"Your angel?"

"Yes, my precious Angel is always in my heart. My precious Angel will answer anything I desire. My precious Angel is without wrong. My precious Angel will surely bring me happiness as long as I follow!"

Right after he finished, Hino's hand convulsed and writhed. Kanzaki seemed to be on guard against his hand's movements.

"Yes, my precious Angel is always right! My precious Angel opened the gas stopper; my precious Angel said if I use an ambulance, my precious Angel said I could get away in the confusion."

Kamijou looked at Jinsaku Hino's stomach. The words CALL AN AMBULANCE had been carved in English into it as wounds with his own knife.

"…A literal translation would be to get an ambulance, nyaa~?" translated Tsuchimikado, following Kamijou's gaze himself.

I see, he thought. Originally, the riot police were the ones who were supposed to come in here, not Kamijou and the others. And those riot squad members would be decked out in perfect defensive gear with their helmets and body armor.

Jinsaku Hino would retreat to a place with a sturdy structure, like the bathroom. Then, when the riot police broke in, the gas would light up and explode. Then he'd steal the equipment and clothing from the fallen officers. After that, if he pretended to be injured and called for an ambulance, he could easily get through the encirclement…perhaps.

His "Angel" would tell him the answer to anything he wanted to do. However, Kamijou thought something about that was strange.

Hino's finger was writing words with such intensity it might break.

In a sharp, cautioning voice, Kanzaki commanded, "Stop your hand, Jinsaku Hino. This is not a warning, it is a threat. If you don't comply, I will take out my katana."

Kanzaki's voice was cold as steel, but Hino's hand did not stop.

Scribble, scribble. Scribble, scribble, scribble as it recorded letters on the floor.

"Hee-eeh-hee. I-it won't stop. I can't stop my precious Angel."

Hino himself appeared to be terrified of Kanzaki's edged voice.

His face looked like it was crying and laughing at the same time, but his right hand kept on moving like a separate creature.

...?

Suddenly, Kamijou was bothered by this situation.

He felt like he'd seen it somewhere before...No, he felt like he'd heard about this sort of thing from someone before.

No, wait, it was his summer classes.

Miss Komoe had said something during his summer makeup lectures, didn't she?

If he recalled correctly, there was research on whether one body could use two abilities—

"—That's right, a split personality."

A person's nerves are all part of one network. When a part of it is blocked off to seal away unbearable memories, for example, it's schizophrenia. And when that blocked-off part of the network is able to move independently, it's dissociative identity disorder—in other words, a split personality.

They said so on TV, too.

Jinsaku Hino was diagnosed with multiple personalities during a previous incident, and there was controversy over whether he had the ability to be responsible for it.

People with split personalities don't necessarily fall under the pattern of the person completely switching between "personality A" to "personality B" like they do in manga and movies. Depending on the case, the two personalities could be "crossed."

For example, there was a story about a split personality patient being scared that his reflection in the mirror would talk to him. From the doctor's point of view, the patient would actually be talking to the mirror *himself.* Personality A wouldn't realize that personality B was controlling his mouth.

Hino's right hand was like that, wasn't it?

What if Jinsaku Hino had a split personality, and his *other* personality was controlling his right hand?

"Hey, Angel Fall's side effect was that the inside and outside of people get switched, right?" Kamijou asked Kanzaki. "Then what happens with a split personality? Does one 'outside' count for two 'insides' in that case?"

"Huh?" Kanzaki looked at him.

"Well, I mean—" He immediately followed up, looking into her eyes.

"—is it possible that in Jinsaku Hino's body, personality A and personality B got substituted?"

"Wha...?" All present froze.

"If the two personalities *inside* Jinsaku Hino's 'exterior' swapped places, he wouldn't appear to be any different from the outside, right?"

Kamijou chose his next words carefully. "What would happen? Should we count someone with a split personality to have 'two interiors'? Or should we count the entire split personality as one 'interior'?"

"..." Kanzaki was at a loss. She looked at Tsuchimikado and Misha. They didn't have an answer, either. After Angel Fall had happened, they hadn't met anyone with the unusual characteristic, so they wouldn't know.

But in reality, it was Jinsaku Hino who broke the silence first.

"Sh-sh-sh-sh-sh-sh-shut up! Y-you're one of them, too! You're saying the same thing as that weird, tattling doctor! My precious Angel is real! My precious Angel is really real! Why don't you understand that?!"

From Hino's point of view, rejecting the existence of his Angel was probably more painful than taking his life. After all, Hino wouldn't hesitate to kill people if it was for his "precious Angel."

Unfortunately, his excuse didn't do anything for him.

In fact, it just made Kanzaki and the others look at him even more sharply.

"By a doctor...A doctor said that? That your Angel is just a split personality? Is that what you were diagnosed with?"

"Hee!" Hino quivered in fear at those words. "S-stop it, don't look at me like that. That doctor didn't understand anything. He just didn't know anything, that's all!"

Hino was trembling like a child, and Kamijou couldn't help but avert his eyes.

Though Hino was a murderer, guilty feelings still pricked into Kamijou somewhere.

"It's...decided, then." Kamijou heaved a heavy sigh. "Jinsaku Hino has a split personality. The reason he doesn't appear to be substituted is simply because personality A was substituted for personality B on the inside.

"In other words—" He finished in an agonizing voice...

"**—Jinsaku Hino isn't our man.**"

7

Everyone present froze.

Jinsaku Hino, who was completely caught up in all this, had passed out. Perhaps it was because of the extreme pain, or perhaps it was the shock of discovering that the Angel he believed in wasn't real.

Any clues they had as to who was behind Angel Fall had now been lost. They had wasted a lot of time, too. They didn't know where to start next, nor did they even know whether they had enough time to be moving around randomly.

"Then if Jinsaku Hino is not the mastermind behind Angel Fall, who could be the criminal?"

"Don't ask me..." Kamijou had nothing to say. They were at a total dead end. They could do nothing but continue to stand there in a daze, without any idea on where they should go from here.

Or so they thought.

"Hm?" Kamijou had looked away from Kanzaki's stare, but he thought he felt something wrong with the scene. He didn't know what it was, though.

He drew nearer to where his eyes were looking—to the cabinet Hino was leaning against.

The cabinet was filled with miscellaneous objects. It seemed like Touya went on overseas business trips quite often; it looked like he had just thrown the souvenirs he had collected from all over into there haphazardly.

Among all of them, there was one single object that couldn't be classified as a souvenir. It was a framed picture. The amnesiac Kamijou didn't know for sure, but he had apparently moved to Academy City after graduating from kindergarten. Therefore, the people in the picture were a child Kamijou and a younger version of his parents—or, at least, it should have been.

"This is..."

The "substitution" didn't apply only to flesh and blood; it extended to photographs, as well. The fact that Blue Hair was able to wear Index's habit just fine probably followed the same logic. Everything related to the person—from their clothes and shoe size to their fingerprints and blood-borne information to photographs and videos of them—had been substituted.

Those memories inside the framed picture had been distorted by Angel Fall as well. Kamijou was still depicted as his child self thanks to the effects of his Imagine Breaker, but in place of his mother was depicted Index, and in place of his father was depicted—

—in place of his father, there was...

"...Wait," he muttered automatically. The sorcerers caught up to his gaze, and they also realized a single fact.

What about Touya?
Why wasn't Touya Kamijou substituted?

The words they had just exchanged came back to him as if from the distant past.

—*There was just one person who evaded difficulty.*

—*Is it so strange to think that this young man is suspicious?*

His strange feeling unearthed more odd feelings from his memories, one after the other.

—*The "distortions" had their epicenter right on you, Kammy. It's spreading out from you.*

—*But despite that, for some reason, you stand at the center, alone and unharmed.*

All of the oddities finally resolved themselves into a single direction and became a question.

—*In all fairness, Kanzaki and I got lucky.*

—*Well, it's the* distance *and the* barrier.

That's right, he thought. If even magicians, even professional magicians in their world, were almost all caught up in Angel Fall, too, then…

"Could it be…Dad?"

Kanzaki knotted her eyebrows at the words he breathed. "What did you say? Are you telling me that he isn't 'substituted,' that he's the real thing?"

Kamijou, however, couldn't figure out where Kanzaki was headed with that question.

But he just needed to think about it calmly. As long as Angel Fall had even substituted photographs and records, then if one were to collect documents regarding "person A" after it happened, the only thing they'd have is data on "other person B." Even if Touya Kamijou were to appear plainly in the data, it would only be appropriate to judge that he was a different, substituted person.

Then, Misha, standing beside him, gave a cold sigh.

"Answer one, a self-answer. Target now specified. All that's left is to prove the theory…Opinion one. It was a very uninteresting theory."

No sooner had she said that than she jumped out of an opened window into the garden and ran off somewhere.

"Wait, Misha Kreutzev! What do you mean by *target*?!" shouted Kanzaki in a panic, but she was already long gone.

Her target.

That was the word she spoke as she looked at the photograph of Touya Kamijou.

"...Tsuchimikado," Kamijou began, taking a deep breath. "Is it really that rare that someone would remain normal like I have in Angel Fall?"

"Well, actually, you *should* be the only one." Tsuchimikado looked at the photograph from his blue sunglasses. "Even if someone draws a circle like I did, and even if you were deep in the lowest levels of St. George's Cathedral or the Mont Saint-Michel Monastery like Zaky here was, you couldn't have completely escaped from its effects. For example, even though I know I'm Motoharu Tsuchimikado, for all intents and purposes, I've been nice and swallowed up by the name tag reading 'Hajime Hitotsui.'"

Right. That was why Touma Kamijou had been mistaken for Angel Fall's perpetrator.

Angel Fall should have spared no one in the world from its effects. If there was just one outlier, just one person who hadn't been affected by the grand sorcery at all, then...

...then, in other words, that was the answer.

If the person who hadn't been affected at all by Angel Fall was the criminal, then...

Kamijou looked again at the framed picture on the shelf. He stared at it hard.

There was a family of three depicted in the photograph.

He knew that Shiina Kamijou had been substituted with Index.

He also knew that he himself hadn't been substituted because of the Imagine Breaker.

However...

Touya Kamijou was not substituted.

And there was no way he had the Imagine Breaker like Kamijou. If it was strange that not everyone the world over was engulfed by the effects of Angel Fall...and if this was just like a computer virus, a man-made "means"...and if only the one who spread it was unharmed...

"Damn it..."

But that was the only possibility that remained.

"Damn it!!"

The criminal was Touya Kamijou.

Touma Kamijou couldn't help but hate himself for having come to that conclusion.

8

Angel Fall was apparently a grand sorcery, a spell that needed a barrier and a magic circle.

So if they just destroyed the magic circle, they could stop Angel Fall.

"...Go back, Kammy."

However, Tsuchimikado, without even trying to look for the ritual site that might be in this house, suddenly came out with that. "I'll look around here. Kammy and Kanzaki, you two go protect Mr. Touya."

Kamijou frowned at his usage of the word *protect*.

These two were members of the English Puritan Church. Until now, anyway, they had cooperated under the pretense of stopping Angel Fall's mastermind, but why did they choose to side with Kamijou now that they knew his own flesh and blood, Touya, was the criminal?

Tsuchimikado looked at his face and smiled bitterly.

"Don't underestimate us, Kammy. Our objective is to stop Angel Fall. If we can accomplish that without killing anyone, that's the best solution, nya~." He did a one-eighty and spat the next words. "That damn Misha is too hasty. It's not like killing him will solve this for sure anyway."

Killing him.

Kamijou's spine froze at those words.

Misha never showed any hesitation when chasing a criminal. She had broken Jinsaku Hino's arm and ruthlessly pressed a saw blade against Kamijou's neck.

Would she do that to Touya Kamijou, too?

He had no idea what sort of logic enabled him to cause Angel Fall...

…but did that mean she would mercilessly bring down hammers and pincers against Touma Kamijou's father?

"Damn it, that's bullshit…"

She would not hesitate.

That was the reason Misha Kreutzev came here, after all.

Because she was trying to solve the problem by killing the criminal behind Angel Fall.

"…That's bullshit, damn it!!" Kamijou screamed.

The person he should have been taking his anger out on was no longer here.

CHAPTER 3
Angel Fall in the World of Injury

1

Kamijou and Kanzaki were silent in the taxi back.

He thought about Misha. They were in a car; she was on foot—it went without saying that they would arrive back at the beach house before her. However, Misha might get a ride midway through.

"..." He shut his eyes, exhausted. The framed picture, in all its substituted distortion, appeared on the backs of his closed eyelids.

It hadn't just happened to that picture. Somewhere, packed away, there was a precious photo album for which the same could be said, as well as for albums belonging to people all over the world.

And perhaps even for all the faded eight-millimeter film passed out at elementary school athletic meets...

...and perhaps even for that one Christmas card with the baby photo on it...

...and perhaps even for that cell-phone picture where a person huddled up with a lover to fit them both on the tiny screen.

They would all be precious memories for those people.

They were all memories that should never be sullied, never be distorted, and yet...

Why...why did that damn father of mine...

Kamijou heaved a long sigh.

Even that sound seemed to wear down on his spirit.

When they returned to the beach house Wadatsumi, it was engulfed in the orange sunset.

It looked like the color of fresh blood or a blazing flame, and it gave Kamijou the creeps.

Misha…Has she not returned yet?

Now that Touya was the criminal, she, who wanted his life, would surely appear.

And not as an agent of the devil, but as a righteous hero.

Nevertheless, Kamijou burst into the beach house, fearing for his father's safety. Good and evil, justice and injustice—these were merely secondary. He was only worried about his father. Above all else, the fact that feeling that way was considered "evil" made him despise this situation.

"Huh? Big brother, where have you been?"

When he entered the house, Mikoto called out to him. She was lying on her stomach in front of a fan and watching TV while licking an ice pop. *Thank goodness*, he thought. At the very least, it hadn't come to the point where the enlightened Misha had taken someone hostage.

"You were gone all of a sudden, so we were all really worried, you know? We were playing in the water, but we called it quits and started looking all over for you. If you were going out, you should have told someone or left a note or something—"

"What about Dad? Where is he?"

Mikoto's eyes grew wide at his sudden interjection. Kamijou didn't know what kind of face he was making, but his own voice sounded like it was on the verge of tears.

"On the beach, I think? I don't know where exactly, since everyone is all over the place looking for you, big brother. Oh, and I'm not slacking off; I'm on telephone duty. Seriously, you should go apologize to everyone."

Kamijou nodded and gave a "yeah."

He was about to go and run down his own father. He should apologize to him for that.

As he looked over toward the beach, Kanzaki, who was next to him, opened her mouth.

"The rest is my job. Please wait here," she said in a serious voice. "I will ensure Touya's safety, so—"

"Not gonna happen," he refused bluntly, croaking it out like he'd been standing out in the freezing rain. "I'll be the one to settle this. I need to be the one to solve this problem.".

"But—" Kanzaki started, then hesitated…probably out of kindness. Her kindness didn't want her to let him stand face-to-face and confront someone so close to him.

But that got on his nerves instead.

"No buts! Who the hell do you think you are?! Touya Kamijou is my father! *My* father! The only one in the world! I can't replace him with anybody! He's my only father!!"

Kamijou's sudden shout caused Mikoto to look at him, startled.

Kanzaki didn't say anything.

"So…"

Touma Kamijou declared, alone…

…without knowing what to do, without any answers…and yet, he declared it:

"So I'll be the one to settle this. I won't let any of *you* get in my way. I won't let any of *you* hurt him. My father, my father is—"

And yet he declared it.

He said it, each word, one by one.

"—I will save Touya Kamijou."

2

Touya Kamijou was walking on the sunset-tinted beach.

Touma could see exhaustion on his father's face. His body was dripping with sweat, too. He'd probably been running all over the place looking for Kamijou, who had suddenly vanished. Tonya was dog tired, but he wouldn't allow his feet to stop. He walked across the beach, almost dragging those legs of his, filled with exhaustion.

He looked nothing like a sorcerer.

He looked nothing like a combat professional, either.

"...Dad," he called out.

The moment Touya turned around, his truly drained expression transformed to one that looked relieved and happy.

It was the face of a normal person.

It was nothing but a father's expression, given after having finally found his missing child.

"Touma!!"

After waiting an ample five seconds, his face finally turned to anger.

"Where have you been?! Why didn't you tell us you were going somewhere?! Your mother is worried sick! In the first place, you said you were resting in the house because you were fatigued from the summer heat. Are you all right? You're not in any pain or about to throw up or anything, right?"

However, not even a second passed before his words of ire shifted into consideration for Kamijou.

Of course.

Touya wasn't angry with him because he hated him.

His father was angry because he was worried about his son.

Kamijou gritted his teeth in frustration.

He didn't want to have to go and *interrogate* Touya if he could help it. He didn't want to ask if he was the criminal who caused Angel Fall. He wanted to treat everything like it never happened, to go back into the beach house and enjoy themselves like they had been until now.

But he couldn't do that.

He needed to bring the Angel Fall incident to an end.

Even if that meant Touya would be his enemy. Even if at the end, he stopped Touya's wish, and his actual father ended up hating him. Even if after this, his father never talked to him like family again.

Because he had made up his mind.

He made up his mind that he would save Touya Kamijou.

He didn't know what Touya wished for. But Kamijou still wished he hadn't gotten mixed up in the bloody world of sorcery. Kamijou knew what sorcerers were really like. He knew how scary they were. He didn't want to consider that various sorcerers, Misha first on the list, would come for Touya's life.

That was all the more reason to end things before she arrived.

He needed to bring Angel Fall to an end.

So Kamijou asked, "...Why...?" while taking care not to let any trembling into his voice and not to break out crying.

Touya frowned at Kamijou, but he continued.

"Why are you here in this abnormal world? You're one of the normal people. What the hell did you go and get caught up in stupid occult bullshit for, Dad?!"

Touya's smile froze at those words.

"What...are you saying, Touma? More importantly—"

"Don't play dumb! I'm asking you why you're pretending to be a magician!"

Touya's expression vanished like a cord had been cut.

It wasn't the expression of a sorcerer who had sensed that he was in danger. It was the kind of look a father would give his son if he'd been caught guilty.

"...Before I answer, just tell me one thing. Touma, I won't ask you where you've been. *Do you feel all right?* Does it hurt anywhere?"

His words were so very unfitting for the situation that Kamijou was taken aback.

Even now that it had come to this, he was still worrying about Kamijou's health.

Like a father would.

"It doesn't look like there're any problems, then." Touya sighed a small sigh of relief. "Now, then...Where should I start?"

Kamijou remained silent.

He couldn't find anything to say to him. There was no reason he could have. But he kept his gaze fixed. He didn't take his eyes off his father for even a moment.

Touya's face was as blank as a toy with dead batteries.

To Kamijou, it looked like the man had suddenly put on ten years.

"I knew it, myself…I knew that trying to grant my own wish with those sorts of methods was idiotic." At last, he began. "Hey, Touma. You probably don't remember this, since you were sent to Academy City right after you graduated from kindergarten," recalled Touya, "but when you were still with us, do you remember what people around us used to call you?"

Kamijou frowned.

He didn't have any memories from the start and couldn't even remember anything from before this July.

Touya swallowed once, like he actually had something caught in his throat, then continued.

"They called you a curse."

He said this looking as if he might bite off his own tongue.

His expression belied his unending regret at the fact that he needed to declare that word to his son.

"Do you understand, Touma? You've certainly been an *unlucky* human ever since you were born. That's why you were called by that name. But do you understand, Touma? It wasn't just benign children's mocking." Touya gritted his teeth. "Even fully grown adults called you that. There was no reason. There was no cause for it. They called you that name just because you were *unlucky*."

Kamijou caught his breath.

The expression vanished from Touya's face.

It wasn't joy, and it wasn't happiness. There was simply nothing there.

"With you nearby, everything around you becomes *unlucky*. Children believed that rumor and would throw stones at you soon as look at you. The adults didn't even stop it. When they saw your wounds, Touma, they wouldn't feel sorry—in fact, they ridiculed you. They would goad you on, asking why you hadn't suffered even worse wounds."

Kamijou couldn't figure out the emotion behind the impassive words Touya uttered.

That was probably the point. All those emotions twisting and turning inside him, so strong that he couldn't suppress them. He thought it was a display of his feeling that he absolutely did not want to show them to his son.

"If you went away, the *misfortune* would go away, too. Children believed that rumor and distanced themselves from you. Even the adults believed the story. Do you remember, Touma? You were once even chased around by a man with a debt and stabbed with a kitchen knife. The people at the television station who heard about it made it the pretext for a supernatural-themed episode and showed your face on camera, without asking permission, and treated you like some kind of monster!"

The world dyed in orange was like the flames that burn in hell.

The single man could do nothing within those flames but stand there with a frozen look.

"That's also the reason I sent you to Academy City. I was scared. Not about good luck, or bad luck, or whatever. I was scared of reality—where people would believe in that and commit violent acts against you like it was the obvious thing to do." Touya's face didn't change one bit as he continued his lament. "I was scared. It seemed like that urban myth would eventually kill you for real, Touma. That's why I wanted to send you to a world where those sorts of myths didn't exist."

So Touya had even severed a bond with a family member.

He wanted to protect his child, even if it meant their family couldn't be together.

"But even on the cutting edge of science, you still came to be treated like an *unfortunate person*. I could tell just from the letters you sent. Though it seems like the malicious acts of violence weren't happening." He smiled. "I couldn't be satisfied with just that. I wanted to destroy your misfortune itself. But that was a wish that wouldn't be granted, either using common sense or the latest scientific methods."

And still…even though he knew it couldn't be granted…
Touya Kamijou never, ever wanted to give up.

"Only one option was left. I decided to sully my hands with the occult."

Touya Kamijou cut off there.
Kamijou considered it—that Touya had executed Angel Fall in order to erase Kamijou's misfortune. But what did Touya want to do by summoning an angel? Was it something so stupidly straight-forward like wanting to have a direct line to God so that his prayers would reach? And to do that, he caught up so many people in it and even went so far as to substitute their insides and outsides…
Then, after having thought that far, Kamijou realized.
People's insides get swapped. In other words, Touma Kamijou's title of "unfortunate human" would be switched with someone else. Indeed, if that happened, he wouldn't have to bear that burden anymore.
The angel didn't matter at all.
What Touya Kamijou wanted was the interior substitution.
"…You moron."
However, it was a double-edged sword.
After all, the "existence" known as Touya Kamijou would be switched for somebody else. Touya's own son would no longer think of him as his father. In fact, a completely random stranger would turn into Touma Kamijou. He would rudely set foot into their family as his own son.
But Touya Kamijou still wanted to protect his child.
Even if it got the whole world wrapped up in it.
Even if his own child would never call him "father" again.
Even if they would never be together as a smiling family again.
But Touya Kamijou still wanted to protect him.
Even if he were to become a criminal, he wanted to protect his own son from the invisible "bad luck."
So Kamijou, unable to endure it, roared:

"You freaking moron!!"

Touya looked surprised. Kamijou couldn't forgive that.

"Yeah, I guess I was pretty unlucky," he spat in response. "I've almost died a whole bunch of times already just during summer break. I even had my entire right arm completely cut off. If you compared me to everyone else in my class, I'd probably be the only one who had such an unlucky summer break.

"But," Kamijou continued. "Did I ever once say that I regretted it? Did I *say* that I didn't want to have such an unlucky summer break, damn it?! You've gotta be joking. Yeah, my summer vacation's been unlucky, all right. But so what? You think I'd regret something so stupid like that?!"

That's right.

The one who rescued Aisa Himegami from Misawa Cram School was Touma Kamijou.

That's right.

The one who saved Little Misaka from the experiment was Touma Kamijou.

And...

The one who protected the smile of the girl in white was probably him, too.

Even if those had been situations he'd been dragged into. Even if those opportunities had just been a series of coincidences brought on by his bad luck. He should be proud of them. Instead, he shuddered at the thought that **he wouldn't have gotten dragged into those situations if he had good luck**.

"Yeah, if I wasn't so unlucky, I think I could have lived in a more peaceful world. I wouldn't have nearly died over and over again just this summer." Kamijou glared at his father. "But would that really be good luck? I would live a relaxed life, and in the shadows, others would be suffering, would be bloodied, would beg for help, and I wouldn't notice any of it! What part of just floating along through life sounds like *good luck* to you?!"

Touya looked at Kamijou, taken by surprise.

Kamijou said, "Don't force your pathetic *good luck* on me! Don't take this beautiful *bad luck* from me! I will walk this path. I've done so until now, and I'll keep doing it, so that I won't ever regret it!"

So don't get in my way.

I don't want your good luck. *If I'd otherwise be living in a daze without noticing the suffering of everyone right next to me, I'll get dragged into however much bad luck that suffering people need.*

So..., said Touma Kamijou.

"Don't look down on my rotten luck! I'm the happiest person in the world right now!"

He was probably smiling.

A savage smile, a barbaric smile, a rough smile, without a shred of panache.

But Touma Kamijou was smiling the best, strongest smile as he declared that.

"..."

Touya...

Words couldn't find their way out of Touya Kamijou's mouth.

In this world dyed in orange, with only the sound of the waves to fill their ears, Touya smiled. He smiled wider, wider, wider, wider, stretching his grin out thin across his face.

He...sighed.

At that time, for the first time for real, Touya Kamijou gave a small smile.

"What, really?" he said in a relaxed voice. "You were happy from the start, Touma?"

Yeah. Kamijou nodded without hesitation.

Touya gave an expression like a huge weight had been released from his shoulders.

"I'm such an idiot. This would have the exact opposite effect. Was I trying to steal my own child's happiness from right before his eyes?" He laughed at himself in relief. "Though it's not like I was able to do anything, I suppose. Boy, am I a moron. I should have known that collecting all those sorts of souvenirs wouldn't change anything. **I should know that occult stuff doesn't have any power at all.**"

"Eh?" Kamijou frowned suddenly at his father's words.

Touya didn't notice his reaction.

"Besides, if your bad luck could be cured just by buying up some folk charms for stuff like home safety or scholastic success from souvenir stands, you wouldn't be proud of it. I'll stop coming back from business trips having bought strange souvenirs. Your mother would be happier with candy."

"W-wait a second," Kamijou interrupted. "You triggered Angel Fall, right? Then where is the ritual area? If you don't want to get rid of my bad luck anymore, then we can put a stop to Angel Fall already, right?"

For some reason, Touya made a dubious face at that.

"Angel Fall? What's that, some kind of new lingo? Name of a band?"

"...Wait...a second." Kamijou looked at Touya's face again. "Hey. **Do you know where Mom is right now?**"

"What are you saying, Touma? **She's gone back into the beach house, hasn't she?**"

Kamijou stood there dumbstruck.

It didn't look like his father was lying to him.

Touya really believed that Index was his wife. But that was odd, then. If Touya Kamijou was the criminal who pulled off Angel Fall, then he shouldn't be under its effects.

Wait. Think about this. Have we missed something? This situation is clearly weird. Judging by the way Dad's talking, it sounds like he was just trying to give protective charms to his unlucky kid.

Touma Kamijou's thoughts were suddenly cut off by the *crunch* of sand being crushed.

Kamijou looked up.

"...Misha Kreutzev."

Just how long had she been there? There was nowhere to hide on this shoreline, and yet a girl wearing a red inner suit and an equally red mantle atop it was just...standing there. Black belts wrapped around her in various places, and she even wore a collar. Touya looked at her in automatic disbelief.

Misha didn't answer Kamijou's call, either.

She silently watched Touya's face.

They were ten meters or so away from each other. Kamijou remembered the night he was first attacked and it sent a chill up his spine. That power of hers, which was so far above even the fearsome Jinsaku Hino's that she crushed him as if she were chasing away a stray cat. A distance this short couldn't be called "distance" for Misha.

However, Kamijou still thought that maybe he could talk to her. That was his mistake. He casually stepped in front of Touya, as if to cover him, and said:

"Wait, Misha. Something's wrong. Dad is definitely not substituted with anyone. But he doesn't realize that other people are, either. Angel Fall is affecting him. I don't know how, but—?!"

He was cut short as his throat froze.

He got goose bumps.

Something was erupting from Misha Kreutzev's petite body—something invisible. Kamijou's feet were glued to the ground, a pressure settled into his stomach, his breathing became ragged, his heartbeat rushed about, and it felt like painful sparks were bursting in the back of his head, and his thoughts stopped.

He almost thought it was like there was nerve gas spewing from her pores, but that wasn't quite right. Misha wasn't doing anything. She wasn't doing something in particular—her very presence was constricting Kamijou's body.

Intent to kill.

With just that malicious aura, Touma Kamijou felt himself turn to stone.

Whump!! He felt an oppressing fear like the gravity here had ballooned to ten times its normal strength.

Misha's slender hand slowly wavered toward the belt on her waist. What she took out was the L-shaped nail puller. He saw the half-baked sharp tips, and behind him, Touya gulped. Yeah—the wild shape of the tips looked more heinous than a poorly made knife.

Despite that, Kamijou managed to call out to her again. "Wa...it. ——Misha...listen to me!" However, she did not answer.

The wind simply blew. Her bangs fluttered.

Behind them were glaring, squirming eyes, utterly devoid of all emotion.

Kamijou gave a start in spite of himself.

Compared to Jinsaku Hino's eyes, embellished with violent, passionate emotion, Misha's eyes were the direct opposite. They were no longer human eyes. Human eyes cannot have that sort of color. Two eyeballs, which looked like nothing more than glass or crystal balls, as if they had cut off all psychological phenomena.

Misha Kreutzev said nothing.

She simply brought the nail puller straight out to the side and looked at Kamijou with eyes like security cameras.

He froze.

His voice stopped.

This small girl in front of him, wearing a red inner suit wrapped in a mantle, did not look human. He felt like it was something completely different, writhing around inside human skin.

Misha slowly, slowly readied the nail puller as one would ready a shinai.

That torture device she had used to break Jinsaku Hino's wrist with but a single flick of the hand. Could he possibly keep Touya safe while evading attacks from something like that? Kamijou was trembling, and his palms moistened with a disgusting sweat.

Nonetheless, he could not back down.

Kamijou finally balled his quivering right hand into a fist—

—when suddenly he heard Kanzaki's angry shout from out of thin air.

*　　*　　*

"Get away from there, Touma Kamijou!!"

Whoosh came the cry of the wind.

Something that could be called an invisible slash ran across the sand and glinted between Kamijou and Misha. The earth that was whipped up from the straight cut rose to form a wall of sand. Misha, who was just readying her pliers then, averted her attention for a moment, and in that moment Kanzaki stepped between them.

Then, next to the murderously posed Kanzaki, he saw Tsuchimikado. When did he get back?

"Good work, Kammy. You really did well. You settled things, right? Back off, then—battle is our job."

He didn't know what means he had used, but he had been watching from close by?

Touya looked at Tsuchimikado and worked his mouth. That was understandable. If he was under the influence of Angel Fall, then he would appear to be a sketchy idol surrounded by rumors to Touya's eyes.

But it didn't seem like there was any free time to clear up the misunderstanding.

Kamijou, still astonished, nonetheless looked toward Misha, who was acting strange.

"Hey, Tsuchimikado. What the heck is up with her?"

"Well...When we gave it some thought, it was strange before." Tsuchimikado grinned savagely. "We'd figured someone from a different church would use a fake name to refer to themselves with, but Misha didn't actually do that. We should have been on our guards right then, nya~."

"?"

"You see, 'Misha' is, well—" Kanzaki stared at Misha without faltering. "—In Russia, **it's a name given to boys**. It's far too strange to even use as a fake name."

On the other hand, the Misha in question said nothing.

She narrowed her eyes and adjusted the aim of her nail puller from Touya to Kanzaki.

"What? Why would she do something like that...?"

"When we put in an inquiry to the Russian Catholic Church about it, we learned that there's a Sasha Kreutzev, though. The one she's substituted with is probably Sasha."

Kamijou looked at Misha's face.

That's right—if she was under the effects of Angel Fall, she'd have to have been swapped with someone. It would be strange otherwise. But if that was the case, **then who was this girl who had substituted in for Kreutzev?**

"They exist, Kammy—people in this world who can become either a man or a woman. Their genders are always indeterminate, and they are present in the myths as both neither and both. A name, for them, is their objective itself, for which God made them. They would never be able to exchange names."

Kamijou frowned at what Tsuchimikado was saying, but he asked:

"Kammy, did you forget? **What's this grand sorcery called again?**"

In that moment, Misha's eyes shot wide open.

With a *roar* loud enough to shake the earth—

—the sunset, enveloping them in orange, cut to a night with a star-filled sky before he could blink.

"Wha...?"

Kamijou automatically looked above him. Touya's breath froze.

Night. As if a light switch had been flipped, the sunset transformed into night. An ominously giant, full blue moon loomed overhead. However, that was strange. At this time of the month, the moon should be half full.

"Wait...What the hell is this?!"

"Can you not tell by looking? That *thing* has changed twilight into the darkness of night," Kanzaki responded easily to the awestruck Kamijou.

It changed from evening into night. That was simple as wordplay, but that would mean she had freely changed the positional relationships between whole heavenly bodies, of the Earth and the sun. No, looking at the phase of the moon being incorrect, she might even be able to control that and other planets.

Celestial manipulation.

If that mad term doesn't give a good picture, then think of it as the power to end the world. For example, if the Earth's axis were just changed by ten degrees, one-fourth of all creatures would die out. If the Earth's rotation stopped, the entire world would collapse. Those standing on the planet cannot feel it, but the Earth is a celestial body that revolves at an amazing speed of 1,666 kilometers per second. If that revolution were brought to a sudden halt, then the dreadful power of inertia would work the same way as the inside of a car when the driver slams on the brakes. The entire crust of the planet would be completely blown away.

This all meant…

…that at a whim, Misha could break this world, whenever she wanted, and from wherever she wanted.

"Wait. Hey, wait a minute! Sorcery can do this kind of bullshit?!"

"No, **not by man**."

The cold, sharp, bladed voice belonged to Kanzaki.

"So this is a *night* meant to strengthen her own attributes. Looking at the placement of the moon and its principal axis, yes. I see, I understand. The one that oversees the blue as a symbol of water, and the one who protects the rear as a guardian of the moon. The one who rained down arrows of fire upon the corrupt city of Gomorrah in the Old Testament, and the one who proclaimed the conception of the son of God to the Holy Mother in the New Testament."

After all this, Kamijou finally remembered it.

He remembered what this grand sorcery was called.

Angel Fall.

Because it was called that, a certain existence must surely come falling down.

"—Known as the POWER OF GOD. A winged archangel who sits at the right hand of God, was it?"

The one who served God answered not the question of the one who slayed gods.

As if a shell was broken by an invisible force, as if shedding an invisible skin...

Like that, *it* awoke.

3

The angel didn't make any movements in particular.

As Kanzaki moved into a position to shield Kamijou and Touya, she reached down to the katana on her waist.

"An angel is a power that knows neither good nor evil. If it obeys the will of God and saves people, it is respected as an angel, and if it falls to the Earth and is tainted with mud, it is feared as a demon," Kanzaki explained sourly. "It's exactly like the legends in the Old Testament. POWER OF GOD...Would you go that far to return to your original place?"

Kamijou looked at Misha—no, the angel called the POWER OF GOD—in astonishment. Her reason for trying to stop Angel Fall was likely the simplest of everyone here.

Angel Fall is a technique to drop an angel to Earth.

So it's only natural that the dropped angel would feel like it should return to where it came from.

The POWER OF GOD said nothing.

No longer offering any explanation, she waved her L-shaped nail puller into the air above as if to begin.

A shivering chill settled over him like a nail of ice had pierced his heart.

The moon overhead radiated a huge, striking blue light. A ring of light appeared around the brilliantly glowing moon, like when a camera lens tries to chase the sun.

The lunar corona, with the full moon as its center, expanded in a blink and disappeared past the edges of the horizon in the night sky.

Then, various strands of light shot through, as if inscribing compli-cated symbols on the ring's inside.

It wasn't simply giant. When Kamijou looked more carefully, he saw that each and every one of those specks of light drawing those lines was a separate magic circle. Like a school of fish swimming through the sea, like a line of ants parading across the ground, the millions, *billions* of magic circles floated into a regular pattern and constructed one large circle.

But. There's…There's such an incredible amount of light.

Kamijou couldn't help but be amazed when he stared at the cluster of sparkling lights in the night sky.

It would be incorrect to look up at the stars at night and think them frail or transient. Things that are farther away appear smaller—even an elementary school student understands perspective. For exam-ple, if one lives in Japan, they've probably at least seen an SDF or USFJ jet fighter flying through the air before. However, even if they can see the vapor trail running through the sky, would anyone have ever seen the color of the flames spurting from its engines?

That's how it is.

It means that there is enough distance so that one can't see the level of light from a combat fighter's jet engines. In fact, artificial light that can be picked out in the stratosphere is probably limited to the rocket propulsion light when sending up a satellite.

Even Kamijou, who was not well versed in sorcery, could under-stand it.

This was phenomenal.

Bzzt. From inside him came a trembling sensation.

A spongy bead of sweat appeared on Kanzaki's cheek as she looked up at the night sky.

"Are you insane, Power of God?! You would bring out a tech-nique above even the levels recorded in the Old Testament just to aim for one person? Do you plan on purging this world?!"

Both her tone of voice and her words were extraordinary.

Kamijou couldn't help but squeeze in a question.

"What? Hey, what the hell is that angel about to start…?"

"It's the torrent of fire arrows that once burned an entire corrupt civilization. If something like that is activated, the history of mankind will end right here."

This was so colossal that Kamijou couldn't get the sense that it was real.

However, the words *fire* and *torrent* left an unpleasant feeling in his mind.

Arrows of fire...are gonna fall? Wait, could that be those lights in the sky? Those billions of clusters of lights that are as bright as a fully fueled rocket...are gonna all come down?!

Petrified, Kamijou looked up into the sky. Considering it simply, those billions of sparkling points of light were basically all the rocket flares from missiles aimed at the ground. This wasn't on the level of a simple carpet bombing. Enough missiles would come raining down on them that even though each one would lock on to a different person, there would still be some left over.

He didn't know the scope of attack. Was it this city? Was it this country? If it were everything under the night sky, then perhaps it would reduce half the planet to rubble.

Kanzaki, looking like her heart would stop beating any second, said, "Angels cannot kill humans without an order from God, and yet...have you even forgotten that, POWER OF GOD? The number of souls to be judged during the 'final judgment' in the New Testament is decided ahead of time. You would understand that killing people so carelessly now would equate to bringing that judgment to ruin! You told us that!"

He felt like he'd heard that from Tsuchimikado before.

He said that God would come down to Earth at the end of the world, then decide on a case-by-case basis who would go to heaven and who would go to hell. The results were actually set in stone from the beginning, so if an angel killed people imprudently, then those results would go wrong or something.

Leaving religious notions behind, the logic was a sort of time paradox. If it killed someone who was never originally supposed to be killed, their children would never be born. And then their grandchildren and their great-grandchildren—none of them would be born. Just like how someone who uses a time machine is a transcender who can bend history to his will, this angel, who was out of position with the history of mankind, had the power to change mankind's future and its ultimate end.

A transcender.

Kanzaki gave a heartrending cry for her to stop this massacre, but the servant of God didn't budge an inch.

It did not go mad with rage, nor did it smile in scorn, nor did it feel any guilt.

It simply did not budge.

Kamijou shuddered at the sight. Logic likely would no longer work on this angel, on the POWER OF GOD. It was like it had gone off some sort of rails at the very moment Angel Fall activated.

The angel before them now had only one directive—to return to heaven.

It was not giving the most minute of thoughts to the effect it would have on the world as a result.

It was like...all it wanted to do was put something proper back in its proper place.

Just like a person who has received another person's organ during a transfusion, but the organ is unsuitable—even though he knows he'll die, his body will reject it anyway.

Had it only been moving with Kamijou and the others until now just to ascertain its target?

After an overwhelming bombing run, it can be difficult to judge whether the target is dead when they're hidden underneath a mountain of wreckage and corpses. So did she need to know her target's face beforehand?

Kamijou bared his canines and looked skyward.

His right hand could erase any abnormal power, even if it was a miracle from God himself. But the magic circle was placed too far away from the start. The stratosphere is too high to be reached even by jet fighters.

Therefore, he turned his glare to the POWER OF GOD.

If he couldn't stop that magic circle, then all he could do was stop the one using it. It was the same with Angel Fall. If the sorcery was still incomplete, then if he stopped the practitioner, it should be able to obstruct its activation.

"Damn it..."

However, presented with the simplest answer before his eyes, Kamijou gritted his teeth.

That would make him no different from that angel.

"You bastard!!"

The POWER OF GOD just looked intently at Kamijou like that, without adjusting its expression.

With eyes that looked like they were staring at an insect wriggling around in the mud from one spot higher up.

The archangel who had prepared enough power to destroy the world without moving a single fingertip said nothing.

Her gaze had no sense of danger. He couldn't even feel any compassion.

There was no reason to feel pain over squashing one bug, after all.

"Damn it! Say something already! Listen up—I'm really mad right now. I'm pissed out of my fuckin' mind! We're not negotiating any of this one bit—shut up and stop this damn spell!" yelled Kamijou at the angel shorter than him, but his voice seemed to be trembling.

Touya appeared to be shocked by his own child flinging obscenities more than anything else in this situation.

Kamijou thought back. He thought about the speed at which she had driven away Jinsaku Hino right before his eyes. Her weight. Her timing. Her construction. That power, though camouflaged. The mere Kamijou could do nothing but be made to dance in her hands, like in the preestablished harmony of a contrived chessboard in the newspaper. That GODLIKE POWER.

And now it was even more than that.

Her stiff, uncomfortable true character had already been unmasked.

"..."

A muddy sweat broke out on him. He stepped in front of Touya to cover him. That attitude certainly appeared heroic, but its essence was nothing but rashness. The gap in strength between him and the POWER OF GOD was no longer something that could be closed by human hands. It was like he was being told to fight a nuclear missile with his bare hands.

"Touma Kamijou."

Then, Kaori Kanzaki quietly turned around to him.

"I will hold back the POWER OF GOD. You take Mr. Touya and flee as soon as possible."

At that moment, Kamijou was unable to understand what it was that Kanzaki had just said.

She declared it so simply.

She asserted it in a situation like she was being told to fight a nuclear missile with her bare hands.

Without any hesitation, nor any reserve, nor any mercy, nor fear, nor exhaustion.

Kanzaki turned her back to Kamijou and confronted the angel, who was like a god of death.

"Wh...y...?"

That was the only question Kamijou could pose.

But to that barely squeezed-out question, Kanzaki did not even turn around.

"I don't have a reason. I only stand here because there is something that I can do," replied her back, in a voice that sounded truly uninterested. "A *purge*, is it? How worthless. How truly worthless. By such a worthless method, the destination I aim for is far and unreachable," she spat, taking a step forward.

Kamijou couldn't stop her back. He couldn't catch up to her back. The distance, not even spanning one meter in length, felt infinitely large. She wasn't strong, nor frightening, nor sharp, nor heavy, fast, cold, or hot.

She was just...different.

The back of she who confronted the POWER OF GOD was incredibly different, as is fitting for someone in that role.

The god slayer spoke.

"The war we are about to conduct now is *different*. While you flee, please take the utmost caution not to be caught up in it."

He was told to run away, but Kamijou couldn't understand.

Where should he run to at this point? Mars?

Then, without turning back to face the confused Kamijou, Kanzaki said:

"Think about it and look. This *purge* of the POWER OF GOD. If it conducts it, it can end things quite easily. Why do you think, then, that the angel watches what we are doing indifferently?"

When she said that, Kamijou finally figured it out.

If it could perform its "purge," then it should just do it now. The POWER OF GOD would have no reason to hesitate to do so. After all, it had but one objective.

Why in the world would she not carry it out despite that?

"It is not that it *isn't* carrying it out, but rather it *cannot*. It may be called the POWER OF GOD, but a technique on this scale will take time to complete. It is nothing unusual. There was, generally speaking, such a wait time for the heavenly judgment that came down upon civilizations in the past, as well." Kanzaki's back spoke. "—About thirty minutes or so, in terms of time, I see. He-heh, that's cutting it a bit close to get all the animals onto the ark."

Kamijou was speechless.

Thirty more minutes. After thirty minutes, the purge would bring arrows of fire down on about half of the world. Just at a guess, how many millions of missiles might come down? Kamijou's Imagine Breaker couldn't cover the entire world, of course.

But on the other hand...

If they could stop the POWER OF GOD in thirty minutes...

"Well, then, I can't just run away! I'm in this, too! My right hand can at least do a little against an occult opponent like that, can't it?!"

"Please leave. If a professional were to let an amateur protect her and be wounded, she wouldn't even have the right to commit *seppuku*," answered Kanzaki in a cool voice.

"Why are you so calm? That thing can't tell right from wrong right now. You all kept saying how angels couldn't kill people and every-thing, but look at how reliable *that* was!" Kamijou was shouting as if to stop someone from leaping to their death. "I can't leave you to fight that thing by yourself! I can fight, too! How can I run away at this point?!"

"Listen to me," Kanzaki's back said, however, coolly. "That thing exists outside of human standards in the first place. Thinking that you will fight it, or that you will win against it, is already mistaken."

Kamijou caught his breath and fixed his eyes on her back.

"Do not get me wrong, though. I have no intention of dying a pointless death. I will not lie and say I will win, but I also will not say I will lose. The only thing I can do is *hold it off*, equally and evenly.

"Touma Kamijou, while I am holding it off, I want you to take Mr. Touya and undo Angel Fall," she told him quietly.

"Wait, hey, what?"

"Have you forgotten the POWER OF GOD's objective? It created this purge in order to stop Angel Fall. In other words, if you stop Angel Fall before the purge is carried out, it will no longer have any neces-sity to do so. Do you not think so?"

Her final phrase sounded like it was directed not at Kamijou but at the archangel.

The chilling angel did not respond.

The POWER OF GOD didn't care one way or the other. In any case, the purge that would destroy Angel Fall's caster, Touya, in thirty minutes would resolve everything. If Kamijou could find another way to stop Angel Fall before that happened, the angel shouldn't have a problem with it.

Therefore, the POWER OF GOD silently stared down its target, Touya.

As if to say that whatever they chose, and however the cookie crumbled, they'd get the same result, it didn't even need to raise an eyebrow.

Like it was carefully considering which route to take: its purge or the more brutal stoppage of the Earth's rotation by means of celestial manipulation. Like it was absentmindedly rolling its options around in its hand.

Kamijou shot a glance at Touya. It was certainly far too dangerous to leave him close to the POWER OF GOD. But still…

"But what about you? You can't go up against the POWER OF GOD…"

"Who knows? However, this is the most beneficial option. You would not be able to hold that off. Please carry out your own role properly and undo Angel Fall as soon as possible. Your efforts will raise my chances of survival."

Kanzaki took yet another step toward the POWER OF GOD.

"And above all, not a hair on my head wishes to make a sacrifice of a civilian in a sorcerer's battle. I will not let Touya Kamijou die— even if it should cost me my life."

"…Are you seriously okay with that?"

"Yes. I apologize for being rude, but I will try trusting you. If you can save my own life in the same way you once saved that child before my eyes, I would appreciate it."

Kanzaki's back didn't say anything more than that.

Kamijou thought about saying something, but he couldn't find any words.

If he was to try and stop her, they'd lose that much more time. Each and every pointless act surely brought down her chances of survival.

He clenched his teeth.

"I'll leave it to you, Kanzaki! I'll trust you, too!!" he shouted, grabbing his clueless father's arm and darting back toward the beach house, half dragging him. Touya cried, "Wait, what's going on here?" but Kamijou took no notice of it.

The POWER OF GOD's gaze passed through Kanzaki and shifted toward Kamijou.

Kanzaki slid in the way to cut it off.

"Your opponent is right here. Listen to what I'm saying. The role of an angel, to begin with, also includes delivering messages between God and man, and yet you…" Then, Kanzaki smiled a little. It didn't match the situation. "But even still, he said he'd trust me. Me, of all people. My word—I can't make fun of Stiyl's report for saying how that threw him off during the Misawa Cram School battle. That one utterance was certainly ideal. My chances of survival have doubtlessly been raised because of your words," she soliloquized, reaching a hand for the hilt of the sword at her waist, the Seven Heavens Sword.

The Power of God, for its part, keeping a silent eye on Kanzaki, finally breathed, in an inhuman voice:

"————qFOolIshrw."

Kaboom! The angel's back exploded.

What came out of its back was like wings, but they were not the elegant white ones of a swan.

They were like the wings of a peacock, as if made from carved ice.

The wings were sharp and rough, seeming to have been made from shaved crystal, and there were dozens of them all sticking out like a pincushion. Tons and tons of ocean water rushed against the angel's back.

Its back and the seawater made contact, and they transformed into giant wings of water.

Each one of the giant, watery wings protruding from it was anywhere from fifty to seventy meters in length, and they slashed out behind the Power of God.

They appeared to form a wall that no number of people could breach, and they looked like sharp, crystalline fan blades that would cut off your finger if you touched it.

The dozens of frozen wings stretched their blades toward the heavens.

At the end, a single drop of water appeared over the Power of God's head. It drew a small circle and stabilized as a ring floating in the air.

Each and every one of those drops looked like the ocean surface in the dead of night—a deathly blue, soiled with black.

Those wings, which had Telesma going through them from the ends of the feathers to the beginnings without a single gap, were each a single, divine judgment attack that could blow away entire mountains, rip into the lands, and create valleys. Normally Kanzaki had enough power that her enemies would fear her on the battlefield and open a way for her, but even she found her body tingling with nervousness. A normal person might have forgotten to breathe just from the pure malice radiating in this place.

"My, I've made quite a rash promise for such an extreme position." Kanzaki lowered her center of gravity just slightly—and then noticed something. "? Tsuchimikado, where are you? Tsuchimikado?"

He wasn't here.

At some point, he had shrewdly vanished from the battlefield.

Exasperated at Tsuchimikado's having upheld his policy of infidelity even in this extreme situation, she muttered, "Well, that's the kind of person he is. I can throw him away and he'll still survive. Now then, I must survive through this with my own power. Now, along with the use of my Single Glint, I give one name."

Then, Kaori Kanzaki declared…

…her other name, engraved upon her own body and soul.

"The hand of salvation for those who cannot be saved—Salvare000."

4

Meanwhile, Tsuchimikado ran alone, cutting through the dark of night.

Now, then…This has gotten pretty bad, yeah, pretty bad. Though it was unavoidable, I should have blasted the whole thing to smithereens sooner.

As if distancing himself from the battlefield…as if running from the fight.

Many errors should be forgotten—clearing my head with positive thoughts. Aight, Kanzaki is holding it off, and she was getting in the way from a certain point of view, so I should think about how I'm able to move freely now.

As if heading to a new battlefield, as if an insect diving into the fire.

Heh-heh-heh. Now, then, time to start the captivating betrayal. Sorry, Kammy, it seems like saving this problem is gonna take at least one person to be a sacrifice.

Smiling enjoyably, Fallere825—the backstabbing blade, Motoharu Tsuchimikado—dashed through the darkness.

5

Kaori Kanzaki and the POWER OF GOD faced each other with ten meters between them.

However, if you knew even a little about Crossism, that sentence would sound reckless. Not on the level of Kanzaki being weak or the archangel being strong, mind you. A more fundamental part, at its very roots, was altogether different.

Roughly speaking, this is a rule that applies to mankind's religions the world over, but…

Humans cannot go against God.

Aside from heretics who serve different gods, those of Crossism cannot go against angels of the same Crossism. It's an obvious rule when you think about it.

In other words, as soon as Kanzaki aligned herself with the Church, she was absolutely unable to win against the POWER OF GOD.

It was like a game of rock-paper-scissors where she could use nothing but scissors—as soon as rock came out, she would lose for sure.

That was why this was all absurd.

However, the angelic girl didn't speak a word. It didn't even show a smile of compassion.

The POWER OF GOD simply raised on high one of the water wings coming out of its back. There was close to ten meters distancing them, but that had nothing to do with it. For one of those wings, which were seventy meters in length, it was almost *too close.*

Those water wings, which enclosed Telesma all the way to their tips, just one of them could be said to be divine judgment that would crush a city. With one downward flap, this beach would blow away, and it would be able to dig a crater into the Earth and create a bay. Just like how the gods' power shaped the lands in the era of myths.

The POWER OF GOD did not hesitate.

Even knowing what would happen should it unleash that destructive force on a powerless human.

The archangel presiding over blue didn't hesitate for a moment—it swung down that raised seventy-meter-long water wing.

It resembled a tower collapsing. The sliced air changed into a windy fist and ravaged the surroundings. Then, suppressing even that, the watery wing came down straight upon Kaori Kanzaki's head at a terrifying speed.

That was it.

That should have been it.

Slash! came a smart sound as the water wing was severed with a flashing horizontal stroke.

Who could have predicted that to happen?

The POWER OF GOD abruptly stopped; Kanzaki only inhaled and answered it.

The nearly two-meter-long katana hanging at her waist.

As soon as it was plucked out, the giant seventy-meter-long water wing was severed like a bamboo shoot. That wasn't all. The wreckage of the sliced-off wing immediately blasted apart into very small pieces like it had been blown away by an explosion and disappeared off into the nighttime darkness.

Kanzaki didn't try to say a single thing.

Her katana's blade was already resting in its black sheath again.

The POWER OF GOD's bangs flapped in the wind. The glassy eyes behind them writhed, staring at her, as if to search for a weakness. It swung another one of the water wings on its back like it was testing something.

This time, a ferocious gale, seeming like it would wipe away everyone standing on the Earth with a single, flashy horizontal stroke, whipped up.

However, even that...

Slice! Kaori Kanzaki's single katana easily cut off the fifty-meter-long wing.

To add to that, Kanzaki also wasn't thrown around by the drawn katana's speed or its weight. The blade, which had been unsheathed a moment ago, was a moment later resting quietly in the sheath again.

At a distance of ten meters, Kaori Kanzaki silently fingered the katana's sheath.

The angel's movements ceased...

...as if carefully rewriting its tactics, wondering how best to cook the prey in front of it.

"If anything—" she taunted, "I, for one, did not expect you to be surprised at that. Perhaps you have underestimated this Kaori Kanzaki creature a bit, no?"

The POWER OF GOD didn't respond. This time, it crossed two of its watery wings, on the left and right, like scissors.

Roar! The two wings delivered a shriek as they assailed her...

...but with one attack from Kanzaki, who spun her body like a tornado, they were cleaved at the same time and destroyed.

"..."

Its bangs waved in the night wind. The eyes behind them rotated at her, as if to confirm a single fact.

Not just one or two of them had been sliced—in all, it was four. That wasn't a coincidence but rather a necessity. And one pregnant with contradiction. A disciple of Crossism shouldn't be able to go against its angels.

To her, Kanzaki said in a cool voice...

"Your first mistake was thinking I was just a disciple of Crossism."

She showed calmness enough to go all the way to show her own trump card. "My techniques are of the Amakusa-Style Crossist Church. It is a form of Crossism unique to Japan, created to believe in God even when its believers were being oppressed during the world of Edo."

During an era when oppression was so severe that being in possession of a cross or an image of Mary warranted execution, believers would liken Shinto wooden tags to "crosses" and images of the Buddha to "images of Mary." Amakusa-Style, which conducted camouflage in this way using Shinto and Buddhism, at some point became too intertwined with these fake faces of Shinto and Buddhism, and it started to get difficult to tell where the actual Crossism started. They had constructed an arranged version of the original.

The diverse fusion of religions with Crossist technique—Amakusa-Style Crossism.

In other words...

If she couldn't win against an angel with Crossism techniques, she would not use Crossism techniques. She would take the roundabout route of using techniques of a "religion in which angels do not appear," Buddhism and Shinto, and attack the angel that way—that was all.

What can't be done with Crossist techniques can be dealt with using Buddhist ones.

What can't be done with Buddhist techniques can be dealt with using Shinto ones.

What can't be done with Shinto techniques can be dealt with using Crossist ones.

Amakusa-Style covers for the weaknesses of each religion's techniques by using other ones. In other words, it can break through the major premise that one cannot defeat "angels" in "Crossism."

"..."

The POWER OF GOD's eyes froze. It waved three of its water wings up, one to the left, one to the right, and one straight above.

However, they were once again easily cleaved by Kanzaki's Single Glint.

"Also, a large amount of gods appears in Japanese Shinto, even when compared to other polytheistic religions. The *Yaoyorozu no Kami*, the eight million gods residing in every object in the world; the *Tsukumogami*, which form even in worthless objects given a long period of time; the man-made *Inugami* that, though hastily created, are made to protect people's homes; the *saru-kami*; the *hebi-kami*. There is probably not a religion in the world that consists of as many gods as Japanese Shinto. Therefore—" She touched the Seven Heavens Sword at her waist as if to emphasize it. "And this may come as difficult to believe for an angel to a monotheistic religion, but there are ways to interact with the gods of the polytheistic Shinto—in other words, ways to fight against gods. Stories that describe such legends as people killing sorts of evil gods who go berserk, demanding a sacrificial girl and wreaking havoc, with but a normal sword exist in great quantity, you know. There is a restriction in Shinto that says one mustn't wound a god, but...**why do you think they needed to create such a law?**" she asked in a singsong voice.

She said it so that this one-sided match with the angel would not end.

"..."

The POWER OF GOD just remained silent and sized up its "enemy." The severed water wings took in seawater anew and began to return to their original form and size.

On the other side, Kanzaki needed no preparation. All she had to do was lightly touch her finger to the hilt of the long katana that hung from her waist. She wove mana within her body using a certain type of unique breathing method, then reconstructed her own body into "the one who kills gods."

Then there was silence.

After that silence, which was so short—one-thousandth of a second—that a human couldn't detect it...

The POWER OF GOD and she who slays gods began their bout of life and death.

*   *   *

Thud!! came a powerful bellow.

It was the sound of Kanzaki, ten meters away, cleaving through the fifty-meter water wing that the archangel brought down on her head.

However, the POWER OF GOD did not move, for it could mend its shorn wings however many times it needed to. Before Kanzaki replaced her katana in the sheath and regained her balance, it waved another wing toward her for a strike from the left side.

As soon as Kanzaki cut that one apart, another wing flashed across on the right, aiming for her back.

There was a distance of ten meters between the POWER OF GOD and Kanzaki. The angel seemed to be trying to maintain that distance. It repeated its flurry of wing attacks, not letting Kanzaki draw near.

Kanzaki twisted her whole body, turned around, and cleaved the wing coming at her back in two. As if aiming for that moment, the servant of God swung three watery wings down on her from directly overhead, leaving time gaps between each.

The time gaps, however, were one-hundredth of a second—the realm of godlike speed, a gap undetectable by humans. However, Kanzaki reacted to it. The human body apparently needs 0.18 seconds to deliver a command from the brain to the fingertips, but Kanzaki, having transformed into the god slayer, was temporarily in a state above human domain, and that kind of common sense wouldn't work. Her blood vessels, muscles, nerves, organs, and skeleton—they were all recomposed so that they were able to kill gods due to the technique she used.

Slash! Kanzaki sliced through the first of the three watery wings by unsheathing the katana.

Before the next one-hundredth of a second elapsed, Kanzaki already had swung the Seven Heavens Sword back in its sheath and was prepared for the next strike. *With time to spare*, she thought, giving a smile in that one-hundredth of a second, but at that moment—

—the second watery wing spontaneously shattered.

Thousands of blade shards, like fine glass fragments, shot directly toward her.

"Wha...?!"

Kanzaki immediately attempted to deal with this downpour of blades, but at that moment, the third wing unexpectedly overtook the downpour, as if to scatter it.

"...Kuh!"

She managed to cleave the third surprise one. But she didn't have time to resheathe her katana. If she did that, she wouldn't make it in time to deal with the bladed downpour. With no other choice, Kanzaki gave up on her *iai* attack, and without returning her unsheathed blade, she began to intercept the downpour.

However, there was no way a single katana could cut down every last one of the thousands of edges.

The mere seventeen fragments that slipped through (the fact that she sliced all of the rest spoke volumes about her own skill) fell to the beach around Kanzaki. *Pow!!* came the roar of the explosive shock wave as the sand all launched into the air.

It was a wall of sand, blanketing her whole vision like a desert storm.

She cut through it like paper, and then more wings came at her from the left, right, and diagonally right.

The state of battle stabilized there.

There were ten meters between Kanzaki and the POWER OF GOD. In other words, that meant that Kanzaki's attacks would not reach the angel and the POWER OF GOD's would one-sidedly storm her.

To add to the bargain, because of the angel's repeated, rapid strikes, Kanzaki wasn't allowed to even resheathe her katana. Her specialty, the unsheathing skills, had been negated, and she was completely on the defense, wildly swinging her katana. Anyone looking at her wouldn't have seen anything but the inferior party.

Kanzaki gritted her teeth.

She was one of the top ten sorcerers, even in London.

She could count the number of times she had lost in one-on-one combat in her life on both hands. "One-on-one" wasn't limited to just "man vs. man," either, but also "man vs. beast king" and "man vs. weapon."

But it seemed she had come to the moment of the century.

Those "records" that she could count on her fingers seemed about to become endless.

Of course…

It was pretty doubtful as to whether this nonstandard angel *should* be really counted in that.

Sparks from the forty-five slashes per second burst with a *ckk-kk-kk-kk-kk-kk!!*

It was as if a large war sword of durable make was being steadily chipped away at amid an exchange of blows.

The angel made no attempt to move back. Absorbed in this protracted battle, like it was slowly but surely draining away Kanzaki's stamina, it began to send out rapid strikes with its watery wings at even more incredible speeds. Not allowing Kanzaki even a hundredth of a second's rest, it worked its dozens of wings like they were each a separate creature and assailed Kanzaki from all different angles, directions, with varying speeds and margins.

Then, something in Kanzaki's hands glistened, bathed in the moonlight.

Hyun!! came an air-splitting sound as seven wires cut through the sky.

Seven Glints.

Of course, against those watery wings filled to the brim with Telesma, from their tips to their roots, wires wouldn't be of any use. They were world heritage–class steel cords that a sword smith, inheriting the signature of Samoji, had forged, but nonetheless, they were easily sliced through like silk by a single-winged strike and met their ends.

But by cutting those sharp strands, the wings slowed their speed.

It was only a minute act of resistance, and though they did slow, it was only by one-tenth of a second.

However…

In this battle, she could unleash four or five moves in the span it took her to blink an eye.

"————, lkcURsEs!"

The POWER OF GOD's eyeballs squirmed and rolled. Cutting the wires carelessly had reduced its wings' speed. Kaori Kanzaki wasn't one to let those 0.1 seconds escape from her. She readied her lengthy katana at middle guard and pushed off with force—

—but when she tried to run, her leg collapsed with a *thud* underneath her.

…?

The angel, its drive returned, swung three watery wings down at her, one after another, but Kanzaki still cleaved them all with staggering agility and precision. However, it was then that the POWER OF GOD saw it—

—the feverish sweat breaking out all over Kaori Kanzaki's body.

Though god-slaying techniques may exist, the thing is that not everyone is able to use them. And no, it isn't a matter of talent. More crucial is that the burden they would place on a human body is just too large.

It wasn't that Kanzaki's unsheathing techniques were her specialty.

They were simply techniques that would rack her body to the point of destruction if she did not settle bouts within a moment's time.

As the angel threw out its merciless strikes with its watery wings, it looked at Kanzaki once again. Though she was performing rigorous movements ten times beyond that of a normal person, her face was not flushed, but rather it had gone blue, as if icy water were soaking all the way down to her neck. It could also make out a slight quiver in the hand that gripped her katana.

The price for that hard work had already begun to gnaw at her body.

The POWER OF GOD continued swinging its water wings around.

The results of the protracted battle were finally starting to show. At this point, the angel just needed to draw their duel out and Kanzaki would destroy herself. Kanzaki's body was finally beginning to waver at its rapid attacks, to which it added even more variation in speed.

The angel of blue commanded the watery wings on its back to deliver the killing blow—

—but Kanzaki pierced straight through the POWER OF GOD with a sharp sparkle in her eye.

"...Too slow!!" she thundered, batting down that winged attack that would have finished her off.

Her motions, so relentless as to be utterly impossible for a human being, raised her body temperature to abnormal levels, disrupted her blood flow, and ate away at her oxygen. Not only her muscles, but her very *bones* shrieked. Her pain was not that of a fever. It might have been easier on her had she imbibed *poison*.

Despite that, Kanzaki didn't stop.

With the look of a fierce god, she cut down the watery wings without yielding even a step.

Though Kaori Kanzaki was overwhelming the angel, she had already been driven to the precipice of death.

With every single action she performed, she vividly felt her own body being destroyed. Each time she swung her Seven Heavens Sword, the price for that excessive movement forcefully stretched out her joints; made her arteries squeal; and her organs, which weren't being properly supplied with oxygen, hit her brain with screams of a fuel shortage in the form of pain.

On top of that, she didn't know how long even *that* would hold. If just one of her arteries, squealing eerily in some kind of rhythm, was torn, then Kanzaki's life would surely end from just that.

"But—" She gritted her teeth, then sliced two wings coming at her from the left and right out of the sky like a tornado.

She moved her lips, which could no longer sense the muddy taste of blood.

"—are you saying that matters?"

She cut through an even more innumerable amount of wings, swinging her long katana around like a raging storm.

I cannot let it break through.

If Kanzaki went down here, the POWER OF GOD would doubtlessly set out to destroy the Kamijous, father and son, who would try and stop the purge descending upon the world.

I cannot let it break through!

Outside, she cut away the watery wings, while on the inside she was exposed to her own collapse, and she was in tatters. Despite that, she clenched her teeth and readied her blade yet again. Against the seemingly unreasonable slicing attacks from the water wings coming dozens of times per second, she sliced away the absurdly rapid attacks coming dozens of times per second, while she again readied herself for its next move.

The taste of blood and her fading consciousness stirred memories of days long past.

It was back when Kaori Kanzaki was still called the Priestess of Amakusa-Style. It was back when she was adored and referred to with a name far above a young twelve-year-old girl. Kanzaki had always harbored doubts. As she had listened to passages from the Bible before sleeping as if from a picture book, she always harbored doubts.

Heaven and hell.

When a person dies, God is said to decide whether to raise them to heaven or drop them to hell. Therefore, a human should do many good deeds during their life to prepare for going to heaven.

But...

If God has the power to save all people, then why would a hell be necessary?

If he could save all people, then he should save every one of them. If there are those who have somehow strayed from the path, then he should just lead them back to the correct one. If the hand of salvation really existed, it would be the best if it became something everyone could use to smile with each other equally.

Why did only some people become happy?

Why must those who were not chosen go to hell?

Kanzaki was ever one of those who were chosen. However, because of that, nobody around her was chosen. If a plane she was on were to crash, she alone would survive. No one else would. A bullet from an assassin's gun would never hit her even when aimed. The stray bullet, however, would shoot down somebody else. When a bomb would blow away an entire room of a building, person after person would fall on her to block the impact. There was even a child not even ten years old among them.

And in so doing, those people who were not chosen even at the very end would all look at Kanzaki's face and smile.

Ah, thank goodness, they would say.

I'm so glad you're safe, they would say.

As they stroked her head with the last of their strength, trying to caress the young, crying Kanzaki.

They would close their eyes happily, and the strength in the hand stroking her head would vanish.

They were all her fault.

God must have mistaken the distribution of "good luck." That's why Kanzaki, **someone who wasn't even strong**, was blessed. And that's why there were people who suffered, caught underneath her. So Kanzaki never thought about using her strength for someone who was chosen. The chosen ones should just live with their *own* strength. It was wrong that only the chosen ones monopolized the strength.

If this undeserved power was something she had stolen from those who were not chosen, then she must have to return it to them.

Because those who wish for the hand of salvation…

…would be those who were unchosen, coldly looked over by fate.

Therefore, Kanzaki could not kill. However vast her power was, she could not kill anyone. There was a time as she chased down the Index of Forbidden Books and confronted a single young man. Obviously a fight between a pro and an amateur was not a real fight. After settling it within some tens of seconds, the wounded young man asked one question of her. *Why don't you kill me?* The answer was pretty simple. It wasn't that she wouldn't kill him—it was that she couldn't. Because what Kanzaki was trying to protect were people exactly like that young man, who had gone through such unjust violence and sought salvation.

That's why she felt this way.

She would fill her blade with but one conviction and carve out her own path with that one sword.

God, if you say you will only save those you choose...

...then everyone else you did not choose—I will save every last one of them.

"—Ha-aahhhh!!"

Kanzaki let out a long breath and brandished the Seven Heavens Sword high above her head, slicing apart the two watery wings. Then, as she brought the katana back, she cleaved through three wings coming at her from the side, sending them flying sharply. Kanzaki, layering offense over defense, over and over, knew that this equilibrium would shatter soon.

Kanzaki would likely lose. Regardless of her god-slaying body, created by assembling the essence of Amakusa-Style techniques, she wouldn't be able to take one of the angel's water wings and come out safely.

However, she still didn't quit. The moment her body was sliced apart—in that very moment—the movement of the POWER OF GOD's watery wings would dull. In that moment, if she unleashed one last, desperate attack, the god-slaying power-filled Seven Heavens Sword might be able to slice through both the external Sasha Kreutzev and the internal archangel all at once.

Kanzaki's face scrunched up bitterly.

Not because she had so easily and certainly been able to predict her own defeat.

Kanzaki didn't even wish to slay the POWER OF GOD. She really did want only to hold it off. Unlike her Seven Glints, the steel wire technique she'd used as a feint, she couldn't hold back the unsheathing technique Single Glint of her Seven Heavens Sword. Just considering the possibility that she might accidentally slip up and the blade's edge would pierce through the POWER OF GOD nearly made the strength flee from her fingertips.

Even though she understood that, however, she could not stop her sword. The moment she ceased using her full power, she'd be shorn in two by the POWER OF GOD. Kanzaki's defeat equated to the Kamijous' deaths.

In order to help them, she could not take a hand off of this for a second.

However, if she let her hand proceed to the end, the blade might reach to the POWER OF GOD.

This was another reason for getting Kamijou away from here. If the amateur Kamijou and the POWER OF GOD fought, Kamijou would be instantly killed 99 percent of the time. However, his right hand was the Imagine Breaker, which could negate any and all occult powers. If worse came to worst and Kamijou's right hand touched the POWER OF GOD, whose very existence was a clump of occult abnormality, it might completely destroy the POWER OF GOD just like that.

Kanzaki wanted to save everyone who was not chosen.

Since she was saying that already, it wasn't as if the angel in front of her was standing here before the jaws of death because it wanted to.

Because when Angel Fall occurred...

...the fact that it ended up being her to fall, rather than any other of the angels, was unmistakably because of *bad luck*.

Therefore—

...*Other than having Touma Kamijou remove Angel Fall, I cannot bring this battle to an end with no casualties. Please, before this insane duel comes to a close, hurry—*

With an expression sad and bitter, Kaori Kanzaki swung her Seven Heavens Sword around.

As if she, driven one step short of death, was offering a prayer for the sake of the POWER OF GOD, which had driven her there. She whispered the prayer of a trembling child in her mind.

—*so please,* **save this angel, Touma Kamijou.**

CHAPTER 4
The Last Sorcerer in the Single World

1

As Kanzaki and the POWER OF GOD continued their upper-dimensional warfare with wild attacks occurring on the scale of a hundredth of a second, Kamijou and Touya were finally able to burst into the beach house.

However, they hadn't *fled*, per se.

The POWER OF GOD and the purge both could, if desired, kill the two of them no matter where on the planet they ran to. That's how far removed from their world they were.

Touya, unable to take in the situation well, his shoulders heaving up and down with ragged breath, demanded:

"T-Touma! Wait just a minute; can't we take a rest? What is that thing? What is going on here right now? I feel like I've seen that man who was with us before on TV— Is this the filming for a movie or something?"

They were inevitable questions from Touya, to whom nothing had been explained. But even now, Kamijou couldn't let himself be convinced by the face of the incident's perpetrator who didn't understand anything.

But as he was about to automatically yell at him, he suddenly noticed something odd out of the corner of his eye. Someone was balled up, collapsed, in the shadow of a round table placed on the floor, as if hiding.

It was Mikoto Misaka.

"Wha…? Hey, wait, are you all right?! What happened?!" cried out Kamijou without thinking, drawing closer, but there was no response. There should be about thirty minutes of time left before the limit, but were the effects of this strange *purge* already starting to show?

Kamijou noticed something at that point.

The strange, subtle smell wafting to his nose—and when he realized what it was, he panicked and stopped breathing.

$CHCl_3$. It was chloroform.

"Kh…ah…"

It seemed the chemical compound that he had breathed in only a little of entered into his brain, because his consciousness blurred for a moment. But it seemed it was an extremely minute amount, because he managed to barely avoid passing out.

"Hey, Touma, what's wrong?! Hey!"

Hearing Touya's voice of worry, Kamijou waved one hand to answer that he was fine. *But who would have done this?* he thought. Chloroform is the most harmful of all the trihalomethanes, with even carcinogens detectable from it. There's no way Mikoto would have inhaled something like this on her own.

Who did…?

$CHCl_3$ is extremely volatile, so if left alone, it should evaporate within a matter of seconds. In other words, the person who put Mikoto to sleep might still be around here somewhere.

Kamijou suddenly started to worry for Index, who wasn't here. Even though he knew this wasn't the time nor the place, his feet nonetheless carried him up the stairs to the second floor.

He dashed up the stairs, ran down the hallway, and flung open the door to Touya's room.

When he did, Index was likewise collapsed. This time, he didn't try to sniff out the scent. After he observed her sleeping breath was regular, extremely regular, he reached a conclusion. Somebody had put Index to sleep with medicine. This kind of deep sleep would not be lifted by simply shaking her.

Then who?

He didn't know who it had been, and he didn't know their goal. Touya finally caught up with Kamijou, who was on his guard for no apparent reason. He looked at the fallen Index—no, rather, it appeared to him to be his wife, Shiina—and he blanched.

"T-Touma, what is this? What the hell is going on here?!"

"That's what I should be asking!" Kamijou remembered the thing he had to do right now. "Listen up, Dad. People are going to die at this rate. People will all die, every one of them. To stop this from happening, we need to cancel Angel Fall. You did it, so you stop it!"

"Touma, this is no time for games—"

"I know! This is no time for games! If you don't know how to stop this, then fine! Just tell me where you did Angel Fall in that case! I'll handle the rest!"

However, Touya looked at Kamijou incredulously.

It was as if he were trying to say that he had absolutely no idea what he was being told.

"Touma. I'm asking you, what is this Angel Fall? Some kind of metaphor?"

When he heard that, Kamijou lost all sense of what was going on.

It didn't look to him like Touya was lying. He honestly seemed like he had nothing at all to do with sorcery. *Could we have…made some kind of terrible mistake?* he wondered.

"Give it a rest, Kammy. He *wouldn't* know anything."

All of a sudden, a voice came from the room's entrance.

Kamijou turned around. Touya did as well, and they were stunned at who they saw there.

Motoharu Tsuchimikado.

He probably looked like an idol from TV to Touya. He looked nonplussed at the man who had suddenly appeared.

"Ah, I was the one who put them out. I can't get civilians involved in this carelessly, y'see."

Tsuchimikado's voice was different from usual.

His form, which should have been within normal life, seemed to have cracks running through it.

"Hmph. From the look on your face, I suppose you haven't caught on yet. Well, guess it's only natural, y'know? Kammy, you're an amateur when it comes to sorcery, after all."

The cracks expanded and shattered like a sheet of glass.

The one who stood there was not the Motoharu Tsuchimikado who Touma Kamijou knew.

He was something stranger, someone he couldn't ascertain the true identity of.

He was but one sorcerer.

"Hey…wait, Tsuchimikado. You realized there was something weird about Dad? Hey, could it be that the one behind Angel Fall is a different person—"

"No, the criminal is Touya. There's no way we can be mistaken. It's just that the man himself activated Angel Fall unconsciously and doesn't realize it," he said. Touya looked enraged.

"Wh-who are you calling a criminal?! How dare you, saying something like that the first time we meet! Do all performers act like this?!"

Kamijou looked at the way Touya was acting, mystified. If he was the criminal behind Angel Fall, it would be strange if he was under its effects, but…

"Yeah, that's right, Tsuchimikado. My dad is a normal person. He's not a sorcerer like you guys. There's no way he could pull off some complex technique on this planet-wide scale. Besides, you were the one who said there needs to be a magic circle or a ritual site or whatever for grand sorcery, and I don't see anything like that any—"

"It's in the house. It's in your house, Kammy. Did you not realize it?"

Kamijou fell mum at Tsuchimikado's statement.

He didn't understand what those words meant.

"I told you, didn't I? I specialize in feng shui. And feng shui is a sorcery that involves building circuits via the placement of room arrangement and furniture."

"What...?"

"To put this as quickly as possible, basically it's a technique to create a magic circle by placing furniture and rooms in certain positions."

Kamijou didn't understand the meaning of those words.

He had absolutely no idea what he was saying.

"You...What are you talking about? Are you an idiot? There's no way that normal house could be some crazy ritual site! With one movement of a piece of furniture, you can create a magic circle? That's...That's absurd!"

"I'm telling you, that's not a normal house. There were occult goods all over the place—all kinds of charms and folk pieces. Each one of them by itself is just a meaningless, mass-produced souvenir on its own. They might as well not contain any power at all. But you can't treat simple replicas so recklessly, either. If they're arranged properly according to feng shui or Onmyou, they start to feed off one another." For some reason, he sounded like he was having fun. "For example, there was a short Japanese cypress tree planted near the entrance, wasn't there?"

"How would I know?"

"There was. It was a small tree with a birdhouse in it. For little birds to come and rest. And in Shinto shrines, there is a deep meaning in placing a resting tree at the entrance to the grounds. Do you get it, Kammy?"

"G-get what?"

"It's a *torii*. The very word we use for that red arch means 'the place where birds are.' The things were originally for giving rest to the sacred birds who served the gods. When I think about a cypress *torii*, the Ise Grand Shrine comes to mind, but man, this is some crazy coincidence." Tsuchimikado laughed pleasantly. "There's still more. There was an ornament on a red mailbox at the south-facing entrance. The color attributed to the south is red. In the bath, there was a toy turtle, the guardian beast of water. Atop the refrigerator and microwave in the kitchen, there were tiger toys or something. The white tiger—the guardian beast of metal. Each one of them is cheap nonsense on its own, but there were more than three thousand charms in that house altogether. With that much, the synergistic effects turn into a huge force. The house itself is transformed into a temple."

Kamijou couldn't believe what he was being told.

In fact, he heard what Tsuchimikado had to say as nothing but false accusations.

"Hmm. It's more than likely that the *ritual site* was completed at the moment the Kamijou couple left the house to come here to the *ocean*," said Tsuchimikado, seeming highly interested. He turned a cruel smile on Touya. "Sheesh. Kammy's right hand is one thing, but Touya is something else altogether. This is the most beautiful coincidence I've ever seen. It made me feel like I was looking at a naturally formed diamond, it did. Though I can't say whether such a wonderful coincidence was good or bad luck, I suppose."

"Quit it…with your bullshit! That's stretching the truth no matter how you think about it!!"

"Yeah, it's stretching the truth—which is why I couldn't lay a hand on it carelessly, either."

Finally, Tsuchimikado's sense of relaxation vanished.

Kamijou thought it suspicious, and then Tsuchimikado said:

"You know, Kammy. Everything I just said *is* a stretch of the truth. Just false accusations. But Angel Fall *did actually activate*. This is exactly what a miracle is. Oh, by the way, Kammy, do you believe in miracles? Can you trust in a one-in-a-million coincidence?"

"What are you talking about? Of course not! I don't know shit about sorcery, but electrical circuits and precise instruments won't work if they're all over the place!"

"But, as a matter of fact, Angel Fall is active. So can you not think this way, Kammy? **That there is some method to draw out a one-in-a-million miracle with one hundred percent certainty?**"

Wh...at...? Kamijou's thought processes slammed to a halt. Tsuchimikado grinned at him.

"There were all kinds of souvenirs in the Kamijou residence. They weren't placed in order to create Angel Fall in particular. From the amateur Touya's point of view, it was just by chance, placed as decoration just wherever. Angel Fall's magic circle is nothing more than something created by accident from those countless *replicas* that were placed there. However—" He continued, "Even if Angel Fall hadn't happened, some other grand sorcery *would* have. If the placement of the souvenirs were just a little bit different, the *circuit*, the magic circle, would have changed"—he turned over the palm of his hand—"and therefore, there is no such thing as 'failure' for that magic circle. **Whatever way those souvenirs were arranged, some sort of grand sorcery would have absolutely occurred.**"

And this time, it just so happened that Angel Fall was the one that activated.

If it hadn't been Angel Fall, a completely different incident would have happened—that's what he was saying.

"Kammy, why do you think I didn't tell you any of this while we were at your house? It was because we couldn't break that magic circle now that it had somehow stabilized for the moment. It's far worse than Angel Fall itself—there are Tactical Circles in there for all sorts of things, like Earth Shaker, Phantom Hound, and Cocytus Replica, and if any of them had been activated, one or two entire countries would have their region wiped off the map...And on top of that, there were even Original Circles present, of which I don't even know the essence of. Understand? You're one thing, being an amateur, but those are magic circles that a sorcerer—and even the feng shui expert, Tsuchimikado, at that—understands. We mustn't let them activate. They're of the sort that must absolutely never be brought to fruition."

If Kamijou had touched one of the souvenirs and stopped Angel Fall...

...then at that exact moment, a different grand sorcery would have activated, as if he had flipped a switch.

"Thinking on it now, that was a pretty damn dangerous situation. Touma Kamijou, Kaori Kanzaki, Misha Kreutzev, Jinsaku Hino, and Motoharu Tsuchimikado—if any one of us had moved even one of those souvenirs in your house, Kammy, it would have shifted to a different circle right then and there."

Kamijou finally recalled it. So that was the reason Tsuchimikado seemed to be urging them to get away from the house as soon as possible. This was that reason.

But still, Kamijou tried to grope for some factor he could deny.

"But, but...That's right, my father is a normal person. He's just an ordinary office worker. Don't you need mana to use sorcery? My father wouldn't have any idea how to use mana!"

"He doesn't need to, Kammy. I told you before—feng shui is something that moves *shikigami*, the 'formulaic gods,' by converting the earth's 'spirit' into energy. A person's mana has nothing to do with it." Tsuchimikado waggled his index finger. "Well, it basically took a route like a cycle: electrical generator to transformer to circuits—the earth's spirit to Touya Kamijou to the souvenir technique. Though that doesn't change the fact that Touya is an important 'accomplice' here."

Was he saying that was likely why Touya Kamijou was only partially under the effect of Angel Fall?

Touya was *one* of the criminals who perpetrated Angel Fall, but he wasn't the master but rather the slave.

Angel Fall wasn't something that occurred by human hands.

The master, the main criminal, was the world's own mechanisms, set up in a devilish way thanks to feng shui.

Damn it all. Kamijou was speechless.

Tsuchimikado didn't stop to take any note of him.

"That house is like a railroad with more switch levers than stars in the sky. By destroying one of those souvenirs, it would change over to a different rail—a different magic circle." He spoke smoothly. "So that's why I couldn't just say something like I'd destroy the souvenirs one by one. I would have needed to destroy the entire magic circle in one blast. So I would have gotten you away from the magic circle for now, Kammy, then secured that old dude, compromised with Kreutzev as well, asked for Kanzaki's assistance, and returned back to the house to destroy the magic circle...but that was the very best-case scenario, though. The schedule got a wee bit compressed, and now we're in this situation."

Damn it. Kamijou swore.

"What...the hell? How did this happen? Dad really doesn't know anything about sorcery at all. So why, how did everything turn out so—"

"Don't think there *is* a reason," Tsuchimikado interrupted calmly to the despairing Kamijou. "No reason, no origin, no logic, no theory, no cause, no objective, no meaning, no value—it was just totally nothing. Kammy, you would understand that."

So he said, but Kamijou couldn't understand any of this.

Kamijou's face like that of a lost child, Tsuchimikado smiled at him cruelly.

"In the end...it was just a case of damn bad luck."

Kamijou didn't understand the meaning of those words.

His frozen brain, however, slowly, with time, restarted his thoughts, like melting ice.

Because his luck was bad.

Because he had rotten luck.

So what did that mean? Was that a conclusion? He just happened to be attacked by Jinsaku Hino, the POWER OF GOD started to rage, half the planet would be burned to a crisp after not even thirty more minutes, Touya Kamijou was treated like the incident's perpetrator, and the reason for all that—could be summed up in just those few words?

"...That's...total bullshit."

Kamijou shook his head. He didn't know what sort of emotions to feel, nor what kind of expression to wear.

He still felt like he'd needed to stop Angel Fall despite that.

Because his luck was bad…Because of his rotten luck…

This problem couldn't be resolved with a few cheap, shitty words like that.

Angel Fall's magic circle was Kamijou's house itself. He couldn't ask for much. He didn't know what magic circle would be activated next time, but for now, if they went to his house and destroyed the Angel Fall circle…then at least they would be able to stop the POWER OF GOD from cleansing the planet!

"Give it a rest—it's too late," declared Tsuchimikado coldly. "Do you remember how far we are from your house, Kammy? You couldn't make it if you started running now."

"Then what the hell do you want me to do?! It doesn't matter if I can or not—there's no other choice!! Or what, you got some other method or something?!"

"Well, of course I do."

Tsuchimikado grinned. He grinned and answered immediately.

He took a step into the room with a face that asked, *Why don't you even understand that?*

"It'll be fine if a certain somebody here is sacrificed."

Kamijou was dumbfounded.

Though he was unable to understand the meaning of what he had just been told, his body moved to protect Touya. Despite Touya not understanding the situation, he seemed to be catching on to the fact that he was in ever-increasing danger.

Tsuchimikado watched Kamijou and grinned.

He grinned, then said:

"Well, man, thank goodness. Kanzaki's holding off that stupid angel and all. She's not someone who would let a murder happen in front of her eyes. If I told her about this, she'd definitely come running in to stop me without asking the specifics."

As he spoke, he took another step into the room.

Enduring the bowling ball that had just dropped into his stomach, Kamijou backed up a step, pushing his father with his back.

"You get it, right, Kammy? Now that it's come to this, we can't solve it without sacrifice anymore. What? The sacrifice is only gonna be one person. I guarantee it. So there's no need to worry...for **you**."

As Tsuchimikado grinned, both of his hands swayed. Those long arms with an abnormal reach, fitting for the man's height.

"But I'm in kind of a bind here, too. After all, I can't use sorcery right now. Man, the Church must think they're funny or something, making me do this job while I'm in this state. Don't you think so, too, Kammy?" went on Tsuchimikado, amused—truly amused.

That made Kamijou finally remember what Tsuchimikado had been calling himself.

A spy.

"Damn...it. Don't give me that shit," Kamijou growled, gritting his teeth. "I'm no fool. I won't let you kill him for some stupid reason like that. I won't let you!"

"Hmm. I don't really think it's anything you oughta get your panties caught in a bunch for, Kammy. To hell with other people. To hell with them, am I right?"

Tsuchimikado's words sounded like they were seriously making fun of him.

Who would sit back and not care about their own father going to be killed in front of them?

"You bastard...Get out of the way, Tsuchimikado. Don't get in my way! I might be able to break the magic circle with my right hand if I go back to my house right now!!"

"You don't get it, do you? That won't work. As long as you don't destroy the entire magic circle's 'circuit' or kill its power source, the user. Besides, even if you try your best, you won't get to your house before the limit is up."

"We don't know that until we try!"

"You telling me to trust in something so uncertain? You're telling me, a traitor?"

Kamijou bit down on his teeth so hard he thought he might break them.

Tsuchimikado rejected something they wouldn't know until he tried right off the bat and was aiming to resolve everything using the easiest and worst method. Kamijou doubted that saying any more was going to help. He doubted that anything he said would get through to him.

Kamijou balled his right hand into a fist and took a step forward.

Tsuchimikado watched him, then smiled sadly and quietly said, "Give it up, Kammy. You're only gonna get hurt."

"Shut up. I can't waste another second! I'll bury you with one shot!"

Kamijou was certainly not making light of this "sorcerer" species. Kamijou, when presented with the powers of Stiyl and Aureolus Isard, had the fear of them sunken into his bones.

But right now, Tsuchimikado couldn't use magic.

He, who had undergone Academy City's Supernatural Ability Development, should no longer be able to use magic.

"Hmm. Are you thinking *that* will close the gap between a professional and an amateur?" mused Tsuchimikado instead. "I'm gonna ask you one more time, Kammy. **Even if this were the only possible way**, would you still try and stop me?"

" . . . "

Kamijou clenched his teeth.

Out of the corner of his eye, he could see Touya making an anxious face.

Most likely, Touya wasn't grasping the meaning of what Kamijou and Tsuchimikado were talking about. He had probably only guessed that it was an emergency situation and that he was involved in it somehow.

Then, after he looked at the color of Touya's face, Tsuchimikado gave another cruel smile.

"Ah, it must be tough on you, too, being left behind without any idea as to your own position. Even if I told you all about how this worked, I don't think you'd understand, so let me just give you the conclusion."

Kamijou stood, dumbstruck.

"Sto—" He hurriedly tried to check Tsuchimikado's voice, but he was too late.

"Simply, in less than thirty minutes from now, a lot of people are going to die. Touya Kamijou, it is all your fault."

"Stop it!!" screamed Kamijou at that moment.

But that urgent shout itself hit Touya Kamijou with a heavy shock.

Tsuchimikado stared at the two of them, amused.

Seriously amused.

"Now what will you do? Stop me or not?"

If they didn't put an end to Angel Fall as soon as possible, the POWER OF GOD's cleansing would scorch the world.

Kanzaki, too, who was trying to hold the POWER OF GOD back, would be in ever more danger the longer their fight lasted.

If there was no other way, then…

If there was really no other way, even if he searched every corner of the world, then…

"…That should be obvious."

And so, Kamijou made his decision.

"**Obviously I'll stop you!**" he howled like a beast. "I won't accept it. If there's some cruel rule that says that someone needs to be sacrificed, then first, I'll kill that stupid fucking illusion!!"

"I see." Tsuchimikado smiled.

His expression looked, just for a moment, like a child's smile.

"Then let's do it this way, Kammy."

His smile disappeared instantly.

There were a little more than three meters between them. Each of them completely within the other's zone, Tsuchimikado said, extremely lightly…

"Ten seconds. If you can withstand it for that long, I'll give you a compliment."

*　　*　　*

Slam!! came Tsuchimikado's fierce footstep.

Tsuchimikado closed the three meters in the blink of an eye. Those footfalls, however, were not the sound of him stepping on the floor.

His feet.

It was a grand, slamming noise of him breaking the rules and stomping on Kamijou's big toe.

"Gah…ah?!"

The intense pain felt like a nail had been hammered into him, and he tried to retreat, but his feet were tied. His body jerked to a halt, and Kamijou instinctively cast his gaze down upon his feet.

That, however, was a fatal mistake.

His downward gaze having created a blind spot in his view, Tsuchimikado brought down a head-butt from above. His hard forehead rocked the crown of Kamijou's defenseless skull.

Crack-thud!! went the impact as Kamijou's legs gave out. The shock was like a concrete block or glass ashtray had been brought down onto his head at full force.

However, Tsuchimikado didn't stop.

His right hand finally moved. His fist swung wide out to the side, looking like it was trying to aim for the side of Kamijou's head. In boxing terms, it would be a hook. It was a one-hit, one-kill pugilist skill targeting his temples, with a curving path parallel to the ground.

With his foot pinned down, he couldn't back away. His hazy awareness wasn't able to ascertain the attack or consider avoiding it. Kamijou instantly brought up his own hand to protect his temples—

—and with a *whoosh*, the fist caught the air.

…?

The pause didn't even last a second, but Kamijou was puzzled. They were at such close range their noses could touch—there was no way his fist could miss. Then why had he made it miss?

Yes—he didn't **miss**, he **made it miss**?

The answer came to him not a second later. Tsuchimikado's fist, having passed by his temple, went around and was going straight for the back of his head. As if wrapping his hand around his neck to hug him.

The back of his head.

The vital spot judged by even karate and boxing to be against the rules, since it had a chance of leaving lasting aftereffects.

Clomp!! came a magnificent impact.

"Gah—ba…ah?!"

The strength in Kamijou's body all flew out of him at once from that one hit. His body sank straight down. Tsuchimikado's next blow passed overhead the fallen Kamijou, by coincidence or otherwise.

However, Kamijou couldn't turn that into a chance to attack.

Because of the so extremely savage, rule-breaking blow, he fell to the floor, unable even to pick himself back up. His two arms trembled irregularly. His sense of balance was shot, and he didn't even know which direction he would stand up in. The strength left his gut, and the contents of his stomach nearly came back up.

If Aureolus's and Accelerator's attacks had them punching him uniformly with a giant metal plate over his whole body, then Tsuchimikado's one strike was like he had rammed an iron nail straight into a weak spot inevitably created in a person's skeleton.

Forward, backward, left, right, up, down, far, near. Tsuchimikado certainly should have been standing in front of him, but Kamijou was under such an illusion that he was being punched by a whole bunch of people all at once.

"So you can't even last three seconds," said Tsuchimikado playfully, as if looking down his nose at Kamijou.

This was the gap between Kamijou and Tsuchimikado.

It wasn't about a professional going easy or not being careful enough because they were up against an amateur.

That unbreakable wall of skill, even when he did show an opening, was the difference between an amateur and a professional.

Even an ace elementary school baseball player couldn't stand against a real major-league player.

Even the captain of the judo club in middle school couldn't put up a fight against an Olympic gold medalist.

"...Ugh...ah...!!"

Kamijou, despite all that, desperately tried to make it back to his feet.

He was in a state where moving one fingertip was a feat—and yet he still tried to stand.

"It's no use. Kammy, there is certainly a place one can't force his body to reach, no matter how much training you pile up, because of the construction of the human body. If you want the details, then check the *Tar Heel Anatomia* or something."

In other words, that was his weak spot.

"Y'know, Kammy, you can't get through AIDS with fighting spirit, and you can't cure Ebola with guts—everyone knows that. This is the same thing. Right now it has nothing to do with your idealism or whatever. You can't currently stand from an anatomical sense."

A move against the rules.

All those techniques that would make a good human heart hesitate to use because of its oh-so-cruel destructive power, despite their many predecessors admitting to their effectiveness—Tsuchimikado had dared to choose them as his own weapon.

He wouldn't bat an eyelid if he were told they were cowardly or dirty.

He put his life on the line on the battlefield—

Because for Tsuchimikado losing meant that he would lose everything important to him that he was trying to protect.

"...———ugh."

Kamijou gazed up at his grand "enemy" looking down at him.

In response, Tsuchimikado bore an inappropriately gentle smile as he looked down at him.

"Hey, Kammy. I don't have anything right now. I really don't. Any talent for sorcery I once had has long since rotted away, and the supernatural abilities I wanted as a stopgap were stopped at the impotent Level Zero. I may be in Academy City to infiltrate it, but Tsuchimikado was no longer a sorcerer. I was no longer in any condition to fight."

"But," he continued, "even so, my enemies didn't wait up."

"So," he declared, "I needed to win, no matter what the cost."

Kamijou could feel a rather cold chill in those quietly spoken words, and he unwittingly shrank away from them.

The genius from birth was no longer anywhere to be found. Nothing he put in the effort to do would be rewarded. But his hellish conviction that he still needed to win was itself Tsuchimikado's strength. He tempered his fists on battlefields like purgatory, trained them in death matches like hell, and what he received in return for countless wounds were rule-breaking special moves, decisive and deadly.

The fact that they were against the rules was the entire point.

Because Motoharu Tsuchimikado wanted to grasp victory even if it meant breaking them.

"———kuh..."

What was the reason he went so far to achieve victory?

Kamijou knew why, even without going through the motions and asking the man himself.

Tsuchimikado probably had something he wanted to protect.

Even if he had to crawl through the mud or stain his hands with blood. Whoever he was tricked by, whatever he was betrayed by, he still must have had something he wanted to defend. So Tsuchimikado didn't flinch away from a job, no matter how dirty. Never.

"...———hah———"

Tsuchimikado watched the dazed Kamijou and slowly said, "Can you beat me, Kammy?" as if admonishing an unreasonable child. "Do you still think you can win? **Not even on the petty level of 'professionals' or 'amateurs,' either.** Do you fucking think the high school student Touma Kamijou, constantly soaking in lukewarm water, can beat me, Motoharu Tsuchimikado?"

Kamijou couldn't answer him.

He just couldn't answer.

"Go to sleep, *amateur*," Tsuchimikado spat. He straddled Kamijou, who had already lost, and took a step toward Touya.

Damn…it…!!

Kamijou, glaring at Tsuchimikado's back, tried with all his might to stand up. But simply quivering his own arms was all he could do. He was nowhere near able to support his entire body weight. In fact, he fell, under the impression that blood would leak out of his head if he stressed his body carelessly.

But he still needed to stand up.

He needed to stand up, and yet…!!

"That's enough," came a sudden voice to Kamijou.

It wasn't Tsuchimikado's.

It was kinder but somehow reassuring. It was the voice of his own father.

"That's enough. You don't need to get up. Touma, this isn't the place for you to get hurt."

"I see. You are a very understanding person, Mr. Kamijou."

He couldn't see Tsuchimikado's face. But he was doubtlessly grinning.

And yet, even though he saw that…

…Touya Kamijou didn't back off even a step.

"I don't understand the situation, but if you've got something to do with me, then I'm yours. But do *not* lay another hand on Touma. He's got nothing to do with this. No—even if he did, I wouldn't let you. Absolutely not."

"…Huh," went Tsuchimikado pleasantly.

Of course, Touya had to be scared. He was just an office worker. He was an amateur who would shake in his boots even at a back-alley brawl, to say nothing of professional combat.

"I'll say this again. Do not lay another hand on Touma. I will not accept it. Mark my words, I will not accept it. If you do, I won't forgive you for the rest of my life. Got it? *The rest of my life.*"

Nonetheless, Touya spoke. He stood up directly against a professional sorcerer.

There was no need to explain his reasoning. It was because he was the form of the father in Touya's mind.

"You make me laugh. You don't seriously think you can beat me just by getting angry, do you?"

"No, I don't." Touya chuckled deprecatingly. "I'm just a middle-aged man. My lungs and liver are a mess because of cigarettes and alcohol, I've got a terrible case of lack of exercise, and my body's starting to get pretty banged up after all. However—" Touya stared straight at the sorcerer. "I will still never forgive you. Even if I'm no match for you, no matter how many times I lose, I won't forgive you. **I'm an amateur, and that means I don't have the room to give up or negotiate.** If you don't seem to understand, then let me tell you something," he said, bringing himself one step forward, as if to challenge him.

In order to stand at an equal position with the sorcerer, Motoharu Tsuchimikado.

"I am Touma Kamijou's father. I live with pride in that fact every day."

Kamijou heard those words.

And he thought.

Touya Kamijou bought nothing but weird souvenirs, was all over his wife even at this age (though she was Index at the moment), had a somehow unreliable impression, and probably wouldn't be a single bit of help as to either Kamijou's own amnesia or the world of magic. This middle-aged man was, to put it bluntly, probably physically weaker than an average middle school student. As for combat—that was out of the question.

But Touya Kamijou was his father.

There was no other father stronger and more dependable than he was.

"...!!"

Could he watch and listen despite that?

Could he watch him silently be killed by this **goddamn sorcerer?**

...I won't...forgive you...

His fingers twitched.

...for this bullshit...

He clenched his teeth. He forced his muscles, which weren't listening to him, like they had snapped, to move.

He fueled his fingers with strength so that they could grab the floor.

I will not forgive you for this bullshit!

Scritch came a noise from within Kamijou's body that sounded like it cracking apart.

But Kamijou didn't care. It's not like his body was in a condition to let him feel pain anyway.

Critch. He barely managed to lift just his upper body like he was doing a push-up.

"Stop, Touma!" pressed Touya. For someone who wasn't letting his eyes off of the professional sorcerer for a minute and had just declared war against him, he appeared to be on the verge of tears when he looked at the wrecked Kamijou.

"Don't worry about me. From your conversation, I understand that I've wrought something terrible. So, Touma, it's all right— you don't have to stand up anymore," he pleaded with a pained expression. There was no way he would stop Kamijou at this point, though.

Kamijou wormed and writhed with creaking and cracking like a puppet whose cogs were misaligned. Touya, seeming unable to stand it, continued. "It's all right already. There's no one you can save by protecting me so desperately. So, Touma, don't stand up. Please, just stay like that—"

"Don't...give me that shit," interjected Kamijou.

Touya's face looked surprised; Kamijou bit down on his teeth and said:

"Someone I can save? He's right here. I'd be happier if you lived!!"

*   *   *

The movement vanished from his father's face, as if time had stopped inside his body.

That's really all it came down to in the end.

Touma Kamijou simply wanted Touya Kamijou to live, even if there was every reason not to.

Because Touya hadn't done anything wrong, right?

Of course, he knew that this wasn't the dimension of problem that could be forgiven just by saying he didn't have any ill intent. He was also well aware that there wasn't the time to ask him each and every thing about that.

But Touya hadn't done anything wrong.

It was just because his own child had rotten luck. Because he had been unlucky for no reason, for no wrongdoing, ever since he was born. He just wanted to do something about it, so he bought up tons of charms, and yet…

Touya Kamijou wanted to protect his child.

That's all it was.

That's all it was…and yet…!

And yet Touya's feelings, by some accidental coincidence, gave way to Angel Fall, and now he was being called a criminal for no reason and people were *unfortunately* trying to kill him.

Unfortunately.

Unfortunately, unfortunately, unfortunately, unfortunately!!

"Kh———"

For such a moronic, stupid word, Touya was going to be killed? He couldn't stand it. No, no matter what the reason was, he couldn't allow it. Kamijou funneled power into his own legs. Into those legs that shouldn't medically be able to move anymore. As if to say that he would stand back up even if he were to become a corpse.

He glared at the sorcerer who looked down on him with those eyes, with that glint in them.

———*If you don't seem to understand, then let me tell you something.*

————*I am Touma Kamijou's father. The fact is I take pride in that fact every day!*

"Ohhhhhhhhhhhhhaaaaaaaaaaaaaaaaaahhhhhhhhhhhhhhhhhhhhhhh!!"

Howling toward the heavens, Touma Kamijou stood up.

Just doing that sent creaks and screams from every muscle, bone, organ, and vein in his body.

But so what?

Were you thinking something like that would be enough of a reason to stop Touma Kamijou?

The enemy before him…

He wasn't an object of terror, and he wasn't a wall of hopelessness.

He was an enemy who he needed to defeat with his own hands.

"Did it misfire…? Or wait, was the result of his guts for having taken a step forward in the face of Brain Shaker?" Tsuchimikado muttered to himself, looking a bit surprised, but Kamijou could no longer answer.

Tsuchimikado watched the spark in Kamijou's eyes, then turned up the corners of his mouth and smiled.

"Huh, looks like you've gotten serious, eh? That's what it means to be equals. All right, I'll accept ya. From this point forward, Touma Kamijou is Motoharu Tsuchimikado's **enemy**," he remarked with a relaxed expression, turning to face Kamijou.

As if to say that Touya, between them, was a nuisance, he thrust him to the side. Touya still tried to stop Tsuchimikado, but…

"Don't you fucking touch my father with those dirty hands! You want your head stomped in, punk?!"

Touya's movements came to a halt, not from the actions of the "enemy" Tsuchimikado, but from the words of the "ally" Kamijou.

Kamijou and Tsuchimikado sized each other up in the cramped space of the room. Considering Kamijou's condition, Tsuchimikado only needed to buy some time and he'd self-destruct on his own, but it didn't look like Tsuchimikado was considering that.

He would definitely kill his enemy. He would kill him given so much as a blink of the eye.

As if to tell him that this was the courtesy given to those he stood against, the smile had vanished from Tsuchimikado's face. He loosely readied his long arms into a boxing pose, but Kamijou grinned a little bit at him instead. He would come at him with full force. That's why he grinned—because he could tell that it was Tsuchimikado's way of respecting him.

Kamijou made a fist without too much power and quietly readied himself.

There was a blank of one second.

Kamijou and Tsuchimikado lightly touched their fists to each other only once and—

In that moment, they commenced.

With a loud *stomp*, Tsuchimikado dove right in at Kamijou in one step.

This time, Kamijou had pulled one leg behind him so his foot didn't get crushed.

However, it didn't change the fact that he had closed in on him.

At super-close range, so close their noses could touch, Tsuchimikado let loose a fist. It was a wide right hook, tracing a sideways half-moon—camouflaging a Brain Shaker!

"...!!"

Kamijou immediately moved his left hand to the back of his head to protect it. That strike had directly shaken his cerebellum, which controlled his sense of balance. It was a true killing blow, and if it hit him, death from the single attack was inevitable.

However, contrary to his expectations, no impact came to strike his guarding left arm.

When he looked, he saw that Tsuchimikado had returned his swung right hand to himself midway through and was transitioning into a different attack.

A feint?!

Killing moves—he was naive to think that they were skills that would always defeat an enemy when used. It was a perfectly absolute technique that just by giving the name of, the enemy would tremble and yield the path without him even having used it. *That*'s why it was crowned with the term *certain death*.

But by the time Kamijou realized it, it was too late. He had purposely brought one hand behind him at super-close range. He was defenseless, just asking for Tsuchimikado to hit his unprotected body.

On the other hand, none of Tsuchimikado's motions had any waste.

His other hand, his left, didn't create a fist. His flat hand, left open, arced through the air at terrifying speed and slammed into Kamijou's ear. *Bang!* A direct impact ran straight through his ear to his eardrums and ear canals, and the strength evaporated from his legs. His sense of balance had been destroyed.

"Geh...gh, ah————?!"

His strength faded with that one attack. A cold sweat broke out all over him.

Tsuchimikado's right arm came flying toward Kamijou, whose knees were about to give out with a jerk, without wasting a second. It wasn't a fist; it was a hammer-like elbow strike. Even though Kamijou could see it, he couldn't send orders to his exhausted limbs. Tsuchimikado's intense right elbow didn't hit his face or his chest—it was stampeding toward his throat.

Thud!! came the impact.

Kamijou's breath stopped. The fact that his windpipe hadn't been crushed was nothing short of a miracle.

His knees collapsed.

However much he persevered, however much he tried to endure through it, he couldn't muster up any more strength.

"...Gah-aahh!!"

Despite that, Kamijou clenched tight a fist.

Crumpling toward the floor, he nonetheless bit his lip and flung a right fist toward Tsuchimikado's face.

The desperate fist, with all his power behind it, collided directly with it.

However, it didn't make any more noise than a *pop* sound.

He simply didn't have any more strength than that.

If he stopped and watched, Kamijou would fall down onto the floor. However, Tsuchimikado rammed his knee into him, showering him with blows from below to the pit of his stomach, directly upward.

Kamijou's body, the knee kicks hitting it like a raging bull, floated up into the air.

He couldn't maintain the balance of his hovering form, and he slammed back down onto the floor.

Tsuchimikado spoke.

"That's ten seconds. I'll compliment you for that, Kammy."

Kamijou couldn't answer.

He couldn't make a single fingertip move this time. He couldn't even make it twitch. No, it was strange that he had been able to stand until now in the first place. Tsuchimikado's attack just now was like he was delivering a knee kick to a patient under anesthesia in the operating room with his chest open for surgery.

In this situation, where his being alive was miraculous...

Kamijou still didn't give up, and he glared at Tsuchimikado, looking down on him.

"   .   !!"

Touya shouted something and drew closer. He crouched down next to Kamijou's face and was yelling something, but it didn't reach his ears. All he knew was that his face looked ready to burst into tears. *Idiot*, thought Kamijou. *The thing he should be most worried about right now is his own life, so why?*

He didn't want to lose him.

Kamijou thought. He dug deep into his mind and thought. He didn't want to lose this father. While his own life was about to be taken even now, his moronic father couldn't think of anything but his own child. He was someone Kamijou never, ever wanted to lose.

And yet not a single fingertip on his body would move for him.

As Touya shouted something, Tsuchimikado dove in, fist at the ready. Kamijou could watch, but without the ability to operate his limbs, he could only grit his teeth in anger. Tsuchimikado, as if swatting away an insect that had flitted in front of him, gave the approaching Touya a sideways smack. With just that, Touya's body swayed to the side, then collapsed down to the floor.

It looked like a merciful strike—but that would be incorrect. Tsuchimikado had precisely hit Touya's ear, sending direct damage to his eardrums and ear canals and knocking him out.

Touya, now with the added impact within his body, didn't move.

He no longer moved.

"…!"

Still broken on the floor, Kamijou glared at Tsuchimikado, who instead looked down at Kamijou and declared, "Hey, Kammy. That's it. This is the deadline. It's now impossible to reach your house within the time limit even if you drove a Ferrari there. The only remaining way to stop Angel Fall is to sacrifice someone. You get it, right? You really get it? And despite that, you can't accept this method, can you?"

He shouldn't have been able to hear anything, but for some reason, his voice reached Kamijou's ears loud and clear.

So he responded.

"…Of course I can't…accept it." He didn't know whether he could be heard or not, but he continued. "Why do I have to accept some bullshit like that? I don't want to accept any ending other than everyone smiling and going home together!"

"I see," replied Tsuchimikado.

That was it.

"—Ladies and gentlemen, tonight you will enjoy magic brought to you by tricks and devices. (Now demarcating locale. Utilizing paper blizzard to purify the present world of corruption and establishing locale via ceremony.)"

*   *   *

Tsuchimikado took a film case out from his pocket, opened its lid, and scattered its contents.

A huge cloud of paper scraps about one centimeter long blew all over the place, into four corners.

"—This will be today's stage. First I need to do some tiresome preparations. (Binding barrier. Stabilizing the four directions, arranging the four seals, and acquiring most valuable assets.)"

Keen!! The air around them froze.

The air changed. It changed from a seething-hot tropical night to the center of a spring in a deep forest.

"—Now, then, I will introduce my assistants. (Folding origami, converting to descended kami, and forming an environ for the visitation of shiki.)"

Without regard for it, Tsuchimikado muttered even more and opened four film cases.

Turtle, tiger, bird, and dragon. He threw the film cases containing those small origami about the room.

"—Get to work, idiots. *Genbu, Byakko, Suzaku, Seiryuu.* (I command thee, four beasts. Northern black shiki, western white shiki, southern red shiki, and eastern blue shiki.)"

In response to Tsuchimikado's words, the four walls around them began to shine faintly.

Black, white, red, blue. The four walls began to radiate the color of the origami from the film cases.

"—Pistol complete. Now loading with bullets. (Offering locale for firing the shiki. Enshrining locale to call forth sectional shiki.)"

*   *   *

It's sorcery, thought Kamijou somehow or other.

He could easily kill a man with only a fist, but it was like he was showing it to the powerless Kamijou.

"—The bullets will be totally brutal bullets bordering on ridiculousness. (The variety of shiki used for the wicked, nail-pounding priestess at the hour of the curse.)"

But wait a moment.

Kamijou sensed something odd and reflexively looked at Tsuchimikado's face.

"—Now applying barrier to pistol. (This barrier as the puppet.)"

Tsuchimikado was smiling.

Motoharu Tsuchimikado was smiling like he was truly enjoying himself.

"—Now applying shikigami to the bullets. (Firing shikigami as the nail.)"

From the corners of Tsuchimikado's gleefully smiling lips trickled down blood.

Despite that, he didn't stop talking.

"—Your hand on the trigger, now. (Using my fist as the hammer.)"

Espers cannot use magic.

Tsuchimikado had told him that from the beginning. With his body that mustn't be using magic in the first place, he was already overstraining himself to combat Angel Fall. He had said that if he used magic one more time, his broken body would meet its death.

So then why was he trying to use sorcery of all things?

An amateur like Touya should be easy enough to kill with one of those fists.

"I told you, Kammy." Tsuchimikado was smiling. "There are two ways to stop Angel Fall. One is to kill its caster, and the other is to completely destroy the magic circle."

Could he be...? thought Kamijou.

There was no need for him to go all the way and use magic to kill Touya, the caster.

So then, the "resolution" Tsuchimikado spoke of...

"Kanzaki's too nice," he said in fragments. "If I told her I'd be using something like this, she'd definitely stop me. That's just...who she is, y'know?"

As if being cut by an invisible knife, blood flowed from various spots on his body.

That's right—Tsuchimikado was saying that. In order to stop this situation, someone had to be sacrificed.

But Tsuchimikado never once...

He never once said that he was going to kill Touya Kamijou.

Tsuchimikado was being ripped apart in a matter of moments, but he was still grinning.

Even though he was the one who should understand best what happens to espers who use magic.

Even though he had betrayed so many times and learned so many rule-breaking moves precisely *because* he understood it so well.

"Stop...it...," whispered Kamijou in spite of himself.

However, Tsuchimikado said, "Kh-he-heh. Well, I thought you'd say that. I thought you'd say that, and that's why you can't move anymore, eh? Kammy, you and Kanzaki are a lot alike, you know? If you knew I was going to use this kind of method, you'd have stopped me with all your might, no doubt. Right? **If that wasn't right, there'd be no reason to protect you.**"

He grinned like a child.

What...an insane story.

He thought Tsuchimikado had gotten strong for something

important to him, but it was nothing that exaggerated. All he wanted to protect was the school life he was leading, even though he knew it was a fake and he was even faker.

"Ha-ha, what? It'll be okay. Something Angel Fall's level—I can blow away the entire ritual site from super-long range. My specialty is the Black Style. Unfortunately, the POWER OF GOD has stolen that away from me. But I'm cool with using the Red Style every once in a while, too," he stated simply. However...

"Sorry for beating you to a pulp, Kammy. I probably should have used chloroform right from the start, but you wouldn't pass out right when I pressed the soaked handkerchief onto your mouth; it takes a few minutes. With you around, Kammy, I could never look optimistically at those few minutes, after all. I don't have many pachinko balls left, either, so I took the liberty of using some hard-line measures. I can't have this spell failing. That right hand—if the Imagine Breaker gets in the way...which is not probable anyway, but it's definitely not zero, am I right?" Tsuchimikado slowly narrowed his eyes.

"Hey, Kammy. People die pretty easily. They can really end up dying easily. I know that. So in the worst case—if there's a hundredth of a percent chance of failure—then I most certainly need to crush that possibility. That's what human life is worth, right?"

Therefore, so that this magic wouldn't have even that slim chance of failure, so that it would succeed no matter what...

"Kammy, you don't need to worry 'bout nothin'," he declared.

But that was...

If Motoharu Tsuchimikado, who was all shot up inside right now, used magic one more time...

"Ah-ha-ha. 'If there's some cruel rule that says that someone needs to be sacrificed, then first, I'll kill that stupid fucking illusion,' huh? That one was good. It wasn't being directed at me, but it still got me thinkin'," Tsuchimikado said, recalling something.

He put on a quiet smile, like that of a sick person about to pass away.

"Idi...ot. Stop..."

Kamijou desperately tried to reach out his hand. But it didn't reach. As a matter of fact, he couldn't even move a finger. Despite Tsuchimikado being right in front of him. Despite needing to stop him right now.

Tsuchimikado watched Kamijou and said...

"Sorry, I can't listen to your request and stop."

He said, as if really giving his final words to a friend,

"Did ya forget, Kammy? I'm actually a huge liar, nyan~."

Just like that.

Before Touma Kamijou's eyes.

Motoharu Tsuchimikado chanted with his voice, the same way as always, the final incantation.

A blinding white light washed over them, and only the roar of something being unleashed into the night sky exploded into his ears. The boom, sounding like a beast's cry, cut through the night sky and flew away toward a single point.

Was that the direction of Kamijou's house?

Would he end everything with this one last attack?

The damage he took from the numerous blows seemed to finally begin to resound within him late, and Kamijou's consciousness began to fade.

He heard the sound of something slowly falling. *Thump*. Like a doll discarded out of boredom, Tsuchimikado's limbs sprawled and he collapsed onto the floor.

The night sky, a giant full moon floating in it, began to return to the burning twilight.

The night, which was transformed by the POWER OF GOD's spell, changed back into the glow of evening.

Next to a certain young man lay a single girl.

It was the form of Index, having been drugged to sleep—$CHCl_3$.

Her figure grew blurry and vague. Then, in the blink of an eye, the form of Index, who was lying on the floor, transformed into that of a different girl. Shiina Kamijou. The certain boy's mother.

The substitution began to clear.

Angel Fall began to clear.

"Tsu...chi...mikado?"

The young man, the pulp beaten clean out of him, said right before losing consciousness at the end of his intense pain.

There was no answer.

In the gap between Tsuchimikado's face and the floor, red liquid was gradually flowing out.

His body silently sank into the sea of blood.

And despite that, Tsuchimikado did not move.

He did not move an inch.

FINAL CHAPTER
My Betrayer in the World of Normalcy

When he came to, he was in a hospital room.

As far as he could tell from checking the equipment and things, this was a hospital in Academy City. *Well, suppose so*, thought Kamijou. He was an esper, and for his Development, all sorts of medicines had been used on him. If even a drop of his blood were sampled, then there was a possibility that industry secrets he didn't really understand would be leaked. He couldn't be brought to a normal hospital.

As he lay there on the bed, he looked out the window.

It was early in the afternoon, though the sunlight in the August sky was too strong to call it that. Beneath it were walking parents taking a child for a visit, an old man being pushed around in a wheelchair by a nurse, and others. On the television, the newscaster lady was conveying the report of Jinsaku Hino's rearrest.

Atop the side table was something that looked like a letter, written on loose-leaf paper. On it was a single sentence: "I suppose I should say, welcome home, Touma Kamijou?" and a small sticker of a tree frog was stuck on the edge of the letter. *He's my doctor again?* Kamijou thought as he sank deeper into the bed, then silently closed his eyes.

A world in which everything was back to normal.

A world in which everything was back to normal? *Don't make me laugh.*

Angel Fall had definitely lost its effect. The people in the city, the people all over the world, all of them were probably back to the way they used to be. He didn't think they'd even have realized they'd been caught up in something strange. It seemed like people's memories of the incident, including those of the angel's purge, had been rewritten, maybe because of a side effect of the spell being interrupted.

But there was still something that would never come back.

A certain young man had resolved himself to his own death, and he still grinned at Kamijou.

"…What the hell? Damn it," said Kamijou to himself, alone in the hospital room.

Motoharu Tsuchimikado had apparently been trying to protect Touma Kamijou's normal life.

But was he thinking that this world, which was now missing just one person, could really be called normal?

"Damn it, what the hell?!" shouted Kamijou at this abnormality.

The moment he let loose his wail of lament at the normal life that would never come back—

"Hey, been a while, nya~! Kammy, you doin' all right over there?"

In an absolutely impossible event, Motoharu Tsuchimikado came storming into the room.

"—…Hey, huh? Just a minute! What is this? Some spare cloned body?!"

"Huh? Good ol' Tsuchimikado's got enough personality not to overuse a cliché trick like that, y'know."

The young man, flashing a toothy grin, had on bandages here and there.

When Angel Fall activated, Tsuchimikado should have become the super-good-looking idol Hajime Hitotsui…Did his wounds and memories from its active duration not return to the idol? Or had Tsuchimikado been an exception because of how he resisted the spell using some weird magic?

No, there was something more important here.

How was he alive in the first place?

Kamijou decided he'd throw the pillow at him for now.

"Ah, damn it, it hit you! It didn't go through?! So then I'm not in some dream world seeing illusions?!"

"I'm neither illusion nor ghost, nya~. I'm the real thing, Tsuchimikado in the flesh, okay?"

"But, but how?! What was all that explanation for about you having a body that would die if you used magic one more time because your circuits are different because you're an esper?!"

"Oh, that was a lie."

"Uh?!"

"I mean, c'mon, good ol' Tsuchimikado is fundamentally a liar," he said, waving a hand dismissively. "Good ol' Tsuchimikado's power is the weak Level Zero 'Auto Rebirth,' y'see. I could use magic four or five times and come out all right, but it's a real pain in the ass. If I came out and said it, the Church would demand I use magic as much as I possibly could, and it gets honestly tiring. Sorry 'bout that. ♪"

"Ubhaaaaaah!!"

A moment later, Kamijou reflexively hurled the futon covering him at Tsuchimikado.

He dodged it easily, with only a half step's movement, and continued.

"Whoa, there. Kammy, this is the scene where you're supposed to get all choked up and moved to tears, you know?"

"Shut it! A professional *moron* is what you are! So what? Why the hell did you beat the crap out of me, then?!"

"Well, I mean…Gotta keep up the act until the show's over. And, Kammy, even if I had said, 'Hey, it's okay, I won't die,' you'd've stopped me anyway. You probably would've said something about fixing everything with nobody getting hurt and sprinting to your house and using Imagine Breaker or something. I couldn't risk your right hand busting up my shiki, nyan~."

Kamijou grunted and fell mum.

Taking the lack of argument as a good thing, Tsuchimikado forced the conversation onto a different topic.

"Yes, yes, let's leave the moving reunion scene here, shall we? But man, Kammy, we both managed to barely live through this one, too, huh?"

"You almost *killed* me—and you look fit as a fiddle!"

"Oh, you don't hafta worry 'bout Zaky. She ain't in the best of health, but she's already slicing the skins off apples with her stupid long katana and stuff in rehab."

"Listen to me! I mean, I'm happy she's safe and everything, but—"

"But there's one problem still left." Tsuchimikado wasn't listening. "Now, this whole incident…We gotta figure out who should take the responsibility for all this."

"…"

Kamijou clammed up.

In the end, whether there was an evil intent behind it or not, Touya was the one who had caused the trouble with Angel Fall. It meant that the world was thrown into chaos, the remaining sorcerers were jumping around with blood in their eyes, Jinsaku Hino was gravely injured by a stray blow, and Kanzaki ended up being forced to fight a real-life angel.

So then perhaps part of the responsibility *did* lie with Touya.

But how should he take that responsibility?

Kamijou knew of an alchemist. Aureolus Isard. He caused a bunch of commotion in Academy City, and he mastered the secret art of Ars Magna, something no one else in the world had ever accomplished. He'd ended up on the list of targets for all sorts of organizations and agencies seeking that mystique. Right now, he'd be living as a different person after some plastic surgery.

Wasn't Angel Fall in the same vein?

So then, waiting for Touya now would be…

"…Well, see, from my position as a spy for English Puritanism infiltrated into Academy City, I've got a duty to report the truth to the Church if they ask me," explained Tsuchimikado, looking worried—though only a bit.

*   *   *

"But that would be a huge pain, and good ol' Tsuchimikado here is fundamentally a liar, so I'll just make up something and tell them that, nya~."

"Hey!" Kamijou blurted out automatically.

Was it really okay to push things forward so easily?

"It's fine, it's fine! Well, the English Puritan Church is at the forefront of witch-hunting and inquisitions, so liars are the first ones to be tortured, but you can't work as a spy saying things like that." Tsuchimikado clucked his tongue and waggled his index finger. "Oh, and Kammy, one more thing. That was another lie. I said I was a spy undercover in Academy City, but **it's actually the opposite**. I'm a double agent pretending to be the English Puritan Church's ally while I dig up *their* secrets. So I have no hesitation lying to them—none at all, nothing!"

"Wha…?!"

"In addition, that was a lie, too. I actually take requests from other agencies and organizations besides the Church and Academy City, so I'm not a double agent—I'm a spy for hire."

"Who are you?! Wait, that just means you can't keep your damn mouth shut, doesn't it?!"

So he's like an informant who different organizations solicit the services of, in a way? Kamijou wondered, tilting his neck.

"That's why I came here today, too—to make sure our stories line up. Whaddaya wanna go with, Kammy? Should we stick with something Asian and say we survived some remnants of Tachikawa-ryu, nyan~?"

"I can't believe this guy! I don't wanna share a secret with you!" shouted Kamijou half seriously, face in his hands.

"A-ha-ha." Tsuchimikado laughed at him lightly. "But still, nya~, for good ol' Tsuchimikado, anything goes—whether it's tricking, lying, tattling, or betraying—but I make sure my work life and personal life are separate, nya~. I don't bring my job lies into my private life, so rest assured."

"…"

Kamijou stared at him dubiously for a few moments.

Then, he sighed, as if he'd finally gotten tired.

"Well, since Dad's face has already been identified, I guess I've got no choice but to trust you. I'm saying this once—thanks. You saved my dad's life."

"Nah, I didn't do nothin' that worthy of praise. I mean, after all, I did blow your house into bits to put an end to Angel Fall, nya~."

Eh?

"W-wait. Tsuchimikado, what did you just say?"

"Huh? I said I blew your house to kingdom come with my shikigami. There were all those souvenirs making up the pillars for a temple there, so since I needed to bust 'em all up in one shot, then I needed to blow the whole house up, get it?"

"Don't 'get it' me! This is terrible! Is my whole family homeless now?! The mortgage on it is definitely not even paid off yet!"

"Ah, right, another thing." Tsuchimikado wasn't listening. "There was another problem, wasn't there? Kammy, all those memories of people who were substituted during Angel Fall—it was set up so they would go back to their former locations. So if Alice was substituted into Bob, then Alice's memories of her time spent as Bob would go back to Bob. Couldn't hurt to remember that, nya~. Well, Kanzaki and I both used a couple of techniques, so we're sorta like exceptions, I guess."

"Don't change the subject!! What the hell am I supposed to do about my house?!"

With Kamijou's pained shriek, Tsuchimikado laughed heartily and exited the hospital room.

Damn, I really can't trust him! Kamijou shouted internally, but since he was pretty badly wounded, he couldn't get out of bed. Unable to do anything, he stared out the opened door, mouth agape, when suddenly someone entered the room with a ghostlike gait.

It was the sister in white, the silver-haired foreign girl, Index.

In contrast to her usual leaden mood, Kamijou automatically forgot all about Tsuchimikado and fixed his stare on Index. She was hanging her head, so her bangs were getting in the way of her face; he couldn't see her expression.

"Wh-what's wrong, Index? Did you get sunstroke? Jeez, it's because you insist on wearing those long-sleeved robes in this damn heat. You shouldn't underestimate Japan's summers—"

"...—it me," she said suddenly, cutting him off.

What? Kamijou furrowed his brow at Index's words.

"Touma, you hit me!"

Whaaat?! Kamijou's shoulders jerked at Index's words, meaning unknown. Touma Kamijou would assert that he had absolutely no recollection of committing any acts of domestic violence.

Despite that, Index stared at his face, half crying, and said:

"We finally, finally, finally got to the beach, so I was looking forward to it so much, but when we got there, when we were there, Touma, you never even looked in my direction, and whenever I butted in you would seriously hit me, and on top of all that when all I did was call out to you from behind, you buried me up to my head in the sand! Just what do you have to say for yourself?! Mmgyaah!!" she shouted, causing Kamijou even more trouble understanding what she was talking about—

—*Oh.* Suddenly, he remembered something he should not have.

—*Kammy, all those memories of people who were substituted during Angel Fall—it was set up so they would go back to their former locations.*

Now that he thought of it...

Now that he thought of it, while Angel Fall was happening, Blue Hair was standing in for Index.

—*So if A was substituted into B, then A's memories of her time spent as B would go back to Bob.*

*   *   *

Then, what? Blue Hair's memories of his time spent as Index were changed into being Index's own memories?

He certainly remembered he had slammed the door shut in Blue Hair's face when he came out wearing that habit and, reflexively, without thinking, buried him in the sand. **Did that mean…?**

Kamijou looked at Index.

She was baring her teeth and drawing closer, half crying and red-hot with anger.

"Uh, wait, hold on a second. PLEASE HOLD ON A SECOND, MISS INDEX. There's a very good reason for this, and, well, actually, the world was having a huge crisis while you didn't know, and——?!"

"Be quiet! You stupid Oedipus complex! You were staring at your own mother so much like that and paying attention to her, so why did you treat *me* like that?!"

Kamijou distinctly felt the tip of her words driving themselves into his forehead.

Caution: Incidentally, during Angel Fall's active period, his mother was standing in for Index. ☆

"That's why I'm telling you there's a really complicated circumstance here—and how did it come to this? I tried my best! I really tried my best for your sake!"

Kamijou's excuses turned into complaints halfway through, but Index didn't stop to think about it.

She said, "I'll never forgive you, Touma! I shall crush your skull with my teeth!"

With a bit of this and that, Kamijou's daily life resumed with rotten luck and a cry of pain.

AFTERWORD

To all the returning patrons of my series: It's good to see you again.

And to all the bourgeoisie out there who bought up all four volumes at once: Nice to meet you.

I'm Kazuma Kamachi.

We've gotten to the fourth volume before I realized it. But when I look back on it calmly, I haven't even been active for a year yet, huh? Well, thanks to that, my work has managed to get to the point where it can be called a "series," but when I think about that, I get the keen realization that a year is really worth a lot and can't be taken lightly. When I sit down and think about it, I realize I've poured a hundredth of my total life span into this *A Certain Magical~* series, haven't I? If you take that sentence out of context, it sounds pretty high-handed and ceremonious, though.

In any case, as those of you who have finished reading the book will know, the theme this time was "summoning spells." There's plenty of varieties of "summoning" bundled up in just that word, from the necromancer who places dead souls into bodies to talisman accessories imbued with the power of Mercury—there's apparently a whole lot of methods of summoning and lots of different things that can be summoned.

When I thought about summoning angels or demons, I would get this image of praying into an eerie magic circle, but it seems that actual Christianity (in its legends) is a bit different. Like how there's an angel and a demon that come as a pair for every single person, even if you don't go through all the trouble to call on them, and things like that. The entire concept that I see in comics a lot is of "a tiny angel and a tiny demon spinning around your head and arguing with each other whenever you're stimulated by things like worldly desires." If you try to trace this back to its roots, you'll run into some unexpectedly serious references.

To my illustrator, Mr. Kiyotaka Haimura, and my editor, Ms. Miki, thank you, again and again, and sorry for all the trouble. It wouldn't be an exaggeration if I were to say that all of the merits of this book were thanks to you two. I look forward to working with you in the future.

And to all my readers—the fact that you're all allowing me to publish at such a high pace, rivaling that of weekly manga tankobons, is the result of you having purchased my work. I would like to bow my head to you twice; at the same time that I wish you a great "thank-you," I also ask for your continued support in the future.

Now then, for the time being, as this page of my work is closed, and ever wishing that the continuation of the work remains in your imaginations,

today, here, I rest down my pen.

...Summer vacation is so long, this work isn't turning out to be a school drama.

Kazuma Kamachi

HAVE YOU BEEN TURNED ON TO LIGHT NOVELS YET?

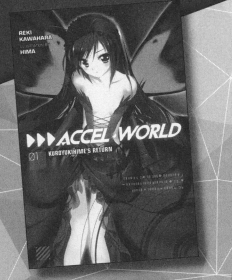

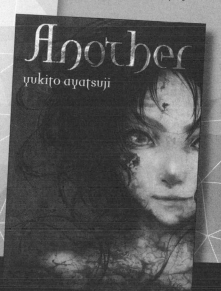